THE
SPANISH
LETTER

Kate McCabe

HACHETTE
BOOKS
IRELAND

First published in Ireland in 2014 by HACHETTE BOOKS IRELAND
First published in paperback in 2014 by HACHETTE BOOKS IRELAND

3

Cataloguing in Publication Data is available from the British Library

ISBN 978 1 44472 633 6

Typeset in AGaramond by Bookends Publishing Services.
Printed and bound in Great Britain by Clays Ltd, St Ives plc.

Hachette Books Ireland policy is to use papers that are natural, renewable and
recyclable products and made from wood grown in sustainable forests. The logging
and manufacturing processes are expected to conform to the environmental
regulations of the country of origin.

Hachette Books Ireland
8 Castlecourt Centre
Castleknock
Dublin 15, Ireland

A division of Hachette UK Ltd
338 Euston Road, London NW1 3BH

www.hachette.ie

This book is for:

Antoinette and Paddy Daly,

Donal Byrne, a good Samaritan,

And my newest fan, Sam Patton (aged one and a half).

PROLOGUE

Fuengirola, Spain, 1980

It was a balmy night, with just a hint of breeze drifting up from the sea. The sky was studded with stars and the sweet scent of flowers floated across the square to where the young woman was waiting.

From a nearby bar, the sound of guitar music spilled out to the table where she sat, a coffee cup before her. It was a lively tune, but instead of lifting her spirits, the music made her sad. This was her last night in Spain. She had said goodbye to her friends. Her bag was packed and her airline ticket tucked safely into her purse. Tomorrow at noon she would catch the Aer Lingus flight back to Dublin.

She closed her eyes and let her thoughts drift. It had all begun four months earlier. She had just finished her college exams and the long summer stretched ahead. She had no idea what she was going to do while she waited for the results, probably get a job stacking shelves in the local supermarket. Then she had spotted an advert tucked away in the personal columns on the back page of the paper: *Au Pair Wanted for Spanish Family.* She scanned the announcement, her excitement mounting. They wanted someone to teach English to two little boys, aged six and eight, the children of a doctor and his wife who lived on the Costa del Sol. She would have her own room, some free time and a small salary. It would be a marvellous opportunity.

She imagined the long summer days, the blue skies and warm sun. She thought of the novelty of living in a different country, the chance to experience a new culture and meet interesting people.

She had studied Spanish at college and spoke it quite well. This job would give her the chance to improve her fluency and earn some money. She had no doubt that she could do it. What was more, she knew she would enjoy it. It would be the perfect way to spend the summer while she waited for the exam results. She took out some notepaper and immediately wrote out a reply to the ad.

Ten days later she had a response. Dr Gomez and his wife were coming to Dublin to interview her. She could barely contain her excitement as she put on her best dress with a light jacket and set out to meet them in a city-centre hotel.

They were a nice couple, the husband in his early forties and his wife a little younger. They drank coffee while they questioned her about her background and studied the references she had brought. Then they explained exactly what her role would entail. When the interview was over, they told her she had got the job. Dr Gomez shook her hand, saying he would send her an airline ticket and take care of all the formalities. In the meantime she should make sure her passport was in order. If everything went to plan, she would start work in two weeks' time. She was beside herself with joy as she made her way home and began to prepare.

The days passed quickly, and before she knew it, she was striding out into the vast arrivals area at Málaga airport. Dr Gomez drove her to his home, a modern villa with a beautiful garden on the outskirts of Fuengirola. He showed her to her room with its en-suite bathroom and introduced her to the boys – six-year-old Pedro and his eight-year-old brother, Alberto. Then they all went out for a special meal at a restaurant on the seafront to welcome her to Spain.

From the very first day, she loved her job. It was exactly as she had envisaged it. Dr Gomez and his wife went off to work each morning at nine and she was left in charge of the boys. They were polite and well behaved but, like most little boys, they had a tendency to mischief. She was well able for them, though: Dr Gomez had told her to take no nonsense so she quickly let them know who was in charge.

She spoke English to them all the time, using Spanish only to explain difficult words or phrases. She taught them from nine o'clock till one when they broke for the lunch Señora Gomez had prepared and left in the fridge. Then she took them for a walk to the nearby park or the beach.

Every day the sun shone. Each morning when she woke, she would hear the birds singing in the trees outside her window. There was rarely a cloud in the sky. It was a completely different world from the one she had left in Ireland. She wrote to her friends to tell them how happy she was and how much she enjoyed her job. Most of them envied her good fortune and wished that they, too, could be in Spain, with its sunny climate and relaxed Mediterranean lifestyle.

It wasn't all work. Each evening when the Gomez parents came home, she was free to do as she pleased. In the first week, she was so tired after caring for two energetic children that she went to her room after dinner and read for a while before falling into bed. But she soon got over that and began to spend her evenings exploring the town.

At first, she knew no one in Fuengirola, apart from the Gomez family. Then, one evening, she stumbled across an Irish bar in a back street of the old town near the port. It was called the Emerald Isle. She went in, ordered a beer and soon fell into conversation with the people crowded around the counter. They were mostly holidaymakers but it was great to hear Irish accents again, to listen to the banter, the jokes and the news from home. She fell into the habit of calling into the bar several evenings a week.

One person there was neither Irish nor a holidaymaker. Alejandro ran the place. He was in his late twenties, tall, with jet-black hair and passionate dark eyes. He spoke very good English and had perfect manners. From the start, he seemed to take a shine to her. His face would light up when she came in and he would drop whatever he was doing, come at once to welcome her and set up a free glass of wine at the bar.

She was flattered by his attention. She was twenty-two but had little experience of men. She had certainly never met anyone as exciting as Alejandro. One evening he invited her to dinner. She was delighted to accept. The following night she put on her smartest clothes and set off to meet him. He took her to a lovely little restaurant with a fountain in the courtyard where they dined by candlelight.

When the waiter had poured their wine, Alejandro took her hand and gazed into her eyes. 'Forgive me but I must tell you. You are *muy hermosa*.'

He had told her she was very beautiful. She felt her face go red. No one had ever said that to her before, and certainly no one as handsome as Alejandro.

'Why do you blush? Is it not good to be told nice things?'

'Of course – but you're so direct, Alejandro, and I'm not used to it.'

'But I believe in telling the truth. Every night I see women come into the bar from all countries – Germany, Scandinavia, Britain – and none of them can compare to you.' He stroked her cheek and leaned closer to whisper in her ear, 'So when I tell you that you are *hermosa*, believe me, it is true.'

She was swept away by the young Spaniard's charm, attention, the gifts he lavished on her and the compliments he paid her. He was so sophisticated, so relaxed, so polite. Gradually, a strange feeling took hold of her. She couldn't get Alejandro out of her mind. At night when she fell asleep, she thought of him, and again first thing in the morning. She began to wonder if she was in love. Was it possible that it could happen to quickly? She had known him just six weeks.

She told herself it was silly. She was there for the summer. In a few months, she would go back to Dublin and probably never see him again. This was just a holiday romance. But, deep in her heart, she clung to the notion that it was something more. They would find a way to stay in touch. There was a phone in the bar. She could ring him there. And next summer she could come back and they would be together once more. She decided to fling caution to the wind. Even if it only lasted for a short while, she would enjoy every moment of it.

❁

It was a marvellous summer, one she would never forget. She spent all her free time with the handsome Spaniard. He had a car and took her for drives along the coast to Marbella and up into the mountains to the little whitewashed villages. They went swimming in the warm Mediterranean. They ate delicious meals in little out-of-the-way restaurants. Alejandro introduced her to his friends and they fussed over her as if she was a princess. She had never been so happy.

But the days were ticking past and now her stay was coming to an end. Next week, the Gomez boys would go back to school, their English much improved, thanks to her efforts. Tomorrow she would say goodbye to the family, receive her final salary payment, and Dr Gomez would drive her to the airport to catch the plane home. This would be her last night with Alejandro.

She felt herself tense as she heard footsteps approach across the square. She turned and there he was, beside her, looking so handsome in a light linen suit and tie, his hair neatly groomed and a bright smile on his face. He took her in his arms and kissed her, then presented her with a red carnation.

'This is our last night together, *cariño*, but do not be sad. We will find a way to meet again.' He put his finger under her chin and raised her face till he was looking directly into her eyes. 'I have booked a table at a beautiful little restaurant. Tonight will be special. Tonight we will remember for the rest of our lives.'

He took her hand, put his arm around her waist and led her past the church and out of the square. She let her head fall onto his shoulder. She should have been joyful but her heart was breaking. It was all she could do to fight back the tears.

CHAPTER 1

Dublin, 2013

It was ten o'clock and Sandy Devine was running late. She had gone to a party last night, with some work colleagues, and hadn't got to bed till three o'clock. And today she had an important lunch appointment. But first she had to call into the office to check that everything was running smoothly and to give instructions to her deputy, Patsy Maguire.

Sandy was a successful businesswoman who ran her own company – an agency that fed gossip stories from the entertainment world to the mainstream press. Her office was at Charlotte Quay in the Docklands, not far from where she lived. It took ten minutes to get there and park her red Porsche sports car neatly between the two white lines that marked her designated space. Then she was riding the lift to the third floor.

Sandy's company was called Music Inc and, in keeping with

its hip image, the headquarters was a large expanse of office floor with glass dividers, the walls painted in bright colours and plastered with posters of rock stars and divas. It was packed with desks, computer terminals, television screens and numerous phones. Sandy's lair was the only space that could properly be called an office because it had a door that could be closed to the outside world and thus provide her with a modicum of privacy. This was where she headed first.

She was met by her personal assistant, a twenty-five-year-old super-efficient blonde woman called Stella Jones.

'Any calls?' Sandy enquired.

Stella had the list already prepared and started to read while Sandy took off her jacket, slid behind her desk, fired up her laptop and began to check her mail.

'Blues Junction are launching their new album this evening at eight o'clock at the Sugar Club. They wanted to know if we're sending anyone. I told them we hadn't decided.'

Sandy nodded. She had trained her PA well. It was important to keep all options open in case something more important turned up. 'We'll send a reporter if nothing more exciting happens.'

Stella continued to read through the list till she came to an item that caused Sandy to raise her head. 'Someone called Sam Ross called to say he had booked a table for two at Les Escargots restaurant on Lower Baggot Street for half twelve. He wanted to know if that would be suitable.'

Sandy glanced at her watch. 'Ring him and confirm that I'll be there. Then tell Patsy I'm ready for our morning conference. And be a doll and get me some coffee.'

'Right away,' Stella said.

Stella returned with the coffee, and a few minutes later a

tall, thin young woman with auburn hair knocked on Sandy's door and entered. This was her deputy, Patsy Maguire. She sat down and pushed her hair away from her face. She gave Sandy a schedule and began to read: 'We've got a tip that Josh Carroll, the lead singer with Crazy Monkeys, is about to split. Johnny Kerr is checking it out right now.'

This was a good story. Crazy Monkeys was a popular boy band. All the tabloids would want to buy it. 'What's behind it?'

'The usual egomania. He's grown too big for his boots, thinks he can make a better career as a solo artist.'

'Okay. If he denies it, run the denial. You know how to handle it. Speculation surrounds the future of Josh Carroll and Crazy Monkeys, something along those lines.'

'Done. We're also checking a tip that Sonora is dating Tommy Black.'

This was another good story, guaranteed to sell. Sonora was a teenage blues singer with a huge following. Tommy Black was an established musician with a band called The Outlaws. 'Excellent.'

Patsy smiled. 'I thought you'd like that one.' She continued through her list: a well-known rock singer had been admitted to a rehab clinic because of a drugs problem; an aspiring young actress had broken up with her boyfriend; a well-known television personality had been involved in a brawl in a trendy Dublin nightclub.

Sandy listened to her colleague as she worked her way through the list of stories that constituted that day's news schedule. Occasionally she would interrupt and give instructions. But mostly she just nodded her approval. When the session ended she went out onto the newsroom floor and visited each reporter's desk to read the stories they were working on. Satisfied that everything was under control, she spoke again to Patsy. By now it was almost midday. 'Looks like you're going to be kept on your toes today.'

'That's the way we like it.'

'So we're all on the same page. Now, I have to disappear for a couple of hours. I'm leaving everything in your capable hands. If anything blows up that I should know about, you have my number.'

She called into the Ladies on her way out to brush her long dark hair and put on a little makeup, then examined herself in the mirror. Pleased with her appearance, she left the office, took the lift to the basement and settled once more behind the wheel of her Porsche. A few minutes later, she was in the stream of traffic heading for Lower Baggot Street and Les Escargots.

CHAPTER 2

Sandy hadn't always wanted to be a journalist. That had been Mrs Moriarty's idea. She was the careers-guidance teacher at Holy Faith School where Sandy had completed her secondary education. Sandy had wanted to be a musician. As a teenager, her big ambition was to become a singer and write her own songs. She had been totally absorbed in rock music since she was eleven years old and had first heard a Little Richard record played on a local radio station.

She had been captivated by the energy and sheer wildness of the music. Quickly, she discovered other bands and soon she was spending all her pocket money on CDs, concerts and rock-music magazines. She dreamed of nights on the road, playing to vast audiences in a leather jacket and mini skirt. She longed for a life of fame, celebrity and television interviews. In Sandy's adolescent mind, nothing could have been cooler than that.

When she was thirteen, she saved up for a second-hand acoustic guitar and taught herself to play. She spent hours with it in the sanctuary of her bedroom, practising chords from a primer. Once she had achieved a reasonable competence, she began composing melodies and writing lyrics to accompany them. Slowly, she built up a repertoire of songs. Her next move was to make a demonstration disc.

Her parents would have needed to be deaf and blind not to be aware of her ambition. But Sandy was an only child and they tended to indulge her. Her mother was a teacher and from time to time she would ask, concerned, if Sandy shouldn't be spending more time studying. Eventually, her father decided it was time to have a word with her. One evening, he took her into the sitting room, puffed out his chest and shoved back his shoulders. She had known a lecture was coming.

Her father was easy-going and doted on Sandy. He was the kindest, gentlest man she knew. He never got angry or even raised his voice. So a situation like this was a big event. She sat up and paid close attention to what he had to say.

'Your mother and I are worried about you,' he confessed. 'Rock and roll music seems to be taking up all your time. You think of nothing else.'

'I love it, Dad. I want to be a professional musician.'

'Well, we don't want to discourage you. You could be another Beethoven for all we know.'

Sandy giggled. 'I don't think Beethoven would have liked rock and roll, Dad. He was more into classical music.'

'You're probably right, but the thing is, Sandy, music is a very precarious occupation and not everyone who wants to be a singer actually succeeds. There must be thousands of young girls like you who want to be pop stars. They won't all make it. What are you going to do if you fail?'

Sandy was shocked. Failure wasn't on her agenda. 'I've made a demo disc in a proper studio,' she said, quickly. 'All my friends think it's brilliant.'

'But they're your pals, Sandy. Of course they're going to say that. The big question is: do the people who really matter think it's brilliant, the concert promoters and the recording companies?'

'I don't know.'

'Well, I don't want to stand in your way but maybe you should find out. You're sixteen and soon you'll be finishing school. Your mother and I think it might be no harm to get a good Leaving Cert under your belt just in case.'

Sandy was a little hurt by her father's apparent lack of faith in her but she knew he meant well. She took his advice and sent the demo disc to some people in the music business to get their reaction. She was disappointed by the length of time they took to respond. Many of them didn't reply at all, which hurt her. But those who took the trouble to listen to her songs were unanimous in their verdict. She had a good singing voice, but while the material showed promise, it wasn't of significant commercial quality to interest them.

That was a bitter blow to her morale but Sandy was resilient and soon got over it. Loads of successful artists had had their early material turned down. Even The Beatles had met with rejection before they found success. But she also began to appreciate the wisdom of her father's words. He might be right. It might be a good idea to have a parachute prepared, just in case.

As the Leaving Certificate examinations approached, the

students were scheduled for an interview with Mrs Moriarty. When Sandy sat down across the desk from her and said she wanted to be a singer/songwriter, Mrs Moriarty showed no surprise. 'I suppose you know it's a cut-throat business and you haven't studied music. I'm not saying you won't make it but it's a bit like wanting to be a Wall Street stockbroker without knowing maths. My suggestion would be to choose a career that you can achieve. It doesn't mean you have to drop your musical ambition altogether – you could still pursue it in your spare time – but at least you'd have a qualification that would get you a job.'

'What would you suggest?'

Mrs Moriarty cast her eye over Sandy's recent exam results. 'You've been getting good grades in English. It's your best subject. Have you ever considered becoming a journalist?'

'What would I have to do?'

'Secure enough points in the Leaving Cert to get a place on a journalism course at one of the colleges.'

'Okay,' Sandy said. 'I'll do that.'

❖

For her last year at school, Sandy became a model student. Every afternoon she went to her bedroom and took out her books. She found English easy. She loved reading novels and composing essays. It came naturally to her. But she also put a lot of energy into her other subjects. The result was that she gained enough points to secure a place on the journalism course at Dublin City University. And, somewhat to her surprise, she liked it.

As part of her course she was allocated a six-week stint of work placement with a Dublin daily newspaper. This whetted her appetite further. She loved the excitement of the newsroom, the adrenalin rush when a big news story was about to break, the camaraderie and the competition among reporters to get the best angles. By the time she left the newspaper to go back to college, she was convinced that this was what she wanted to do.

She resumed her studies and secured a good degree. Now she had to find work. But here she encountered a serious setback. There was a downturn in the economy and instead of hiring journalists' most media outlets were attempting to downsize their staff. She managed to get a few freelance shifts but it was hardly enough to keep her going. If it wasn't for the fact that she was living with her parents who were both working, she wouldn't have been able to survive.

Then she had a stroke of luck. While she was concentrating on her journalism course, Sandy had maintained her interest in music. She attended concerts in her spare time and even managed to sell one of her songs to a young singer who included it on her CD, which sold moderately well and earned Sandy some royalties. And she had got to know many local artists and performers.

One day she was surprised to receive a phone call from a young rock singer called Frankie Kelly, whose career was on the rise. Sandy knew him well. She had even been the secretary of his fan club for a while.

'Are you free to have coffee?' he asked. 'I need your help with something.'

'Sure,' Sandy replied, intrigued.

They met in a café in town. Kelly was a young man with brooding good looks that appealed to his many female fans. He looked nervous as he poured sugar into his coffee, which stoked her interest further.

'I've been wondering how to handle this and I've decided you're the best person.'

'Go on.'

'I'm forming my own band. I've got a drummer lined up and a saxophone player. I'm looking for a bass guitarist.'

Sandy tried to contain her excitement. She could see at once that this was a big story. All of Frankie Kelly's fans would want to read about it and so would most music-industry insiders. 'Is your manager on board with this?'

'I've fired him,' Kelly said. 'He wasn't looking after my career. We've been arguing for months.'

The story was getting bigger. 'So you want to get this information into the press?'

'Exactly. I wasn't sure how to handle it until I thought of you. You're a journalist. You know what to do.'

Sandy took a notebook and pen from her bag. 'Okay,' she said. 'Let's go over it from the beginning.'

An hour later, she had all the information she required along with numerous quotes from the singer. She went back home to her bedroom, rang Kelly's manager and got his side of the story. Then she sat down at her laptop and began to compose a news report. She spent another fifteen minutes, honing it to the style she knew the entertainment editors liked. Finally, she started ringing around the newspapers and magazines.

When she had finished, she had sold the story to fifteen news outlets. She counted up the fees she had earned and realised she had made more money in one day than she would in a week spent working daily shifts on the newspapers. That was how her business was born.

Now she stopped looking for freelance shifts and concentrated on writing music stories. She poured her energy into it and spent all her time attending concerts and record launches, picking up pieces of gossip and listening out for stories. As word began to spread that Sandy was the person to go to for publicity, her contacts book began to grow. Soon she had the phone numbers of most musicians, managers and agents on her files.

She also built up a good relationship with the entertainment editors, who quickly realised she could be relied on to provide solid exclusive material. At the end of the first year, her income came to €40,000, and it had all been earned from the comfort of her bedroom. Her only expense was the phone.

Several daily newspapers offered her permanent jobs as entertainment correspondent on attractive salaries but she turned them down. Why work for one news outlet when she could sell material to them all? Besides, she had further ambitions to expand her agency to cover all entertainers: comedians, actors, even fashion models. She felt she was just getting into her stride.

Over the next few years, her business grew till it reached the stage where she couldn't handle it by herself. She needed assistance. She looked around and finally hit on another young journalism graduate, Patsy Maguire. She trained her in what was required and let her loose on the entertainment scene. Patsy proved an inspired choice. She had almost as much energy as Sandy and the same nose for a good story.

With Patsy on board, the agency continued to expand till it became obvious they would have to move out of Sandy's bedroom and find an office. In addition, she would have to acquire the services of an accountant to look after their financial affairs. Sandy was spending so much time dealing with paperwork that she barely had any energy left for the main business of Music Inc.

She made some enquiries among her friends in the industry and was directed to a suave thirty-five-year-old, with a penchant for pinstriped suits, called Freddie Thornton. She was happy to

unload all the messy paperwork onto him and concentrate on
her next objective – finding an office.

She settled for a two-room basement premises in Harcourt
Street and hired a secretary to handle the growing volume of
phone and email traffic. Two years later they had to move again.
By now the business had become very successful. But Sandy felt
there was still room to develop. After giving it much thought,
she decided to take a leap of faith, hire several more reporters
and rent a floor in a new office block at Charlotte Quay.

The gamble paid off. Now Music Inc was firmly established
as the top entertainment news agency in the country with
a network of informants and sources in every branch of the
business. She paid them to feed tip-offs to the central office.
Often she didn't have to pay at all because the subjects were so
anxious for publicity. Music Inc's reporters checked the stories
and wrote them up while Patsy sold them to hungry media,
always eager for more.

By now Sandy had become quite a wealthy woman. She had
her penthouse apartment overlooking the river, bought outright
with no mortgage, and her red Porsche, plus a couple of healthy
nest eggs salted away in various bank accounts. And she was still
only thirty-two.

CHAPTER 3

Sam Ross, the man she was seeing for lunch, was a financial investor. Sandy had met him at a dinner given by one of her music-industry friends a fortnight earlier. He was thirty-six, tall, with close-cut blond hair, blue eyes, and had a sexy look about him. When she had entered the room where pre-dinner drinks were being served, her eyes were drawn to him at once. He looked like a Nordic god and had 'single man' written all over him.

He was standing alone in a corner while the other guests clustered in little groups, chatting together. She accepted a glass of wine and, feeling sorry for him, walked slowly across the floor and joined him. 'Hi, I'm Sandy Devine,' she said.

He seemed glad of her company. 'Sam Ross,' he replied, clasping her hand.

Several people had seen Sandy arrive and turned to her to wave.

'You seem to know a lot of people here tonight,' he said.

'Most of them through my business.'

'And what is it?'

'I run an entertainment news agency. I sell news stories to the media.'

'That sounds interesting.'

'It is, but it can also be exhausting. I work hard and it doesn't leave much time for relaxation. What do you do?'

'I'm in finance. I'm an investor. I'm interested in the music industry. That's why I'm here tonight.'

'I hope you know what you're getting into.' Sandy smiled. 'There's a lot of sharks swimming around in the warm waters of the music business.'

He laughed. 'Thanks for the warning, but I always check everything thoroughly before I commit myself. I think the music industry is ripe for investment. It's a booming sector. I find it very exciting.'

'That's certainly true,' Sandy admitted. 'But be sure to do your homework. Do you know many people here tonight?'

'Just the hostess.'

'In that case, come with me and meet some of the guests.' Sandy led him into the little groups of drinkers and made the introductions, and soon he was chatting happily. Her good deed done, she went off in search of the hostess, a music agent called Minnie Dwyer, and found her in the kitchen overseeing the caterers. 'That guy Sam Ross, where did you find him?'

'He went to school with my brother, Peter. He wants to get involved in the music business so Peter rang and asked if I could help. I decided the best thing was to invite him here. He's bound to meet some people tonight.'

'What do you know about him?'

'Apparently he inherited a pile of money when his parents died. He used it to make a killing on some smart investments in the City.'

'Any other family?'

'I think he has a sister somewhere.'

'No Mrs Ross?'

Minnie allowed a smile to play around her lips. 'Not that I'm aware of. He was involved in a long-term relationship with an actress called Claire DeLisle but I believe it broke up recently. He's quite attractive, isn't he? A good catch for someone. Any chance you might be interested?'

Sandy didn't rise to the bait. 'Just asking, that's all.'

But when it came time for dinner, she found she had been seated next to him. He turned out to be a charming companion with a host of witty stories and a fund of salacious gossip about well-known personalities. When the party was breaking up, he asked for her phone number and she gave him her card. She had heard nothing more from him until three days ago when he had rung and invited her to lunch.

She was looking forward to this meeting and not just because she was hungry. Sandy rarely went out for lunch, preferring to have a sandwich and coffee at her desk. Later, in the evening, she might graze at some music bash where the food was often very good. Occasionally she had dinner with a client or a particularly fruitful source.

But the main reason she was anticipating this occasion was because she wanted to see Sam Ross again. She had enjoyed their first meeting at Minnie Dwyer's dinner and wanted more.

She found him waiting for her when she arrived. He was wearing a navy suit with a blue button-down shirt and his face had a healthy glow, as if he had come straight from the gym. He stood up as she approached, took her hand and politely kissed her cheek. Then he drew out a chair for her to sit down. 'Thank you for agreeing to come,' he said. 'I'm sure you must be very busy.'

'I'm always busy so that doesn't make any difference. I hope I didn't keep you waiting?'

'Not at all, I've just arrived.'

He passed her a menu. 'Been here before?'

Sandy shook her head.

'The food's very good and the service is excellent. I eat here quite often.'

She glanced at the menu. 'What do you recommend?'

'Depends what you like to eat. Fish or meat?'

'I've taken a fancy to fish recently.'

'Then I can thoroughly recommend the sea bass.'

'My favourite.'

'You won't get better in Dublin. And to begin?'

'I'll have the prawn salad.'

'Wine?'

'I never drink alcohol while I'm working.'

'That's a very good principle. But since I'm not working, you don't mind if I order some wine for myself?'

'Go right ahead.'

He summoned the waiter and gave their order, then sat back in his chair and examined her till Sandy felt herself begin to blush. 'Forgive me for staring at you,' he said. 'I was admiring your hair. It's a magnificent dark shade and, with your brown eyes, it gives you a distinctive Mediterranean look. It's very attractive, but I'm sure you've been told that before.'

Sandy found her blushes giving way to a smile. It was always nice when a handsome man paid her a compliment. 'Thank you.'

The first course arrived and they began to eat. The prawn salad was delicious: plump juicy prawns lightly cooked in oil on a bed of lettuce and rocket. The sea bass was even better: a large fish lightly grilled on both sides and garnished with baby potatoes and string beans.

'So, how are your investments coming along? Found anything that attracts you?'

'Yes, indeed,' Sam replied, suddenly animated. 'I've unearthed one or two possibilities. There's a British band I'm interested in called Platform Two. Sounds like a railway station, doesn't it? Ever heard of them?'

She hadn't.

'They're not long out of college but I've been told they're very good. I might take a trip to London to hear them play.'

'Remember what I told you. Be very careful. Bands come and go like the swallows.'

He laughed. 'I've been an investor for some time, Sandy. And I've learned a few tricks along the way. I'm not about to rush into anything crazy.' He turned the conversation back to her. 'So you're the famous Sandy Devine?'

'Famous?' Sandy was secretly pleased. 'Who told you that?'

'They all do. Everyone in the business talks about the *wunderkind* who's turned entertainment journalism on its head.'

'*Wunderkind*? That means a child prodigy, doesn't it? I'm hardly a child any more. As for turning journalism on its head, well, that's a slight exaggeration. There was a gap in the market and I went for it.'

Sam smiled. 'I'm only quoting what I hear. I'm told the people in the music industry like you, Sandy. They think you understand them. They say you're one of the few journalists to appreciate the poor, tortured, artistic souls who hide behind those gruff exteriors.'

It was her turn to laugh. 'Tortured artistic souls? Are you sure we're talking about the same people?'

He shrugged and made a face. 'That's what they say.'

'Well, most of the musicians I know wouldn't recognise art if it bit them on the arse. They just enjoy making music.'

'I hear your agency is highly successful and you built it up from nothing in the attic of your house all on your own.'

'It was my bedroom and it was a fluke,' Sandy replied. 'Like I say, I saw an opening and took it. And I've had a lot of help from my staff, particularly my deputy, Patsy Maguire.'

'I suspect you're being modest. People don't become successful at business without hard work, flair, imagination and a certain degree of risk.'

'I took a few gambles along the way, that's true.'

'And now what do you intend to do?'

'Like I've got lots of time on my hands? I'm so busy I can't think further than the next twenty-four hours.'

'Why don't you delegate more? Why don't you let your deputy run the show? You trust her, don't you?'

'Absolutely.'

'So promote her, pay her more and let her take the strain. Spend more time on yourself, Sandy.'

'I'd miss the excitement.'

A broad smile spread across Sam's handsome face. 'It's true what they say about you.'

'What's that?'

'You're a workaholic. You never stand still.'

'It sounds like you've been making a lot of enquiries about me.'

'Of course. I told you I always check everything thoroughly if I'm interested. And I'm certainly interested in you.'

❖

Sandy had eaten so much that she had to turn down his offer of dessert, even though a tempting selection of homemade pastries and cakes was on offer. The conversation had been so exhilarating that it was almost three o'clock when Sam Ross settled the bill and they finally left Les Escargots, venturing out into the bright March afternoon. He walked with her to her Porsche.

'Thank you for lunch,' she said, as she settled behind the steering wheel and slipped on her seatbelt.

'Not at all. It was my pleasure. I thoroughly enjoyed our conversation. In fact, I wouldn't mind repeating it. May I give you another call sometime?'

'Sure. I enjoyed it too.'

'Good. You'll be hearing from me soon.'

He waved her off. When she checked a minute later, his tall, handsome figure was still standing on the pavement watching her car disappear into the Dublin traffic.

CHAPTER 4

Sandy left the lunch on a high note. It had gone extremely well. Sam had been an entertaining and gallant companion, complimenting her on her looks, particularly her colouring. She often wondered where it had come from because neither of her parents was dark. Perhaps a grandparent. She made a mental note to ask her mother some time.

Thinking of her mother led to a change of plan. Before returning to the office, she would pay her a quick visit at her home in Primrose Gardens, Rathmines. She had been concerned about her. Lately, she had seen worrying signs that her mother might be neglecting herself. Sandy traced the decline to the sudden death of her father three years earlier after a massive heart attack.

She had been with her mother when they got the news. They were having lunch together at the Imperial Hotel, a treat they enjoyed once a week. Sandy always made time in her busy schedule for these little outings, which gave them an opportunity to catch up on news and exchange titbits of gossip.

They had been seated at a table beside the window where they could look out over the garden. Her mother had picked up the menu and begun to study it when Sandy's phone rang. Thinking it might be something to do with, work she clamped it quickly to her ear. But it wasn't work. Instead, she heard a male voice asking if he was speaking to Ms Devine.

Something about the man's tone immediately made her cautious. He sounded sombre, as if he was about to deliver bad news. 'Yes,' she replied.

'Ms Sandy Devine?'

'That's correct.'

'Forgive me for disturbing you. This is Edward Armstrong. I'm the MD of Capital Brokers. I've tried calling your mother but her phone isn't picking up.'

Capital Brokers was the firm her father worked for.

'How can I help you, Mr Armstrong?'

'Your father has taken ill. We think it might be a heart attack. We've called an ambulance and it's bringing him to the Mater Hospital. I'm very sorry, Ms Devine.'

She felt her body grow cold. 'Thank you for calling, Mr Armstrong. My mother and I will come right away.'

She closed her phone and glanced across the table to her mother, who looked up and smiled. 'I think I'll have the roast Wicklow lamb,' she said. 'With sprouts and mashed potatoes.'

Sandy took a deep breath. Her knees were trembling. How was she going to handle this? 'That was Dad's boss,' she said. 'He thinks Dad's had a heart attack. We have to go to the hospital straight away.'

She would always remember the horror on her mother's face, the way her eyes widened and her cheeks seemed to collapse in on themselves. Nor would she ever forget the frantic dash through the Dublin city-centre traffic as they rushed to the hospital where her father had been brought.

When they arrived, they were told that Mr Devine had been taken to the emergency unit and a nurse brought them to a room to wait. She asked if they wanted tea and promised news as soon as it was available. The minutes felt like hours as they held each other's hand and her mother mumbled silent prayers. Sandy thought of her father, his smiling face, his gentle manner, his kindness and generosity, the little trick he had of pushing his shoulders back and expanding his chest when he wanted to say something important.

She thought of all the presents he had given her, the pleasures they had shared, the Christmases and Easters, the summer holidays in Connemara. He had taken them to London when she was ten and they had seen Buckingham Palace and the changing of the guard. She didn't know his exact age. He was older than her mother, quite a bit older, but she knew he was the best father any girl could have had. She loved him, had always loved him. And he had loved her back.

She tried to remember the last time she had seen him. It had been just three days earlier, on Sunday afternoon, when she had called out to their home and found him reading the papers in the conservatory he had built at the side of the house.

He had asked her about her job and when she was going to marry, settle down and give them a grandchild. It was the usual banter they exchanged whenever they met. He had seemed fit and healthy, his eyes bright, his complexion clear. He certainly didn't look like a man who was just three days away from a heart attack.

She closed her eyes and began to pray. Please, God, let him live. Don't take him just yet. Let him stay with us for a little while longer.

At last, they heard hasty footsteps approaching from the corridor outside. Sandy sat up straight and held her breath. The door opened and a doctor in a white gown came in. His face was covered with sweat, as if he had come straight from the operating theatre. He paused and looked at each of them in turn. An icy feeling gripped Sandy's spine.

He addressed her mother. 'Mrs Devine?'

Her mother was staring at him, her mouth open. 'Yes.'

'It's bad news, I'm afraid. We weren't able to save your husband. He died five minutes ago. Cardiac arrest. I'm terribly sorry.'

❀

After the funeral, Sandy took her mother and her aunt Betty to Galway for a break. It was June and the weather was warm and sunny. Galway was packed with tourists and everyone seemed to be having a good time – everyone except them. Her mother was still in a state of shock. She looked dreadful. She barely spoke, picked at her food and every now and then she would burst unexpectedly into tears so that people would stare.

Sandy didn't know what to do. She had never faced anything like this before. Her father was the first person close to her who had died. She knew that her mother needed to grieve – all of them did. People told her grieving was important for the healing to begin. But how long should it continue? And when was it okay to get on with your life again?

In the end her aunt Betty, her mother's older sister, took matters into her hands. Betty had a jovial exterior but it disguised a character that was as hard as nails when required. One afternoon, when they were alone in the garden of their hotel, she sat down beside her sister, held her hands and looked straight into her face. 'You have to let go, Angela. Tom was a good man and a great husband. You had a good life together. You should count your blessings. Do you think he wants you to be sad? I don't. I think he'd want you to pull yourself together and get on with your life. Weeping and mourning isn't going to bring him back.'

After this lecture, her mother seemed to perk up a little. It took a while but gradually she regained some of the life she had enjoyed before the sudden tragedy had struck. She decided to retire from her job as a teacher but she kept in touch with her friends and rang Betty regularly. She resurrected her interest in reading. She went into town one day and spent an afternoon buying a new wardrobe. Sandy even managed to coax her out to lunch again – although they never returned to the Imperial Hotel. But her mother was still not the woman she had been before her husband's death.

It was twenty past three when Sandy parked her Porsche outside 43 Primrose Gardens. It was a modest three-bed redbrick house dating from the 1940s on a street off Rathmines Road. As she stepped out and pressed the remote to lock the car, she noticed a couple of teenage boys casting admiring glances in its direction. They looked at her and grinned.

'Nice wheels, Miss.'

But Sandy was in no mood for small talk. She simply nodded and pushed open the little wrought iron gate that led to the front door. It was about a week since she had been there.

Her eyes took in the front lawn. It could do with a trim, she thought. And the roses needed pruning. Her mother answered after she had pressed the bell a couple of times. 'Oh, it's you,' she said, as if she was surprised to see her.

Sandy was shocked by her appearance. She was in her early fifties with brown hair and blue eyes. She was about five feet six, almost as tall as Sandy. Sandy had seen photographs of her mother as a handsome young girl. But today she looked like an old woman. She hadn't bothered to dress, just thrown a faded dressing gown over her nightie. She hadn't brushed her hair either, and looked as if she hadn't even washed. Sandy's spirits sank.

'Come in,' her mother said, and Sandy followed her into the conservatory where she had last seen her father alive. A large cat was sleeping on the settee. It examined her inquisitively before jumping down and running out of the room.

'Take a seat and I'll make you a cup of tea,' her mother said.

Sandy put out her hand to stop her. 'No, don't bother. I haven't got time. I just called to see if you were okay.'

'Well, that was a nice thought.' Her mother sat down on the settee that the cat had occupied and turned on the television set that stood on a table in a corner. Sandy looked around the conservatory. There was dust along the window ledges and the floor would have benefited from a good session with a vacuum cleaner. Even the garden was dreary. Until her father's death, her mother had made sure it was bursting with colour at this time of the year.

'You haven't rung Aunt Betty for several days.'

'I called her yesterday,' her mother said defensively. 'We talked for twenty minutes.'

'No, you didn't.'

Her mother scowled at her. 'Are you calling me a liar?'

'Of course not! I just think you might have—'

'What?' the older woman demanded.

'Got mixed up.'

'Do you think I can't remember when I spoke to my own sister? She told me she was going to a concert in the Gaiety Theatre. She wanted me to come with her. But I said I was busy. There was a function in the church hall for some charity and I'd told Father Breen I'd go to that.'

As if the speech had exhausted her, she sighed, leaned her head back on the settee and closed her eyes. It was as though she had no energy left.

Sandy had spoken to her aunt earlier. She had suggested that she should call in on her mother because she hadn't heard from her sister for several days. The conversation about the Gaiety concert had taken place the week before. But, rather than contradict her mother and possibly provoke her, Sandy decided to let the matter rest. 'Are you tired?' she asked.

Her mother nodded. 'But I don't want you fussing over me. It's just a phase. I'll get over it.'

'Have you been to see Dr Hanley?' She was her mother's GP.

'I've been to the chemist. I got a bottle of tonic.'

'Maybe you should see the doctor.'

Her mother waved her hand in a dismissive gesture. 'You know I don't trust doctors. All they do is send you for tests and pass you around from one to the other like a second-hand car.'

'She might be able to help you. I'll go with you, if you like.'

'No, I'll be all right. I've probably caught a bug or something. What I need is a good rest. That will build me up.'

'Have you had anything to eat?'

'I had some tea and toast earlier.'

'You have to do better than that, Mum. You have to eat properly, regular meals, fresh vegetables and fruit. Nobody can survive on tea and toast for very long.'

She made a decision. 'Tell you what. Why don't you get dressed and I'll take you out for something to eat?'

Her mother just shook her head. 'Thanks, Sandy, but I really haven't the energy. Maybe we'll go next week.'

'Are you sure?'

'I'm positive. I'll take some of that tonic and go back to bed. A good sleep is what I need. You'll see, I'll be right as rain tomorrow.'

Sandy nodded. There was no point in arguing with her mother when she got into these moods. But there was one thing she was going to insist on. She took out her mobile phone and dialled her aunt's number. When she answered, she gave the phone to her mum. 'That's Betty on the line. Talk to her.'

While Aunt Betty and her mother chatted, Sandy took the opportunity for a quick look around the house. She was sad to see that it was in need of a thorough cleaning. It was so unlike her mother to let things slide. She had once been the most house-proud woman on the street. The windows had gleamed, the door knocker shone in the sun, the rooms were bright and airy, not a speck of dust to be found anywhere.

There was a pile of books on a shelf but none of them looked as if they had been read recently. Her mother had always been a voracious reader. It wasn't unusual for her to get through three books in a week. As for the garden, it had once been her special pride. The lawn had been trimmed to within an inch of its life and all year round, the borders were blooming with bright flowers.

What was wrong with her that she had become so careless? Why had she no energy? Why was she not eating properly? Was she slipping back into the depression that had plagued her after Sandy's father's death? It was breaking her heart to see her mother like this. She stayed till her mother finished talking, then left, promising to call her the following day.

She was still downcast when she got back to Charlotte Quay and the Music Inc office. But she was pleased to find it a hive of activity: phones ringing, keyboards tapping, the buzz of industry that told her the gossip mill was in full throttle and the agency had plenty of material to sell to the panting media.

She stayed at her desk for the next several hours, checking the stories the reporters were writing, dealing with queries and talking to contacts who insisted on speaking directly to her. By nine o'clock, when the papers would be getting ready to print, she decided to call it a day. She turned down Patsy's suggestion that they go out to a record launch party. She'd been out late the previous evening and needed an early night.

But after she had undressed, showered and slid into bed, she couldn't get to sleep. She was still thinking of her mother and the way she was letting herself go. Something had to be done about it. She would have a serious talk with Aunt Betty. If matters didn't improve, the situation might call for action. Together they would compel her mother to seek medical attention.

Gradually her thoughts shifted from her mother to Sam Ross and the wonderful lunch they'd had earlier. He was one of the handsomest men she had ever met and, what was more, he was very good company. He had charm and excellent manners. He wasn't arrogant and spoilt, like many of the good-looking men she had known: they'd thought they were God's gift to women. And he was single.

Minnie Dwyer had said at the party that he would be a good catch for someone. And at today's lunch he had openly admitted that he had been checking her out.

I wonder, Sandy thought, as she finally drifted off to sleep.

CHAPTER 5

Most people who met Sandy described her as beautiful. She was five feet eight inches tall, thin, with long legs and, as Sam had remarked, Mediterranean colouring. She wore her clothes as if she was a fashion model. When she walked into a room, people stared. And, on top of all this, she had a lively sense of humour. She ought to have had lots of boyfriends.

Yet here she was at thirty-two and she had no man in her life. It wasn't that she didn't get offers. Even as a gangly teenager she'd attracted admiring glances and invitations. But back then she'd had no time for relationships. Since the day she had made the inspired decision to set up Music Inc, she had given everything she had to the company. It was her baby. She had brought it into the world and she showered it with a mother's love and protection.

In those early days, she had worked every hour that God sent and had done everything herself. She interviewed musicians and singers. She rang contacts for tip-offs and pieces of gossip that could be worked into stories. Then she typed them up and worked the phone till she sold them. Any free time she had was spent at music events and publicity parties. Even then she didn't relax. She listened, she watched, she observed, she got people's phone numbers. It was all work, work, work.

Even when her little business had grown big enough to stand on its own feet and she was able to hire Patsy, Sandy had had to be kept informed of everything that was going on. She insisted that every story be read to her or sent to her for her approval before being released to the media. She had her reputation for accuracy to protect. Any time that was left over she spent in cultivating fresh sources of information and signing new customers for her despatches. This heavy toll of work left little time or energy for affairs of the heart.

By this stage, Sandy had an army of admirers. She was becoming something of a personality in her own right and she had the money to dress well. There was no shortage of invitations to dinner dates, functions and private parties. But Sandy didn't take them up. How could she afford to dawdle with some man in a bar or restaurant when there were stories out there to be unearthed, written up and sold? It just didn't seem right.

As she got older, her attitude changed and she began to see the advantages of having a partner. But now a new factor came into play. Sandy had built up a successful business almost single-handed. She had gained a reputation for being tough, smart and independent. She soon realised that some men weren't comfortable with that.

They didn't like women who were cleverer than they were or more successful. They preferred women they could talk down to and dominate. Some of her friends said she was too particular, but Sandy wasn't about to sell herself short to please some insecure man. She had high standards and didn't suffer fools gladly. If a man didn't interest her after a couple of dates, she dropped him like a hot potato.

She had had a few relationships but they had soon run into the ground. One was with a young doctor she had been introduced to at a party, Colm O'Brien. He was good-looking, generous and clearly besotted with her. But that turned out to be a problem. He doted on Sandy to the extent that he began to get on her nerves. He was so indecisive it was as if he had no mind of his own. Before he made a simple decision, like choosing a meal in a restaurant, he had to seek her advice. She longed for a man with spirit and initiative. Sometimes Colm was so weak and uncertain that she felt like shaking him. In the end, she had let him go.

Then she'd met a barrister, Charles Fitzsimons. He certainly didn't lack self-confidence. He was full of opinions on every subject under the sun. If they were out somewhere in a group, it was Charles's voice that soared above the rest, laying down the law as if he was back in the courtroom. She was quite fond of him. Unlike Colm, he had backbone. But as time went by, she soon discovered that he had a very disagreeable flaw. He was a control freak.

Whenever they met, he would grill her about her day – where she had been, whom she had met, what she had done – as if he was cross-examining a defendant in the witness box. When they were at a party, he would never let her out of his sight. If he saw her talking to another man, he would immediately get agitated and intervene. His behaviour soon became intolerable. Matters came to a head when he took to ringing her late at night to make sure she was safe at home and not out with another admirer. Sandy had had enough of Charles's paranoid behaviour. She got rid of him too.

She began to think she might never find a man who suited her. Perhaps her friends were right when they said she had set the bar too high. Although she was successful and comfortably off, she was often lonely. After a busy day at work, she would come home to her splendid penthouse by the river and think how pleasant it would be to have the company of a man, someone she could rely on, someone she might fall in love with and marry.

So far, such a relationship had escaped her. However, she consoled herself with the knowledge that she was still young and attractive. She knew she could easily find a man if she put her mind to it. But he had to be the right man. One thing was certain: Sandy knew she could never settle for second best.

❧

The following morning when she got into the office Patsy was already there, with the day's news schedule prepared. 'Late night?' she teased, as Sandy slipped into her seat and asked for coffee.

'No. Just tired, that's all.'

'Maybe you should take a break. You know I'm ready to stand in for you any time you want.'

'I might take you up on that one of these days,' Sandy replied, recalling Sam Ross's suggestion at yesterday's lunch.

They finished the morning conference and Sandy went out into the newsroom to see how the reporters were getting on. There were five of them and she had picked them all herself. Most were graduates of the media schools and they had been trained thoroughly. Although the agency dealt with entertainment gossip, which was not in the same league as high-powered political stories, she insisted on the strictest standards of accuracy and had drilled into her reporters the need to check facts and make sure that everything they wrote could be backed up with evidence and quotes. The last thing Music Inc needed was a costly libel action that put the company out of business.

Happy that everything was under control, she returned to her office and made some calls to her personal contacts. This resulted in several more stories, which she relayed to the reporting staff. Shortly after one o'clock, she began to feel peckish so she sent Stella to the delicatessen for a tuna roll, which she ate at her desk.

The day wore on. By eight o'clock, the staff were drifting off to various parties and entertainment events. This was one of the perks of the job, the opportunity to mix with music stars and celebrities at nightclubs and watering holes. It had the added advantage of often throwing up tip-offs and stories.

Sandy didn't go with them. She stayed at her desk till ten when she left to go home to her penthouse. On the way, she picked up a Chinese takeaway, which she ate in the kitchen with a glass of wine. Then she had a shower, got into bed and fell asleep immediately.

❁

Between keeping an eye on her mother and running Music Inc, Sandy's days were so busy that a week had passed before she realised that Sam Ross hadn't contacted her as he had said he would. Normally, something like that wouldn't have bothered her. People were forever promising to call and forgetting. She often did it herself.

But, gradually, his failure to get in touch began to irk her. She had felt confident that he would call. Her mind kept returning to the lunch at Les Escargots, how jolly it had been and how well they had got on together. She remembered his tall figure standing on the pavement, watching her car disappear, as if he was sorry to see her go. How had he forgotten about her so quickly?

The thought occurred that he had been teasing her, playing with her feelings to bolster his own self-esteem. She knew there were men who behaved like that, leading women along the garden path and dumping them when they grew bored. But when she thought again of the events of the lunch, she was sure that Sam wasn't one of them. He had sounded so genuine and sincere that she found it impossible to imagine he had been trifling with her. He would contact her in due course. She would just have to be patient.

She decided to put the matter out of her mind and threw herself into her work. She spent several nights on the town with Patsy. But even though she was exhausted when she finally climbed into bed, the minute she closed her eyes, Sam Ross's face swam into her consciousness.

It was crazy. No man had affected her in this way before. She began to invent excuses to explain his failure to contact her. Perhaps he had lost her number. But she knew that was ridiculous. If he wanted to get in touch, he simply had to look her up in the telephone directory. The number of Music Inc was prominently displayed.

She thought of other possibilities and dismissed them all. And as the weeks passed without any word, she began to reassess the situation. By now, she was certain that he wasn't going to call. She began to entertain the thought of ringing *him*. She could pretend she was enquiring about his search for an investment prospect. It would give her a chance to hear his voice again. And if he wasn't interested in her, it would give him an opportunity to tell her so. At least it would put her out of her misery.

A few times she picked up the phone and braced herself to make the call but pride stopped her. She had never chased after a man and she wasn't going to start now. In Sandy's eyes it was demeaning and, besides, it would be counter-productive. Sam Ross was a man of the world and he would see through her ploy straight away. She would look foolish in his eyes.

Now she cursed the evening she had met him and allowed his silver tongue and good looks to beguile her. Finally she was forced to accept the inevitable. He had lost interest in her. There was nothing she could do about it. She would just have to put him out of her thoughts and move on.

It was difficult but now she set her mind firmly to the task. She spent her spare time visiting her mother in Primrose Gardens and was pleased to see an improvement in her. She had managed to pull herself together and was reading books again. She had even managed to tidy the garden. But she was still refusing to see a doctor.

As a distraction, Sandy went clubbing with Patsy and accepted invitations from men she knew to go out to dinner or to the theatre. Gradually, Sam Ross began to fade from her mind although he never disappeared completely. He was still the best man she had ever met. Sadly, he didn't seem to feel the same way about her.

Time moved on and she realised it was almost six weeks since that fateful lunch. By now, she had adjusted to the fact she wasn't going to see Sam Ross again. Then came an afternoon when she was in the office struggling with a difficult news story that concerned a famous entertainer who was having an affair with a dancer. It was a big story and they had the exclusive. But before she released it to the media she had to go through it line by line to make sure it was watertight. Suddenly her personal phone buzzed. She clamped it to her ear. 'Yes,' she said, thinking it was someone she had been trying to contact.

'Hi,' a voice replied. 'I'd like to apologise for not calling you sooner but I've been away on business.'

Her heart jolted. 'Sam?' she gasped.

'Yes. I wondered if you'd be free to meet me for dinner some time soon?'

CHAPTER 6

She had flushed at the sound of his voice. He had caught her completely off guard and she didn't know what to say. He had ignored her for weeks and now here he was, ringing her as she tried to sort out a major story. 'I – I …' she stammered.

'If it's inconvenient, I can call back later.'

'No, don't do that. I'm very busy right now. Can you leave it with me for the time being?'

'Sure,' he replied. 'Maybe you could call me when you're free. You've got my number.' She heard disappointment in his voice.

They said goodbye and she returned to the job in hand. But Sam Ross's unexpected call had shattered her concentration and it was some time before she managed to rewrite the story to her satisfaction. At last, she stood up from her desk.

'I'm going out for some fresh air,' she said to Patsy. 'Keep an eye on things while I'm gone.'

'Sure,' her deputy replied.

She took the lift to the ground floor and walked out across the plaza till she came to the water's edge. There was a café with seats outside. She sat down and ordered a coffee while she tried to sort out her thoughts.

She still hadn't got over Sam Ross's call. She had vowed to put him out of her mind and had almost succeeded. And now here he was, back again, as if the previous six weeks hadn't happened. Part of her was relieved that he had finally contacted her. But another part was angry.

He had left her hanging for so long and Sandy wasn't used to being treated like that. She found it insulting. It told her he didn't regard her as very important. And then, out of the blue, he had decided to call, expecting her to jump to attention and go running off to dinner with him. What arrogance. It appeared that Sam Ross was not the man she'd believed he was. He was just like all the other spoiled brats she had come across.

She thought of the weeks of uncertainty she had endured while she waited for his call. She'd be mad to put herself through all that again. And if she gave in this time, it would let him know he could do it whenever he pleased. No, she decided. She would give him some of his own medicine. She would *not* return his call. Instead, she would stick to her commitment to cut him out of her life.

After making this decision she felt cheered. She finished her coffee and left a tip for the waitress, then returned to the office and the comforting turmoil of Music Inc.

❖

But getting rid of Sam Ross didn't turn out to be as easy as she'd expected. A week later, as she was having breakfast in her apartment, her phone rang and she recognised his number. She answered it.

'Hi, Sandy,' he began, in his breezy manner. 'I didn't hear from you and I was beginning to wonder if I'd missed your call.'

This time, she spoke in a steady, confident voice: 'No, you didn't, Sam.'

'How do you mean?'

'You didn't miss my call because I didn't make one.'

'I don't understand.'

'It's quite simple. I've decided that I don't want to see you again.'

Now he was the one at a loss for words. 'But why not?' he stammered eventually.

'The last time we met you undertook to ring me. It took you six weeks to do it. I call that insensitive if not downright rude.'

'I told you I was away on business. I went to London to take a look at Platform Two – the band I said I was interested in? While I was there I took the opportunity to do some research into some other investments. I've just got back to Dublin.'

She hesitated. It sounded like a reasonable explanation. 'You could at least have sent me a text.'

'But I was very busy. It wasn't that I was ignoring you. I was thinking about you all the time but I decided to wait till I was back in Dublin before contacting you. Look, if I've upset you, I apologise. That wasn't my intention at all.'

She paused. He sounded contrite. He had a good excuse and he had apologised. Was she being too hard on him? But she held firm. 'I just told you, Sam. I don't want to see you again.'

'But that's ridiculous.'

'I think it's perfectly reasonable given the way you've behaved.'

'Oh, come on,' he coaxed. 'I'm dying to see you. And I've

got so much to tell you. Why don't you let me buy you dinner tonight at La Belle Époque on Stephen's Green? I can pick you up if you like.'

'Sam, you're not listening.'

'Eight o'clock. You'll regret it if you don't come. The food is magnificent. You'll really enjoy it, Sandy.'

'Sam ...'

'Look, all I'm asking is a break. Won't you at least give me an opportunity to explain myself?'

Her resolve crumbled to dust. 'Okay,' she said. 'But it'd better be good.'

Suddenly his self-assurance was back. 'That's brilliant. You've just made the right call, Sandy. I promise you we're going to have a fantastic night.'

She shut the phone, closed her eyes and prayed that she hadn't made a gigantic mistake.

By the time she left for work her mood had changed and now she felt buoyant. She had made her point and left Sam Ross in no doubt that she was not a woman to be messed about. And he had sounded so relieved to be seeing her again that he couldn't possibly have faked it. She discovered that she was quite looking forward to her dinner date.

She spent another hectic day at Charlotte Quay then left around six with Patsy remaining in charge to make sure that everything ran smoothly. She went straight home and began to get ready. First she relaxed in a warm bath to soak all the tension out of her body. Then she tried to decide what to wear.

She had a bulging wardrobe but tonight she wanted something special. She wanted to have heads turning in admiration when she came through the door of La Belle Époque. She wanted Sam Ross to realise what a prize he had almost thrown away.

In the end, she chose a black cocktail dress that revealed a little thigh and cleavage, hung a simple gold chain round her neck and stepped into a pair of black heels. Then she sat down at the dressing table to apply her makeup. When she had finished, she stood up and studied herself in the full-length mirror in the bathroom. She thought she looked good. No, she looked better than good: she looked spectacular.

By now, it was a quarter to eight. Parking would be difficult around Stephen's Green so she booked a cab for eight o'clock. It would get her there for a quarter past. It was rude to be late but she didn't want to arrive smack on time in case he mistook it for eagerness. Besides, she thought, having to wait for a while would do him no harm.

She wasn't disappointed when she walked through the doors of the restaurant at fourteen minutes past eight. She was slightly out of breath as she spoke to the solemn head waiter at his desk near the door and told him she had an appointment with Mr Sam Ross. His attitude seemed to change and she thought she detected a smile as he gave a polite bow. 'Mr Ross is waiting.'

He snapped his fingers and a waiter appeared at her side. 'Please show the lady to Mr Ross's table.'

Sandy followed the waiter across the carpeted floor. The restaurant was almost full and she was conscious of the eyes of other diners following her as she went. Their looks of admiration gave her a quiet thrill of satisfaction. At last, they arrived at a small alcove set in a corner of the room. Sam rose to meet her, dressed smartly in white shirt and blue tie, dark jacket and navy chinos. He was every bit as handsome as he had been the last time they had met.

He kissed her cheek and the waiter politely drew out a chair for her to sit down. Sam seemed so relieved to see her that his eyes were shining with pleasure.

'You look ravishing. Thank you for coming.'

She gave him a tight smile and sat down.

'Would Madam like something to drink?' the waiter enquired.

'Mineral water, please.'

'And Sir?'

'Could I have a gin and tonic?'

'Certainly.' The waiter gave a slight nod and left them.

As soon as he was out of earshot Sam began to apologise. 'Let me tell you again how sorry I am for the mix-up. I've thought some more about it and I agree entirely that it was very bad form. I should have been more considerate.'

She waited till he had finished then said, softly but firmly, 'I accept your apology but let's get one thing straight. I'm a businesswoman. I trust people to abide by their commitments. When someone promises to call me, I expect them to do just that. Otherwise, I assume they're not serious.'

He hung his head, suitably chastised. 'It won't happen again, I promise.'

'In that case, let's put it behind us.'

He brightened. 'Did you see the reaction when you came through the door? They were gawking at you like you were royalty. You knocked their socks off.'

'Were they?' Sandy replied. 'I didn't notice.'

By now she'd had time to glance around the restaurant and take in their surroundings. The room they were in was very smart but she'd already known of La Belle Époque's reputation as one of the finest restaurants in Dublin. The walls were covered with burgundy flock wallpaper, and discreet lamps cast glimmering shadows across their table. Just the place for romantic intrigue, she thought.

Sam passed her a menu to study. 'What about some oysters to start?' Sam asked. 'I can recommend them. And the roast quail is superb.'

'Is that what you're having?'

'Yes.'

'Okay. Order for two.'

'How about some wine?'

She shook her head and he looked disappointed. 'I thought perhaps we could relax a little.'

'Maybe later,' she said. 'But first I want to hear about your trip to London. Did Platform Two live up to your expectations?'

He sighed. 'That's a difficult question. They sounded good. They've got loads of energy and the audience certainly enjoyed their performance. The problem is, Sandy, I'm no judge of rock music. There were several occasions when I found myself wishing I had invited you to join me. I could have used your expertise.'

She searched his face. Was he serious?

'Everyone I've spoken to has told me the same thing. They all say that no one in Dublin knows the music scene better than you.'

'I take that as a compliment, Sam. But I've told you before, the industry is notoriously volatile and audiences are fickle. Bands break up all the time. Or they're one-hit wonders who enjoy enormous success only to crash and burn a few months later. If you really want my advice, I'd tell you not to get involved with the music business at all.'

'But you don't know me, Sandy. At heart, I'm a gambler. I could never live with myself if I turned down this opportunity and Platform Two went on to become another Rolling Stones or U2. They're playing a gig in Whelan's next week. Would you come with me and give me your honest opinion?'

She hesitated. 'Okay, but on one condition. I will only give you my assessment. You have to make your own decision about investing. I don't want to be blamed if things go wrong.'

He grasped her hand and laughed. 'That's the way I always operate.'

The oysters arrived and soon Sandy was enjoying herself. Sam oozed the same charm and good manners he had displayed the last time they had eaten together. He kept up a steady stream of witty conversation. He plied her with compliments, while his smouldering eyes flirted with her from across the table. She accepted a glass of wine with her main course. By the time the meal was finished, they had drunk a full bottle and she was feeling deliciously tipsy. At last Sam asked for the bill. He seemed reluctant to allow the evening to end. 'How are you getting home?'

'The same way I came. By taxi.'

'We'll share one,' he said. 'You live near your office, don't you? It's on my way home.'

'How did you know where I lived?'

'I made enquiries.'

'So you've been checking on me again.' She made a playful swipe at him with her napkin but she was happy to accept his offer.

A taxi was waiting for them outside and they got into the back seat. Fifteen minutes later, they were drawing up outside her apartment complex. As she moved to get out, his hand detained her. 'I've had a wonderful evening, Sandy. Thank you for coming. I really enjoyed myself.'

'I did too.'

He leaned across to open the door and, as he did so, his cheek brushed hers. Within seconds, his arms were around her and their lips met. Sandy felt a delicious thrill shoot through her from her toes to the roots of her hair. But it lasted only a second, then Sam was out of the taxi and holding the door open for her.

She stood unsteadily on the pavement, intoxicated by the cool night air and the big yellow moon sailing across the waters of the dock. And, most of all, she was shaken by the memory of his kiss.

CHAPTER 7

She woke at seven o'clock with the thought of that kiss still lingering in her mind. Her situation had turned around and now she was bursting with enthusiasm, ready to face anything the day might have in store. She threw the sheets aside and her thoughts returned again to her evening with Sam.

When had she last enjoyed an occasion like that with a handsome man? It was so long ago that she couldn't remember. And then there had been that parting kiss. It had awakened in Sandy feelings of pleasure that had long been buried under the pressure of work and concern for her mother. Now she wanted more.

She felt so excited that she decided to go for a jog to calm herself. She had joined a gym once but had had to give it up because she couldn't find the time to go. She drew back the curtains and saw that a weak sun was struggling to break through the clouds. She couldn't wait to get out into the morning air.

She pulled on her jogging gear and set off. It was early but there were plenty of people abroad, filtering into offices and shops to begin their daily grind. She ran along the river until she reached the toll bridge, then turned back.

She arrived at her apartment shortly after eight, out of breath but feeling vibrant and alive. She had a quick shower, got dressed, and by half past eight, she was driving towards the Music Inc office.

❖

Stella was waiting for her with the schedule of phone calls, messages and a list of that day's invitations. Sandy ran her eye over it, then asked Stella to find Patsy.

A few moments later, her deputy arrived and stared at her before she sat down. 'You have a gleam in your eye this morning.'

'Do I?'

'Yes. You look like a cat that's just had a saucer of cream.'

'It's the product of a good night's sleep and a brisk jog along the river before breakfast. You should try it some time instead of spending half the night in noisy clubs with degenerate wannabe celebs.'

Patsy giggled. 'You won't fool me that easily. It took more than a good night's sleep to put that grin on your face. I've seen it before. It's a man, isn't it?'

Sandy was surprised to find herself blushing. 'My lips are sealed.'

'Oh, c'mon, Sandy! You can tell me. We have no secrets between us. Who is it? Anybody I know?'

Sandy took a deep breath. 'All right. If you must know, I had a lovely dinner last night in a beautiful restaurant with a very charming man who has excellent manners and exquisite taste, the type of man who is rapidly becoming extinct in this town, I might add. But it was purely business. He wanted to get my opinion about a band he's interested in.'

Patsy looked disappointed. 'Is that all?'

'Afraid so.'

'Is he young?'

'Mid-thirties.'

'No hint of *amour* lingering over the smoked salmon?'

Sandy burst out laughing. 'What is this? Aunty Peg's Advice Column? Let's get cracking. We've got a news agency to run.'

The morning flew by with the usual frenzy of phone calls, tip-offs to be checked and stories to be carefully edited. It was almost midday when Sandy finally got the call she had been expecting. When she answered she heard Sam's eager voice. 'I would have called earlier but I guessed you'd be busy. I'm just checking that you're okay.'

'That's very kind of you. And I *am* busy but I enjoy that. Busy is what brings the money in.'

'Damn right. Sleep okay?'

'Like a baby.'

'I really enjoyed our dinner last night.'

'I did too.'

'Are you free to join me again tomorrow evening?'

'What have you got in mind?'

'I've managed to get my hands on a pair of tickets for the Blur concert at Kilmainham Castle. We could have supper afterwards.'

Sandy was impressed. The Blur concert had been sold out for months. Tickets were like gold dust.

'And I promise there'll be no business, just pleasure.'

'Sure. What time?'

'The concert is at eight but we don't want to be late. I could call for you at seven.'

'Seven is fine. You already know my address.'

'So we've got a date?'

She laughed. 'Yes, we've got a date.'

She heard a click and he was gone. She stared off into space. No business, just pleasure, he had said. Sounds like something I might enjoy, she thought.

She sailed through the remainder of the day on a wave of energy and high spirits. She spent two hours dealing with a difficult tip-off then took a phone call from an angry band manager who was trying to kill a hot story they'd got hold of. He had threatened barristers and writs and court action before she managed to talk him down. She even extracted some juicy quotes to beef up the report.

When the rest of the staff began drifting off at around seven, Sandy was still at her desk. She remained there till nine o'clock when the building had fallen quiet. She switched off the lights, locked up and prepared to drive home. But all the time, she couldn't get Sam Ross out of her head. Her thoughts kept returning to the previous evening and the kiss as she was getting out of the taxi. And each time she saw his face, she felt a shiver run along her spine. Finally, she slipped into bed.

Something's happening to me, she thought. The last time she'd felt like this, Sam Ross had been at the centre of it too. But then she had been waiting for his phone call and unsure that it would ever come. Now she felt herself on more certain ground.

There was no doubt about it. He was the one who was doing the pursuing. And she hadn't a scintilla of doubt that she was going to enjoy the experience enormously.

❧

The following morning she was at her desk before the other staff turned up for work. Patsy was the first to arrive. 'You're in early,' she said.

'That's because I'll be leaving early. I have an appointment at three.'

She worked steadily through the morning, then set off for her appointment. It was with the hairdresser, although she hadn't told Patsy that. Patsy had already sensed that something big was going on and she didn't want to give her any more ammunition. She spent two hours in the hairdresser's chair having her hair trimmed and highlighted. For good measure, she threw in a mini facial. It was half past five when she finally opened the door of her apartment.

I'll have to get my skates on, she thought. I have a lot to do and I haven't left myself much time. She tried on a number of dresses, then settled for a knee-length red silk shift. Now she had to find shoes to match. It was approaching six thirty when she finally sat down to do her makeup. She was just finishing when she heard the buzzer sound. She sprayed a small jet of Folle de Joie on her throat and wrists, then ran to open the door.

He was standing in the hall with a single red rose in his hand. What a coincidence, Sandy thought. It matches my dress. He advanced into the room, put the flower on a table, then took her in his arms and kissed her passionately. He smelt of shaving lotion and expensive soap. Sandy felt the same bolt of magic she had experienced the first time.

At last he let her go and gazed into her face. 'You look amazing,' he said. 'You're going to upstage every woman at the concert.'

'That's nice to hear but I think it might be over the top.'

He shook his head. 'Humility doesn't suit you, Sandy. It's the truth. You look fabulous.'

'Thank you. Have we got time for a quick drink?'

He glanced at his watch. 'It'll have to be fast.'

Sandy had a bottle of good white wine chilling in the fridge. She went into the kitchen and poured two glasses, then led him on a quick tour of the penthouse. They finally came to a stop at the vast window overlooking the river and the city beyond.

'Wow, what a view,' he remarked, clearly impressed.

'It's what persuaded me to buy it. There's another penthouse across the hall. It was bigger and cheaper but it didn't have this view.'

'You've got a good eye and sharp commercial sense. You must see my place some time. It's like a dog kennel compared to this.'

He finished his wine, glanced at his watch once more and announced that it was time to go. Sandy turned off the lights, locked up, and two minutes later they were travelling downstairs in the lift to the ground floor.

❖

The concert was being staged outdoors and the venue was filling when they arrived. An area had been cordoned off for parking. Sam slid his black Audi into a vacant spot and they walked the rest of the way to their seats. Sandy glanced around. There were a lot of celebs out tonight. She spotted several people she knew: a well-known fashion designer, a famous writer, several musicians and singers. They had barely sat down when the stage lights dimmed and the concert began. She settled back and prepared to enjoy herself.

She wasn't disappointed. Blur were accomplished performers and quickly had the audience eating out of their hands. It was a balmy night, perfect for the event.

When at last the evening drew to a close, she was on a high.

'Hungry?' Sam asked, as they walked back to the car.

She was starving. She had barely eaten all day but she wasn't about to tell Sam that. 'I could manage a bite of something.'

'Well, I've chosen the perfect place for a nice little supper. I think you'll like it.'

He drove the short distance to Chapelizod village and a quaint restaurant situated beside the river. The night air was still warm and they chose a table in the garden where they could listen to the peaceful sound of the water flowing by. The trees were hung with lamps that sparkled like stars as the moths fluttered in and out of the light. In the darkness they could hear the hooting of an owl.

'What's this place called?' Sandy asked, as she glanced around at the other diners.

'Paradiso. Do you like it?'

'It's beautiful. How did you find it?'

He smiled. 'I make a hobby of discovering good places to eat. Wait till you taste the food.'

They had a couple of glasses of wine, with lobster salad and grilled sea trout. It was true what Sam had said. The food was delicious. This was the third meal she'd eaten with him and each one had been an experience. He was in effervescent form and the time passed in a blizzard of chat and laughter. As the light reflected on his handsome face she felt a surge of admiration. Every encounter with Sam Ross was drawing her closer to him.

It was after midnight when they left to return home and almost one o'clock when Sam pulled up outside her building. There was an awkward pause as the sound of the engine faded away.

'Aren't you going to invite me up for a nightcap?'

It would be the perfect ending to this wonderful evening. Still she hesitated. She had no illusion as to where a nightcap might lead. 'Okay,' she said.

The lift was waiting to carry them to the top floor. Sam stood while she unlocked the door to the apartment, then gathered her up in his arms and carried her into the bedroom. He laid her down and skilfully began to undress her. She didn't resist as his warm mouth closed on hers. And then it was back, the delicious sensation she had experienced when he had first kissed her. It spread through her till she felt as if her whole body was on fire.

'You're beautiful,' he whispered. 'You're the most beautiful woman I've ever known.'

She closed her eyes and let the tide of pleasure engulf her. His mouth travelled down to her neck, her breasts and her thighs till at last he entered her. Sandy surrendered herself to the waves of passion that were washing over her. Her fingers clutched his shoulders and she felt herself give a little jolt as an involuntary cry escaped her.

CHAPTER 8

The morning sun filtering through the bedroom curtains woke her. When she glanced at her watch she saw it was a quarter past ten. The space beside her in the bed was empty. Sam had gone. He had left the rose in a vase on the night table beside a note. Sandy wiped the sleep from her eyes and tried to read it.

> I have an early-morning appointment so I'm leaving you to enjoy your beauty sleep. Thank you for a wonderful night. I will never forget it. Will give you a call later.

His scribbled signature was followed by a row of kisses.

It was a lovely note but it hardly compensated for his absence. Already she was missing him. She put it back on the table and let her mind travel over the events of the night that had just passed and the delicious lovemaking before she had fallen asleep in Sam's arms. It had been wonderful, something she, too, would not forget.

She lay for a few minutes gazing at the ceiling and thinking of how quickly the wheel of fortune had turned. She had spent the last few months alone in her solitary bed and now she had a companion. But not just any companion. She had the magnificent Sam Ross, man-about-town, elegant, witty, handsome and passionate, a man that many women would kill for.

She snapped out of her reverie and threw back the sheets. She had things to do. She was late for work, very late. She never slept till this time, except at weekends when she indulged herself. Patsy was going to be *convinced* that something was going on.

She stood under a hot shower for five minutes, then wrapped herself in her dressing gown and went into the kitchen. She rinsed the wine glasses from last night while she waited for the kettle to boil, then made herself a strong cup of coffee.

She had converted one of the bedrooms into a study with a desk, filing system, phones and a computer so she could work from home if she wanted to and keep in touch with events at the office. She went in now and rang her deputy. She was feeling wide awake.

'*Another* late night?' Patsy said, in a smug tone.

Sandy pictured her colleague's face as she took the call. She would be standing in the newsroom, grinning like a Cheshire cat. There had been the bantering conversation the other morning and Sandy's sudden departure from the office yesterday afternoon. Patsy was no fool. She had undoubtedly joined the dots by now and guessed that Sandy was involved in an affair of the heart.

'I ran into some people in town and slept later than I intended. It could happen to a mother superior.'

'I'm not sure about that. Convents have strict curfews. I don't think they allow the holy sisters to go carousing till the wee small hours.'

'Who said anything about carousing?'

'What else could have kept you in bed till ten o'clock in the morning?'

'No comment.' Sandy laughed. 'Now, enough about me. How are things? Is everything under control?'

Patsy became businesslike. 'Of course. Everything's humming along nicely. We've got a big story about Lee McCoy splitting with his wife. Apparently he's been dallying with one of the backing singers in his band.'

McCoy was a huge star with a massive following.

'Make sure you have it well nailed down. He has a team of lawyers who would take us to the cleaners if we messed up.'

'We already have. He's not denying it. His PR company has promised a statement in an hour's time.'

'Well done. Anybody talked to the girl?'

'She's gone to ground.'

'Keep trying. Sometimes they're so pleased with themselves that they can't keep their mouths shut. Anything else I need to know?'

'I don't think so.'

'Okay, I'm on my way in. I'll be with you shortly.'

She arrived into work at eleven and spent the rest of the morning dealing with the Lee McCoy story. Shortly after one, the phone rang and she heard Sam's voice.

'I'm sorry I didn't call earlier. I've just got out of that damned meeting. People wouldn't stop talking.'

'You don't have to apologise. I know what it's like.'

'Anyway, how are you?'

'I slept a bit longer than usual but I'm feeling fine.'

He lowered his voice. 'That was some night, Sandy.'

'Yes, it was.'

'I can't wait to see you again. How about tonight? I can get tickets to the theatre.'

'Um, I think I may be able to fit that in.'

'Anything you particularly want to see?'

'I'll leave that up to you. Surprise me.'

'Okay. I'll be in touch later with the details.'

'See you.' She cancelled the call and stared off into space. Sam Ross was certainly keen. And she was too. She was longing to see him again.

Just then Stella put her head around the door to say that an urgent call was waiting for her and she got to work.

At two o'clock, a delivery boy arrived with an enormous bouquet of flowers for her and a note from Sam. Everyone in the office stood and stared. Her eyes sought out Patsy, who was grinning. Now the secret was out. Everyone in the office knew that Sandy was involved in a romance. But she didn't care.

That evening, Sam took her to a musical in the Gaiety and afterwards for a romantic supper. Then it was back to Sandy's apartment and another night of passion. After that, they saw each other almost every evening and at weekends. Their free time became a whirlwind tour of restaurants, theatres, concerts. Sandy had never experienced anything like it or felt so happy. And when they weren't out on the town, they were in each other's arms in her bed or at his house in Sandymount.

They had become an item. It was a new feeling, something she hadn't experienced with any other man. Each time they met, Sam was more handsome, more charming, his conversation more interesting, his manners more perfect, his love-making more charged with electricity. She found herself thinking about him all the time, barely able to wait until they could be together once more.

And what made it even better was the knowledge that he felt the same way about her. She could tell by the way he looked at her, the little endearments he whispered in her ear, the presents he bought her, the way he made love to her, the text messages he sent her every day.

She went with him to see Platform Two perform at Whelan's. They were a standard four-piece band who played their own material, some of it quite good. The band members were young and personable, and the audience seemed to like what they played, but Sandy wasn't convinced, and she told Sam so when they went for supper afterwards.

'What's not to like about them?' he asked. 'They sounded good to me.'

'They need to do more work on their material and presentation. The way they are now, I don't think they've got what it takes for stardom.'

'I'm sorry to hear that.'

'It's only my opinion, Sam, but you asked for it. I could be entirely wrong but I didn't see or hear anything tonight that made me sit on the edge of my seat.'

'I accept that they're young and need more experience. That's where my investment would come in. It would allow them time and space to perfect their act and develop their material.'

'Have they got a manager?'

'A man called Tommy Wright.'

Sandy had never heard of him, which was not a good sign. She knew most of the top managers and agents in the music business. 'If you want my honest opinion, I'd have to tell you not to put your money on them. You might not see it again.'

Sam looked disappointed. He lowered his head. 'How would you feel if I disregarded your advice?'

'I wouldn't feel anything. It's your money. If you went out tomorrow and put it all on a racehorse, I'd wish you luck.'

'I'll do a little more research before I make up my mind,' he said.

'Good idea.'

●

Two weeks later, Sam told her he had to go to London for ten days on business but would stay in touch. He kept his word and rang every day, usually in the morning before he began his round of meetings.

In a strange way, she welcomed the break. So far, their romance had been conducted at a speed that had barely allowed her time to draw breath. Now she had an opportunity to stand back and take stock. But as the days slipped by, she realised she missed him desperately and longed for his return.

At odd moments, his face would flash into her mind or some chance remark would trigger a memory of an evening spent with him. And at night, when she crawled into bed after an exhausting day at Music Inc, she would feel lonely, the bed cold and empty, and she would long for him to be beside her, holding her tight.

She wondered if this was it, if Sam Ross was the dream man she had been waiting for all her life. He certainly fulfilled all her requirements. He was good-looking, thoughtful, kind and considerate, and he was a superb lover. Just the touch of his fingers on her bare skin sent shivers of pleasure along her spine. Also, he seemed to have learned his lesson from the incident over the delayed phone call. And every time he saw her, his eyes lit up with pleasure. Unless Sam was a superb actor, he was clearly devoted to her.

Something was definitely happening to her. Some powerful force had come out of nowhere and scattered her senses. She wondered if it was love. But while this exciting new experience thrilled her, it also made her nervous. Sandy was no moonstruck teenager. She was a mature woman of thirty-two.

Besides, she had not spent her entire working life in the entertainment industry without becoming cynical. She had witnessed at first hand the fragile nature of relationships, the way emotions could be manipulated and abused, people tossed aside on a whim. She didn't want that to happen to her.

She knew that love was a serious matter. She knew it made people do crazy things. She knew it could be dangerous and instinct told her to be careful. How well did she really know Sam Ross? What secrets were lurking in his past? She stared into space as the doubts grew. A warning voice told her not to get in too deep in case she got hurt.

CHAPTER 9

While her days were taken up with Music Inc. Sandy continued to keep an eye on her mother. She rang her every morning and visited several times a week. The visits and phone calls were like a lucky dip. She never knew what to expect.

There were times when her mother was sharp and alert. She would talk excitedly about some book that had caught her imagination or some piece of news she had heard on the radio. This might continue for a while and then she would sink into depression again. Sandy would find the house untidy and dishes piled in the sink. Once she had left the cooker on and Sandy had had to sit down and give her a lecture about the dangers of setting fire to the kitchen.

At other times, her mother would become maudlin, reminiscing about the happy days before her husband died and repeating how much she missed him now that he was gone.

'Your father was a saint, Sandy. There's no other way to describe him. You and I owe everything to that man. The things he did for us, you don't know half of it. He was the best husband any woman could wish for. He didn't drink. He didn't gamble like poor Mrs O'Leary's husband, who was forever losing his wages on the horses, leaving his family without a crust of bread and only the Vincent de Paul to feed and clothe them.

'And he was faithful. He never looked at another woman, unlike some I could mention. You and I were the only people who mattered to him. I was a lucky woman the day Tom Devine crossed my path. And so were you.'

Sandy didn't need to be told. She vividly remembered her father's kindness and gentle nature, and missed him probably as much as her mother did. But she disliked her mother talking about the past and tried to steer the conversation to more cheerful subjects.

She began to wonder if there might be something seriously wrong with her mother, something terrible like Alzheimer's disease. Angela was only fifty-two but she was displaying all the signs. Whenever these thoughts occurred, Sandy tried to put them from her mind but they continued to worry her. The person who seemed to have most influence on Angela was Aunt Betty. Whenever Mother had talked to her, she made an effort afterwards to pull herself together. She tidied the house, dressed herself properly and ate more regularly. But she adamantly refused Sandy's request that she see a doctor. Sandy felt it was only a matter of time before she and Betty would have to intervene again.

One morning, as they were drinking tea in the conservatory, Sandy let her eye drift over the garden. It was rapidly getting out of control. Weeds were sprouting in the flowerbeds and the lawns were overgrown. 'We need to tackle the garden,' she said.

'I've been meaning to do it,' her mother replied. 'I just can't summon up the energy.'

Sandy had an idea. 'I'll tell you what. I've checked the weather forecast. It's going to be dry this weekend. I'll call Betty and we'll both come on Saturday. Between the three of us, we'll lick it into shape. If we don't take action soon, it will be a lost cause.'

Her mother's face brightened at once. 'What a wonderful suggestion. I'd enjoy that.'

'Okay,' Sandy said, preparing to leave. 'Saturday at ten, we'll be here. Be ready.'

She rang her aunt, who agreed at once, and Sandy made her way back to the office with hope in her heart.

❋

For once, the weather forecast was accurate. When Sandy rose at eight o'clock on Saturday morning, the sky was clear and the sun was out. A light breeze was blowing and it was a perfect day for gardening. After breakfast, she pulled on an old pair of jeans and shirt, put her wellington boots and a pair of gloves in the car boot and set off for Rathmines.

She arrived soon after nine but when her mother opened the door, Sandy got a surprise. 'What are you doing here?' Angela asked.

Sandy's heart sank. 'Don't tell me you've forgotten.'

'Forgotten what?'

'We agreed we were going to clear up the garden today.'

'Oh,' her mother said, clamping her hand to her face. 'I thought that was next week.'

'No, it's today. You wrote it on your calendar. Look.'

She picked up the calendar from the table and pointed to the date clearly ringed with a red pen.

'I don't know how that happened,' Angela said. 'I usually remember these things.' She went to the window and looked out over the lawn. The grass was at least two inches high and the weeds were luxuriating in the morning sun. The hedge was running amok. 'I suppose you're right,' she said.

'I *am* right. If we don't do something now, you'll have to get professional gardeners in and that will cost a pretty penny.' Sandy looked her mother up and down. Today, she was neat and tidy. She had put on a new dress and her hair had been brushed. At least she's taking an interest in her appearance, Sandy thought, but she was dismayed that her mother had forgotten their arrangement. 'Have you had breakfast?' she asked.

'I had muesli with a banana chopped in it and then I had bacon and eggs and toast.'

'So your appetite's okay?'

'Oh, yes, thank God.'

Angela went off to the kitchen to make tea, which gave Sandy a chance to inspect the house. It seemed presentable. There was no sign of dust, the windows looked as if they had recently been washed and the floors had been swept. She paused for a moment to examine the photo of her father, in its recently polished frame, that sat on the hall table. It had been taken shortly after he and Angela were married. He was handsome with his bright red hair, neat suit and tie, smiling proudly for the camera. She thought again of the mystery surrounding her own dark colouring but this wasn't the time to raise it.

As she was returning to the kitchen, the bell sounded and when she opened the door, her aunt was on the step. Sandy quickly drew her aside. 'Would you believe she'd forgotten we were coming?' she said. 'She thought it was next week. Yet it was clearly marked on her calendar.'

Betty rolled her eyes. 'Maybe it was just a blip.'

'I hope you're right,' Sandy said. 'But it gave me a scare.'

'Don't upset yourself. Anybody can forget things.'

❖

After they had finished their tea, they all trooped out to the garden. The hardest job was going to be cutting the grass so Sandy volunteered to do that. She dragged the lawnmower from the shed and saw that it had become rusty from lack of use. Thankfully, there was a can of oil on a shelf so she sprayed some onto the blades and the axle. After a few attempts she managed to get the blades moving. Meanwhile, her mother and Betty had got out the trowels and clippers and were clearing the weeds and trimming the hedge.

It was backbreaking work. Despite the breeze, Sandy could feel the sweat pouring down her neck. It ran off her forehead, too, and stung her eyes. She had to stop occasionally to wipe her face and catch her breath. But she persevered till at last the lawn was respectable again.

While she was at her task, her mother and Betty had made considerable progress with the weeds and the hedge. Sandy took a short rest, drank a glass of orange juice and rejoined them. It was almost six o'clock when they finished and there were three large bags filled with garden waste.

Sandy noticed that her mother's face was flushed from the exertion but otherwise she looked fine. In fact, she seemed to have enjoyed herself. The exercise should do her good, she thought, and will certainly help her to sleep tonight. Perhaps Betty was right and her memory lapse had been a blip.

They put the gardening tools away in the shed and returned to the house. Sandy went off to make more tea while her mother rested in the conservatory with Betty. She found an apple tart in a cupboard, cut it into slices and brought it in on a tray with the tea things.

'Doesn't it look well?' Angela said, gazing out of the window across the lawn. Already, a flock of birds had descended and were busily pecking at the grass.

'I've been thinking,' Sandy said. 'If the garden is too much for you, perhaps you should get a gardener to drop by once a week and keep it in order.'

Her mother scowled. 'No gardener would do as good a job as me.'

'Just the hard bits, like trimming the lawn. I don't mind paying for it.'

'I'm well able to look after the garden myself, thank you very much. I enjoy gardening. Isn't it one of my hobbies, for God's sake? If it wasn't for that little setback I suffered recently that drained my energy, the garden would have looked as good as ever.'

Sandy exchanged a glance with her aunt, who shrugged. 'Suit yourself,' she said. 'But you'll have to do a little every day. If you don't, the work will just pile up.'

Betty left to prepare supper for her husband, Henry, and Sandy stayed on a while longer to make sure her mother was comfortable and settled for the evening. At eight o'clock she left her mother watching a soap opera on television, and made her way back to her apartment.

She got out of her gardening clothes, poured a glass of wine and heated a microwave meal, then sat at the window watching the dusk creep over the city. She felt tired and her joints were aching from pushing the lawnmower all afternoon. And the visit to her mother had worried her. How had Angela forgotten their arrangement to do the gardening? The forgetfulness, the tiredness, the mood swings – they all formed a disturbing pattern. Was something seriously wrong with her? If not Alzheimer's, might she have a brain tumour? Sandy made a decision. Despite her mother's objections, she must persuade her to visit her GP. She sighed. Looking after Angela was taking its toll. Sometimes Sandy wished she had siblings to share the burden.

CHAPTER 10

When she was very young, some of her little friends had envied Sandy because she was an only child. It seemed to mark her out as special. Adults were forever fawning over her, buying her things and telling her how pretty she was. She had a whole bed to herself, which some of her friends viewed as a luxury. She always wore the nicest clothes and got the best presents at Christmas and birthdays. But that was not necessarily how Sandy saw it.

She was about three when she realised her situation was different from that of most other children. She saw pictures of families on television: a mother, father and heaps of children, five, six or more. And she came across it, too, in the storybooks her parents bought her and some of the nursery rhymes she was learning, like 'The Old Woman Who Lived in a Shoe'. But it wasn't till she started going to school that the full implications began to dawn on her. Everyone seemed to have brothers and sisters. Indeed, there were two sets of twins in the school, one of them, the O'Toole sisters, in her class. Then there were her cousins, Aunt Betty's family. There were four of them, and any time they visited, the house seemed to be in a state of happy turmoil, everyone squabbling and teasing and playing jokes on each other.

A family who lived across the road, the Guineys, had five children, and another, in the next street, had six. Sandy began to realise that big families were not unusual. In fact, they were the norm. She felt like the odd girl out.

She would listen as her friends told stories about what went on in their homes, how it was some brother's birthday or a sister was making her First Communion or their mother had just had a new baby and they had to help her take care of it. To Sandy, it all seemed terribly exciting. There was never a dull moment in those households, always something going on. Now, instead of her friends envying her, she wished she could be like them. In comparison to her cousins and schoolmates, her life seemed very ordinary. There was a settled routine in the Devine household and very little changed from day to day. The family would have breakfast each morning at eight and then her father would leave for work.

After he was gone, her mother would drop Sandy at school and travel on to her own teaching job. She would pick Sandy up again at finishing time. They would go back to their house and her mother would make dinner while Sandy did her homework. Her father would come home from work and they'd sit around the big table in the kitchen, eat and talk about the business of the day. Then he'd read the paper or listen to the radio while her mother knitted or marked essays from school. Sandy would finish her homework, then play with her dolls or read till it was time to get washed and go to bed. It was a placid, peaceful existence where nothing dramatic ever occurred. But it lacked what Sandy craved: excitement.

Only at the weekends did the routine vary. How Sandy looked forward to them. On Saturday afternoons, her mother would take her into Dublin city to go shopping and they would visit all the big stores and make a trip to Moore Street to pick up meat from the butcher, then fruit and vegetables. When they had everything they needed, her mother would round off the journey with a visit to the Regal tea rooms in O'Connell Street to have tea and scones.

Sunday was even better. Her father was a fit man and liked to go walking. He would take her to the Phoenix Park or on the bus out to Howth or Bray, and while they strolled along the seafront, he would entertain her with stories about his own childhood. They would eat ice-cream cones, and when she got tired, he would take her into a café and buy her lemonade before they went home to the lovely Sunday dinner her mother had waiting for them.

As she got older, Sandy felt increasingly lonely. Her parents often talked about subjects she didn't understand. And sometimes they even spoke in whispers so she couldn't hear, which made her feel excluded. She began to daydream about having a little brother or sister. How happy that would make her. She even dressed up one of her dolls, fed it, washed it and talked to it as if it was a real, live baby.

One day she plucked up the courage to ask her mother if she could have a little brother or sister. Her mother stared at her for a long time. Sandy thought she looked sad. Then she sat her on her knee and smiled into her face. 'Why?'

'I would have someone to play with.'

'But you have lovely toys and dolls and picture books to entertain you.'

'It's not the same. They can't talk to me.'

'Are you lonely? Is that what's bothering you?'

Sandy hung her head. 'Sometimes I am. Everybody else has brothers and sisters and they have great fun together. I'd like one too.'

'Well, it's not that simple,' her mother said. 'Do you know where babies come from?'

'God sends them.'

'That's right. You can't just go out and get a baby, like you can buy a loaf of bread. You have to wait. Sometimes God only sends one. Like you. And that makes you precious.'

'What does that mean?'

Her mother hugged her closer. 'It means you're special. It means your father and I pour all our love onto you. We can afford to buy you pretty dresses and take you on nice trips and holidays. You can have nice food for your dinner. In some of those big families there isn't enough money for everyone and they have to do without.'

'I'd still like a baby brother or sister. I don't mind sharing with them.'

Her mother took out her handkerchief and blew her nose. Sandy thought she was going to cry.

'I'll tell you what we'll do. Maybe if you pray hard, God will change his mind and send another. Why don't we do that?'

'All right,' Sandy agreed. 'I'll pray every day.'

So every morning and evening, when she said her prayers, Sandy asked God to send them another baby. While it was nice to be special, she thought it would be much better if she had a little brother or sister to play with. But God didn't seem to be listening. The days and weeks went past and no baby came. In the end, she gave up and accepted her lot. For whatever reason, God had decided she was going to be an only child.

However, it wasn't all bad. Apart from the things her mother had mentioned, she had her own bedroom, her own dressing table and a lovely white bookshelf for storing her books. Her parents doted on her and lavished love and attention on her, although they were careful not to spoil her.

They made sure she got plenty of good presents, useful things that she would enjoy – a bicycle when she was seven, a transistor radio when she was eight, a CD player when she was twelve. And on her fourteenth birthday, she got something that none of her friends had – her very own computer.

By now, she had transferred to secondary school and had learned exactly how babies arrived from a girl whose older sister had one and wasn't even married. Now that Sandy had been made aware of the facts of life, she saw her situation in a different light. She figured out that, for some strange reason, her parents hadn't been able to have any more children. It made her sad to think of the times she had badgered her poor mother for a new baby when she was probably trying hard and not succeeding.

Sandy was too embarrassed to raise the subject so it wasn't discussed again. She got on with her life. But being an only child was already shaping her personality in ways she didn't even recognise. For one thing, it made her extremely independent. As a result, her schoolmates looked up to her. Sandy gained a reputation as a girl who thought for herself and spoke her mind. She was clever but didn't make a show of it. She was good at sports and was made captain of the hockey team.

As she got older, other character traits emerged. She was intensely loyal and expected loyalty in return. She was very

determined and not easily deflected once she had set her mind
to a task. As a result, she was popular. Everyone wanted to get
close to her. People said that if Sandy was your friend, you had
a friend for life. No one was surprised when she was made a
prefect in her final year.

In time, she left school, went to university and then into
journalism. By now, she was fully immersed in the music world
and had all the excitement she could handle. Being an only child
had been lonely but there were worse things.

CHAPTER 11

Eventually Sam returned from his trip to London. She got a phone call one morning at work to say that he had just stepped off the plane at Dublin airport and couldn't wait to see her. Her heart leaped. She took the afternoon off, left Patsy in charge of the office and drove to his house in Sandymount to see him.

Sam's home was nothing like the dog kennel he had jokingly described it as. It was a fine period house, decorated in a smart, modern style, overlooking Dublin Bay. It had three large bedrooms, a big sitting room, kitchen and two bathrooms. There was a small garden at the front and a larger one at the rear, with fruit trees. It was a home that many people would covet.

He answered the door, stood for a moment with a look of delight on his face, then wrapped her in his arms and covered her with kisses. Sandy tingled with delight as she clung to him.

'You don't know how much I missed you,' he whispered.

This was music to Sandy's ears.

'I thought about you all the time. I was like a man in prison waiting for my release day to come round. Just thinking of you kept me going through all those boring meetings. I kept telling myself it was just a few more days and then I'd be back in Dublin and Sandy would be waiting.'

She clung closer to him. 'I missed you too, Sam.'

'Then why are we standing here? Come in.' He picked her up and carried her upstairs to his bedroom, then laid her on the big double bed and frantically began to undress her. She offered no resistance. Next moment, his lips were exploring her mouth, neck and breasts. She shivered as his fingers traced a line along her spine and down along her thighs.

Later, she lay back against the pillows and heaved a sigh of contentment. 'I'd almost forgotten how good it can be.'

'I hadn't. I fell asleep each night with a picture of you imprinted on my mind. And it was there in the morning when I woke up. Sometimes in the middle of a meeting, as some fund manager tried to sell me an investment, my thoughts would wander off and it was you I'd be thinking about.'

She cuddled closer. She felt safe and secure in his arms. This was how she wanted to spend the rest of her life. 'How did the trip go?' she asked.

'Very well. I've unearthed some interesting investment opportunities and made some new contacts. All in all, it was a success.'

He didn't mention Platform Two and neither did she. He already knew her opinion about them. She let her eyes roam around the magnificent bedroom. 'This is a beautiful house, Sam.'

'I like it. I feel comfortable here.'

'How did you come by it?'

'It was our family home. My parents left it to me when they died. Mind you, I had to spend some money upgrading it and having it decorated.'

'Tell me about your parents.'

'My father was a partner in an investment bank. He was very successful and made a lot of money. I probably inherited my talent for investing from him. But he wasn't a very warm man, not the sort to take me on his knee and read me bedtime stories. He was too busy working. When I grew up and we might have had things to talk about, he got a liver infection and died. It affected my mother very badly. Within eighteen months, she was dead too.'

'Something similar happened to my mother after my father's death. She still hasn't recovered although, thankfully, she's alive. What was your mother like?'

'She was very refined, very genteel. She wasn't exactly a hands-on mother. We had a nanny to look after us. But she loved us, Sandy, and that's what matters.'

'What about the rest of your family?'

'I have one sister who lives in Scotland. She's married to a hospital consultant and they have three children. So I do have some nieces and nephews.'

'Do you have much contact with your sister?'

'Not really. We were never very close. We were both packed off to boarding schools and only saw each other during the holidays. We exchange cards at Christmas and that's about the height of it.'

'That's a pity.'

'Well, there you are. That's life, I suppose.'

She snuggled up to his firm, lithe body. 'You're very handsome,' she said, brushing a lock of hair from his face. 'I don't usually say that to men because some of them can get quite conceited. But you're the handsomest man I've ever known.'

He laughed. 'You're embarrassing me.'

'I mean it. Please don't go away again, Sam.'

'I have to. It's how I earn my living. But perhaps the next time I might take you with me, if you can tear yourself away from Music Inc for a few days. In fact . . .' He leaned on his elbow and stared into her face as a thought occurred to him. 'How would you like to come away with me for a holiday?'

She sat up straight. 'How do you mean?'

'I have a friend who's got an apartment in Marbella. He hardly ever uses it so he lets me have it any time I like. We could nip down there for a week or so. It's only a couple of hours on the plane. What about it, Sandy? You've been working very hard. You could do with a break.'

The invitation was so unexpected that it took her by surprise. 'But who would look after the office?'

'Patsy, of course. I've been telling you to delegate more to her. I'm sure she'd be happy to do it.'

Sandy thought of her mother. Was she stable enough to leave on her own? Meanwhile, Sam was continuing to talk excitedly. By now, he sounded completely carried away by the idea. 'You'd love it down there. The sun shines all day long. There are beautiful beaches and loads of lovely restaurants and department stores if you ever feel the need to go shopping. And we'd be away from it all, just you and me, alone together. You could check in with Patsy every morning. Then you'd have the rest of the day to relax. You owe it to yourself, Sandy. You have to slow down. You never stop working. It's a no-brainer.'

Sam had painted such an idyllic picture that she was won over. 'When would we go?'

'As soon as possible. I have no engagements for the next couple of weeks. All I have to do is arrange with my friend to get the keys.'

'Okay. Give me a couple of days to sort things.'

❋

Sandy had never taken a holiday since she'd started Music Inc all those years before, at least not a proper holiday. She had gone off for occasional weekend trips to music festivals and concerts, and once she'd spent three days at a media conference in Glasgow, but she regarded all of those as work. What Sam was suggesting was something entirely different – a break in an exotic location with the man she cared about. He was right. She'd be mad not to go.

She knew there would be no problem with Patsy. She would jump at the opportunity to be in charge of the office. She knew the job inside out. Sandy could go off to Spain in the knowledge that Music Inc was safe in Patsy's capable hands. But what about her mother?

What if she had another muddled spell and left a plug in the sink and flooded the bathroom? Or if she took a dizzy turn and lay on the bedroom floor for days unable to get up? Sandy knew she would never forgive herself if something like that happened while she was off enjoying herself in Marbella. She decided to seek Aunt Betty's advice.

The following morning she rang her. 'I've got a favour to ask,' she began. 'I'm thinking of taking a short break on the Costa del Sol.'

'About time,' her aunt replied. 'I was beginning to wonder if you'd ever drag yourself away from that business of yours.'

'But I'm worried about leaving Mum on her own.'

'Sure I can keep an eye on her. I'll drop over to Rathmines every day and make sure she's all right. Anyway, she's been very good recently. In fact, she's behaving just like her old self again.'

'So you don't mind?'

'Not in the least. She's my sister, for God's sake. It's no big deal. How long will you be gone?'

'I'm not sure yet, probably a week. I'm going with my boyfriend. He has a friend who's lending us an apartment.'

'Well, off you go and enjoy yourself. I wish I had a boyfriend like that.' Aunt Betty laughed. 'I'd be on the first plane out of here.'

'I'm very grateful. I really am.'

'Oh, get a grip on yourself,' her aunt replied. 'It's nothing.'

When she got into work, she took Patsy aside. 'I need to talk to you,' she said. 'But not here. We'll go for coffee as soon as we get the morning news conference out of the way.'

'Okay,' Patsy replied, her curiosity aroused.

At ten o'clock the two women left the office and walked to a nearby coffee shop. By now, Patsy's interest was at fever pitch. Sandy had taken yesterday afternoon off and come into work this morning with a grin all over her face. Now they were having this hush-hush chat. Patsy was convinced something big was afoot. She couldn't wait to hear her boss's news.

'I may be taking a short holiday.'

'Really? Where?'

'Marbella.'

'Lucky you. It'll be lovely down there at this time of year.'

'A friend has the loan of an apartment.'

'Indeed. Is this the same friend who sent you the flowers?'

Sandy smiled. 'How did you know?'

'Well, you don't need to be Sherlock Holmes to figure that

out. You've been behaving like a dizzy teenager recently. What's his name?'

'Sam Ross.'

'What's he look like?'

'He's a hunk, the handsomest man I've ever set eyes on.'

'My God, you sound like you've really caught the bug. Is this a serious romance?'

Sandy nodded.

'Any chance we can meet him?'

'I'll bring him into the office some day and introduce you. Now, the point is, I'm going to need you to run the place. I'll pay you extra, of course. But before I make a final decision, I want to know if it's okay with you.'

Patsy burst out laughing. 'Of course it is! I'd be only too delighted.'

'I'll keep in touch with you every day and you can call me if you need me.'

'Oh, c'mon, Sandy. You're the only person in the office who never takes a holiday. I'm really pleased for you. Go off to Marbella, relax and forget all about work. I'll only ring you if the building falls down.'

Sandy hugged her. 'You're a star, Patsy.'

'This Sam Ross, why don't I meet men like him?'

There was one thing left to do. She had to tell her mother. She drove over to Primrose Gardens after work and found her watering the plants in the front garden. Sandy gave a sigh of relief.

'This is an unexpected visit,' her mother said, peeling off her gardening gloves.

'I've got something to tell you.'

'Come in, come in. Let me make you a nice cup of tea and then we can talk.'

Sandy followed her into the house, which was neat and tidy. They went into the kitchen. It shone like a new pin. Everything was in order, no rings left burning on the cooker or plugs in the sink. 'You look very well,' she said. 'How are you feeling?'

'I'm on top of the world,' her mother replied. 'I slept for eight hours last night and I feel the way I used to, happy to be alive. I told you I'd get better without having doctors poking at me. It was just an infection I picked up somewhere but it's gone now.'

'I still think you should go and see Dr Hanley.'

'Whatever for? I'm fine.'

'It's no harm to have a full health check-up every now and then, Mum, even if you're feeling okay.'

'Waste of time and money. Now let's not argue about it. I'm in tip-top form.'

'I'm delighted to hear it.'

'Go and sit in the conservatory. I'll bring the tea in a minute.'

Sandy left the kitchen. She was thrilled that her mother seemed to be back to her old self again. A few minutes later, she reappeared carrying a tray with teapot, cups, saucers, plates and a large currant cake. She sat down and poured two cups of tea and handed Sandy a plate with a slice of cake. 'Now, what was it you wanted to tell me?'

'I'm thinking of taking a little break.'

'Where?'

'The Costa del Sol.'

'Which part?'

'Marbella.'

Her mother hesitated, her cup halfway to her mouth. 'When are you going?'

'Quite soon. A friend has an apartment he can borrow.'

Her mother looked surprised. 'You never told me you were seeing a man.'

'I've only known him a short while.'

'Is he reliable?'

Sandy laughed. 'I hope so.'

'And is this a serious relationship?'

Sandy smiled. 'It might be.'

'I'm very pleased for you,' her mother said, reaching out and squeezing her hand. 'I was beginning to worry that you'd never find a suitable man. You work too hard, Sandy. You should spend more time on yourself before you're too old.'

'Anyway, I wanted you to know that I'll be away for a while. But I'll still phone you every day. And Betty will drop over and keep you company.'

'Oh, don't be worrying about me,' her mother said. 'I'll be all right. Go off and have a good time with this young man. What's his name?'

'Sam Ross. He's an investor.'

'What's that when it's at home?'

'He makes money investing in stocks and shares and stuff like that.'

'So when am I going to meet him?'

'I'll bring him out some day.'

'I'll look forward to that. Now you just go off with him to Marbella. You'll like it, those beautiful beaches and the palm trees. And the weather will be lovely right now.'

'I didn't know you'd been there,' Sandy said.

Her mother looked at her for a moment, then shook her head. 'I haven't, but I've read all about it in books.'

Now that she was confident everything was under control, she rang Sam and told him she would go.

'That's fantastic. We'll fly the day after tomorrow. Leave the travel arrangements to me. I'll take care of them. You just start packing.'

'How long will we be gone?'

'A week? Ten days? It's entirely up to you.'

'Let's go for a week this time. We can always go again.'

'Okay. Do you want to go out for dinner tonight?'

'No, I think I'll take a rain check. We'll have plenty of time for cosy dinners when we get to Spain.'

'You can be sure of that,' Sam said.

She rang her aunt and Patsy and gave them the details. Already, she could feel the excitement starting to mount. She was looking forward to this holiday, confident she was going to have a wonderful time. She sat down at her desk and began calling up information about Marbella on her computer.

It was exactly as Sam had said. There were pictures of sun-kissed beaches, palm trees, a clear blue sea and bronzed young couples walking hand in hand along the promenade in the moonlight. When she checked the weather forecast she saw that it was twenty-five degrees and guaranteed to stay that way for the next fortnight.

Next, she turned her attention to what she would need to bring. Sun cream, of course, if she didn't want to burn, and shades to protect her eyes. A couple of books to read on the beach. A swimsuit. And enough clothes to last for seven days, including a change for the evenings when they would be dining out in the exciting restaurants Sam had mentioned.

This proved trickier than she'd imagined. She spent an hour rummaging through her cupboards selecting dresses and ended up with enough to fill two suitcases. She spent another half-hour trying to reduce the pile of clothes on her bed and gave up in frustration. She rang Sam again. 'I've got a problem. I'm trying to figure out how many items of clothing to bring.'

'As few as possible. During the day all you'll need is a couple of pairs of shorts, some tops and a pair of walking sandals. You can even go casual to the restaurants. It's very laid back down there. Nobody cares what you wear.' He laughed. 'So long as you can pay, of course.'

'I care.'

'Then throw in some dresses. But, for God's sake, don't bring too much or you'll regret it. We're only going for a week, remember.'

She returned to her task. But it was approaching midnight when she finally had her suitcase packed and fell exhausted into bed.

❋

The following day she was into work early. After the conference, she spent a couple of hours tidying up paperwork, checking accounts, sending out invoices and paying bills so that Patsy would have no distractions and could focus entirely on the news operation. At one o'clock, she took her deputy for a quick lunch while she briefed her on what to expect.

'Just make sure the stories are accurate. If you're uncertain, ring me. And if necessary refer to our lawyer, Jenny Bickerstaff. She'll put you right. You have her number?'

'Of course.'

'As from tomorrow, you'll be in charge. It's a big responsibility and I wouldn't ask you to do it if I didn't think you were up to it.'

'I know that, Sandy. And I'm grateful for your vote of confidence. Now don't be worrying. Just go off and enjoy yourself with this handsome hunk you've managed to bag. Has he any single friends?'

Sandy laughed. 'I'll ask him.'

The rest of the afternoon flew past in the usual flurry of phone calls from contacts and people seeking publicity. At eight o'clock, she left the office to meet Sam for a drink.

'It's all organised,' he said. 'The flight leaves at eleven o'clock in the morning and will get us into Málaga airport around three o'clock Spanish time. I'll pick you up at eight tomorrow morning. Be ready to roll. We don't want any last-minute panic.'

'I'll be ready.'

'How do you feel? Excited?'

'I can't wait.'

'Good,' he said. 'We're going to make sure this is an experience you won't forget.'

She went home. Her suitcase was packed and waiting by the door. The clothes she would wear for the journey were spread out on a chair for the morning. Sandy got into bed with a book she had been reading. At midnight, she listened to the news bulletin, then turned off the light. Ten minutes later, she was fast asleep.

She awoke the next morning at seven. When she drew back the curtains to let in the morning light, the city was grey, dark and blanketed in a heavy drizzle.

CHAPTER 12

It was a different scenario that greeted them when they touched
down at Málaga airport a few hours later. There was a tail wind
behind them, which meant the plane arrived early at half past
two. Once they had disembarked, they made their way quickly
through Immigration and Baggage Reclaim and out into the
arrivals hall. Sandy was delighted to see that the monitor beside
the information screen read twenty-four degrees. She couldn't
wait to get outside into the warm Spanish sun.

But first they had to hire a car. Sam walked purposefully to
a car-rental office, and fifteen minutes later they were dropping
their cases into the boot of a gleaming silver Lexus GS. Once
she was outside the terminal building, the first thing that struck
Sandy was the heat. The sun hung, like a ripe orange, in the
cloudless sky. The next thing she noticed was the profusion
of flowers in their tubs and pots, flaming geraniums, yellow

nasturtiums and a host of plants she had never seen before, all providing a riot of joyous colour.

Sam sat into the driving seat, put on his seatbelt and gunned the engine into life. A few minutes later, they were driving along the motorway heading for Marbella. Sandy gazed out of the window as the scenery flashed by. Down below, she could see the Mediterranean sparkling in the brilliant afternoon light, hotels and villas perched precariously on the parched brown hillsides. There were people relaxing on the beaches and yachts scudding on the horizon. Her excitement mounted. She turned to Sam. 'How long before we get to Marbella?'

'About twenty-five minutes.'

'You know where the apartment is?'

'Of course. I've been before.'

'What's it called?'

'Club Atlantic.'

'Is it near the beach?'

'Ten minutes away. It's also got its own pool and gardens, three bars and two restaurants. It's a self-contained community. It's got everything you could want, Sandy. Some people never leave it.'

'Not even to go shopping for groceries?'

He shook his head and smiled. 'A few live at Club Atlantic all the year round, retired people, widows. It's their home. If they need anything, they ring up the nearest supermarket and get their goods delivered.'

'It sounds idyllic.'

'It is, believe me.'

Soon they were off the motorway and entering the outskirts of the town. The traffic was more congested there and slowed their progress but eventually they saw a sign pointing to their destination. A few minutes later, Sam drew up outside a pair of stout iron gates, took out a zapper and, with a loud clanking noise, the gates slowly began to swing open. He drove the car inside and parked it. 'We've arrived,' he announced.

Sandy got out and looked around. The apartments were built in blocks, each with its own entrance and surrounded by gardens neatly planted with flowering shrubs and orange trees. In the centre there was a Moorish fountain, with water spouting from the mouths of three mermaids. Beyond an archway, she caught a glimpse of a swimming pool and heard the laughter of children playing. Her first impression was of elegance and exclusivity.

Meanwhile, Sam had hoisted the cases from the boot and locked the car. Together, they walked to the entrance of their block. He took out another bunch of keys, opened the door, and Sandy found herself in a cool hall with mirrors, a rack of post boxes and large vases holding an assortment of dried flowers. 'Where do we go now?'

'Follow me.' There was a lift at the end of the hall. He pressed a button and the doors slid silently open. They stepped inside and it began to ascend to the top floor. It came to a shuddering stop and they got out. A door was directly facing them. Sam used his keys to undo the locks and pushed it open.

Sandy entered and found herself in an enormous sitting room. The walls were painted white and hung with paintings. There was a marble floor, a beige settee along one wall, several comfortable chairs and some little tables. Outside the window, there was a large terrace. She unlocked the door and strode out. She caught her breath. The view was of the entire town, basking in the warm afternoon sun. The light sparked off the rooftops and spires and the sea appeared so close that she could almost reach out and touch it. When she turned her head, she could see the mountains and the little whitewashed houses clinging to their sides.

She stood for several minutes taking it all in, then turned to go back inside. She found Sam blocking her way. He was carrying a bottle of champagne and two glasses. He popped the cork and poured. Then he put his arm around her waist, drew her close and kissed her. 'Welcome to Marbella,' he said.

❖

Sandy wasted no time in exploring the remainder of the apartment. Like the sitting room, the main bedroom was painted white, and had an en-suite bathroom with fresh towels set out on a little table. There were two smaller bedrooms, another bathroom and a kitchen. Every room was decorated and furnished with exquisite taste.

'So, what do you think?' Sam grinned when she had completed her tour of inspection.

'I wasn't expecting anything as grand as this. Who is the generous friend who owns this place?'

'He's an insurance broker. He escapes to this apartment from time to time for some rest and relaxation. He works almost as hard as you, Sandy.'

She smiled at his little joke. 'It's magnificent.'

'Think you can stick it for a week?'

She laughed. 'I'll certainly give it my best shot.'

By now, she was anxious to unpack her cases and change into cooler clothes so she returned to the main bedroom and began hanging her dresses in the wardrobe. When she emerged fifteen minutes later, she was wearing a light linen dress and sandals.

'Where do you think you're going?' Sam enquired.

'Out to explore the town.'

'Calm down. Nobody walks around in this heat except the tourists. It's siesta time, Sandy. All the shops are closed and the natives are taking their afternoon naps. They won't emerge again till five o'clock. Are you hungry?'

'Not particularly. I had a snack on the plane, remember?'

'So why don't we just go and unwind by the pool till it's cooler? Then we can think about dinner.'

'That's an even better idea.'

She got changed again into a white swimsuit and packed a bag with sun cream, a towel and a book. Sam put on a pair of swimming trunks and a golf cap to protect his face, and they set off for the pool. A few people were sitting or lying on loungers. They waved in greeting. But the children she had heard earlier had gone.

There were two vacant loungers beside the pool. Sam took out a paperback thriller he had picked up at the airport and started to turn the pages. Sandy applied some sun cream, adjusted her shades and lay down. Twenty minutes later, feeling too hot, she moved her lounger into the shade.

A deliciously cool breeze rustled through the palm trees and bees hummed around the bushes and flowers. Apart from that, there was nothing to disturb the tranquillity. She opened her book and began to read, but after a few pages, her eyelids drooped. The book slipped from her hands and she fell asleep.

She woke with a start when Sam gently shook her shoulder. She looked around. The pool area was deserted. When she glanced at her watch, she saw it was ten to five. 'What happened?'

'You dozed off.'

'I never intended to.'

'You're here to relax. And travelling can be quite tiring even though you're sitting down most of the time. Now it's getting cooler perhaps you'd like to take that tour of the town you planned earlier.'

'Okay, but first I've got to do something.'

She went to the pool showers and washed off the sun cream. Then she made her way to the deep end and dived in. She swam twenty lengths, then got out.

'Feel awake now?' Sam grinned.

'Wide awake and I'm bursting with curiosity to see Marbella. Let's go.'

They returned to the apartment and she changed back into the dress she had worn earlier. Sam had put on a pair of Levi's and a golfing shirt. They locked up and set off.

The town was coming alive, as Sam had predicted. The shops were opening and people were strolling about or sitting at the pavement cafés, chatting and drinking coffee. From the dim little bars they passed, Sandy could hear laughter and chat. Sam led her down a maze of narrow streets, and after ten minutes, they arrived at the promenade.

The beaches were emptying but a few stragglers remained to capture the last rays of the sun. Now the air was much cooler and walking was a pleasure. They strolled past mime artists, and hawkers selling fake watches and bootleg CDs. From the restaurants and bars, they could smell delicious cooking aromas. After a while, Sandy could feel her appetite begin to stir. 'Can we stop somewhere and eat?' she asked. 'I'm starting to feel hungry.'

'Sure, let's find a place that suits.'

Five minutes later, they came upon a restaurant with a large menu displayed outside. They were shown to a table at the window where they could watch the parade of strollers along the promenade. When the waiter arrived, Sandy ordered grilled bass and salad but Sam threw caution to the wind and opted for a barbecued steak. They chose a bottle of house wine to accompany the meal.

'There's something we forgot to do,' he said, when the food arrived.

'What's that?'

'Get in provisions for breakfast, unless you want to eat at one of the bars on the complex.'

'I don't mind. But we should at least get some coffee and milk. I never feel right in the morning till I've got some caffeine inside me.'

'We'll pick up some stuff on the way back. We've got plenty of time. The supermarkets don't close till nine.'

After their meal Sam took her hand and they set off again. The scent of flowers was strong on the evening air and mingled with the salt smell of the sea. By now, the sun was sinking fast into the ocean and a yellow moon was taking its place. Sandy felt contentment settle over her. It was so romantic to be strolling hand in hand with her lover in the moonlight as the waves heaved and sighed on the shore. She laid her head on his shoulder.

'There's something I meant to tell you,' he said. 'When I was in London, I invested in Platform Two.'

She turned to look into his face. His words had broken the spell. He had disregarded her advice and she felt a little peeved. 'Really? You decided it was a good idea?'

'Of course. Otherwise I wouldn't have done it.'

'Do you mind if I ask how much?'

'Not at all. I've invested two hundred thousand euros.'

She was taken aback. 'That sounds like an awful lot of money for a struggling band.'

'But in return I'll get twenty per cent of their recording royalties and concert receipts.'

'If there are any,' she said drily.

'That's the gamble I must take. It's why the contract is so generous. On balance I decided it was a fair risk.'

'Well, it's your money. You can do with it what you like.'

'Precisely,' he said.

She was surprised at his recklessness. In Sandy's view the money was already lost. She had listened to the band and could see no future for them. They walked for a while in silence until he took her hand again. 'You seem upset at my decision.'

'I'm not,' she lied.

'Sandy, there's something you must understand. I don't tell you how to run your business. You shouldn't expect to tell me how to run mine.'

'But you asked my opinion. You brought me to a concert to listen to them.'

'And you said you'd give your opinion and afterwards I could make up my own mind. So I sought many people's advice. That's what I always do. But in the end, I decide for myself. You shouldn't take it personally.'

'You're right,' she conceded. 'It's just that I don't like to think of you losing your money.'

'You're jumping to conclusions. The money isn't lost. It will be used to tide them over while they polish up their act and write new material. Only then will we know whether the gamble has paid off.'

'I hope they succeed, Sam. I really do.'

Privately, she believed he might as well have put the money on a spin of the roulette wheel in the casino.

❀

It was after nine o'clock when they got back to the Atlantic complex after calling into a supermarket on the way and stocking up on breakfast provisions. They decided to drop in at one of the bars and have a nightcap. It was run by a plump English lady called Ivy. They chose a table outside and Ivy came hurrying to serve them. 'What will it be, ducks?'

'I'll have a brandy, large one,' Sam said.

Sandy ordered a glass of chilled white wine.

'I'll be back in two shakes of a lamb's tail,' Ivy replied, and retreated inside the bar.

Sandy looked at their surroundings. The gardens were hung with fairy lights that cast a warm glow on the grass. From the bushes, the sound of chirping cicadas carried to them on the warm night air. 'What's the plan for tomorrow?' she asked.

'Sandy, you're not working at Music Inc now. There is no plan. That's the whole idea. You're here to unwind.'

'What time do we get up?'

He laughed. 'Whenever we wake. Haven't you been on holiday before?'

She lowered her eyes. 'No.'

He was clearly amazed. 'You mean *never*? I don't believe it.'

'Not since I was a child.'

'Incredible. Why not?'

'I never found the time.'

He took her hand and looked into her eyes. 'But you found the time for me?'

'Yes,' she said. 'I found the time for you.'

He smiled and squeezed her hand. 'I suppose that must make me special.'

'Of course it does. Surely you must have realised that by now.'

Ivy was back with their drinks. They sat and chatted as the night grew darker and the moon hung suspended like a yellow lantern in the sky. Sandy felt the warm glow she had experienced earlier on the promenade creep over her again.

It was after midnight when they returned to the apartment and she was exhausted. It had been a long day. They got undressed and Sandy settled comfortably under the cool sheets while Sam slid in beside her. He put his arms around her, drew her close and kissed her. She snuggled into his embrace.

'It's so good to have you all to myself, Sam. This place is perfect.'

'I hoped you'd like it. And our holiday is only beginning. We've got six more days like today.'

They made love and, afterwards, lay in each other's arms. From the window, the light of the moon filtered into the room. Sandy felt so happy she wished it would never end.

CHAPTER 13

When she woke the following morning, it was seven o'clock and Sam was sleeping beside her. It was already light. She got quietly out of bed and slipped into her swimsuit, took a towel from the bathroom and put on a silk kaftan. Then she left the apartment and went down to the pool.

The sun was coming up and already the day felt warm. There was no one about as she made her way across the grass, still damp with morning dew. She plunged into the deep end and began to swim. At once she came vibrantly awake. Fifteen minutes later, she climbed out, towelled herself briskly and flung on the kaftan.

On her way back to the apartment, the smell of freshly brewing coffee drew her to Ivy's bar where she found half a dozen people seated outside, already having breakfast in the sun. The chubby owner smiled when she saw her. 'I didn't think you'd be open so early,' Sandy said.

'Oh, we open at seven o'clock, ducks. Some people prefer this part of the day and they have to be fed. How can I help you?'

'Do you have any croissants?'

'Of course, love. How many would you like?'

'Half a dozen to take away, please. And can I pay you later? I came out without any cash.'

'Of course you can.'

Ivy put six hot croissants into a bag and Sandy proceeded on her way. When she got back, Sam was still asleep and the apartment was silent. She popped into the bedroom to get dressed, then went into the kitchen and made a pot of coffee. Then she poured herself a cup, smeared two croissants with honey and went to eat them on the terrace.

This is so pleasant, she thought, as the sun warmed her face. She took out her phone and checked for texts. Among the plethora of messages, she found one from Patsy sent yesterday evening hoping she'd had a good journey and had arrived safely. She decided to wait till nine o'clock Irish time before contacting her to make sure that everything was okay at Music Inc.

She was just finishing her coffee when Sam wandered out to join her. 'You're an early riser,' he joked. 'What time did you get up?'

'Seven. You were still in the Land of Nod so I decided not to disturb you. I've already had a swim and been to Ivy's for croissants. There are some in the kitchen for you, along with a pot of coffee.'

'Let me take a shower first.'

He returned fifteen minutes later – now shaved and dressed in shorts and a T-shirt – carrying a mug of coffee and the croissants. He stood for a moment looking out from the terrace rail at the sun spreading its light over the town. 'What a glorious morning.' He turned to Sandy. 'I've been thinking. We've got a car. It would be a pity not to use it. We could take a spin along the coast this afternoon, see a bit of the scenery. That would leave the morning free for you to relax outside.'

'I can't argue with that.'

He took a bite of croissant. 'So it's sorted then.'

At ten o'clock Sandy rang her deputy and was pleased to learn that everything was ticking over nicely in the office. She listened while Patsy outlined the stories they were working on, then made a few suggestions and terminated the call. Next she called her mother and her aunt and chatted for a few minutes. They both sounded in good form and pleased to hear from her. Satisfied that there was nothing to concern her at home, she changed back into her swimsuit, packed a bag and they left to pay Ivy, then go to the pool.

When they reached the garden there were only a few people there, exactly like the day before. Sandy spread her towel on a lounger, applied some sun cream and started to read. Today she planned to spend half an hour in the sun before retreating to the shade. She didn't want to ruin the holiday by getting burned. Sam pulled out his thriller and began to turn the pages. 'Now let's see how the hero gets the girl off the railway track before the train runs over her,' he said.

❈

They spent a pleasant morning beside the pool, reading, swimming and relaxing on their loungers. It was one o'clock when Sam suggested they should think of retreating. 'Now what about a light lunch before we take the car out? We can grab something at Ivy's if you like. She does a range of Spanish tapas, nothing too heavy.'

'Okay, let's do that,' Sandy agreed.

At a quarter to two, suitably refreshed and fed, they climbed into the Lexus and set off. This time, Sam stuck to the coast road, heading in the direction of Gibraltar. He let the window down and the cool breeze ruffled Sandy's hair. The first stop was Puerto Banús, a short distance away. It had a reputation as a playground for the rich but Sam said it had been badly affected by the recession. 'A few years ago, properties around here were fetching enormous prices – three or four million euros wasn't unusual. Now the same villas are changing hands for a fraction of that. There are a lot of sorry punters.'

They were strolling along the marina, jammed with expensive yachts, their decks polished and gleaming in the sun. Sandy got out her phone and took some photos. Occasionally she stopped to look in the windows of the chic designer stores at the glamorous dresses and jewellery on display or to read the menus at some of the up-market restaurants. When they came to the end of the promenade, they went into a bar and ordered coffee. It was packed with tourists laughing and shouting as they sipped their wine or guzzled champagne.

Then they were on their way again. All along the road, they could see developments of expensive houses and villas, stretching down to the water's edge. They stopped at San Pedro and strolled along the beach, crowded with people lying on their towels in the sun. It was almost seven o'clock when they arrived at Estepona and they were both hungry.

'I know a nice place to eat,' Sam said, locking the car and steering her away from the main street till they came to a restaurant called La Campesina. It was filling up, which Sandy took to be a sign that the food was good. They were quickly shown to a table and presented with menus.

'What is *lenguado*?' she asked, glancing up at Sam.

'Sole. I can recommend it. It's very good.'

'That's what I'm going to have.'

'I'll join you.'

They called the waiter and gave their order. Because Sam was driving, he contented himself with water while Sandy had a glass of white wine. When the food arrived, they were each presented with a large fish, grilled with garlic and accompanied by potatoes and broccoli. One forkful told Sandy that she had made the right choice. The sole was delicious and melted in her mouth.

When they had finished, Sam glanced at his watch and announced that it was almost nine o'clock. 'Time we were on the road.'

Outside it was dark and the street lights were on. It took half an hour to drive back to Marbella and Club Atlantic, where they sat on the terrace with glasses of wine while they listened to the insects chirping in the bushes. By eleven, Sandy's eyelids were getting heavy. Sam stood up, stretched his arms and yawned. 'I'm bushed. I think I'll turn in and have an early night.'

'Me too,' Sandy said. 'That was another lovely day,' she murmured, as he led her to their bedroom.

'Yes,' Sam replied. 'And there's more tomorrow.'

❁

They spent the rest of their holiday in a similar fashion. Sandy rang her mother a few times but decided to leave Patsy alone. She seemed to be on top of things and probably didn't welcome constant calls from her boss. Besides, Sandy reminded herself, she was here to relax and escape the pressure of work. Why bring it on holiday with her?

All too quickly, the time approached to return to Dublin. As the last day dawned, Sam suggested they visit Fuengirola, another tourist town that lay in the direction of Málaga. 'You'll find it a bit different from the resorts we've already seen along this part of the coast. It's much more Spanish and has a very attractive old town that I think you'll like.'

'Sounds fine,' Sandy agreed.

They set off at what had become their usual time, around two o'clock, after they'd had a lunch of tapas at Ivy's bar. The road, like the others they had travelled along, was dotted with apartment developments, hotels and restaurants. They passed Elviria, Calahonda and La Cala, then drove into the outskirts of Fuengirola. They left the Lexus in an underground car park and began to walk along the seafront towards a restored Moorish castle that had once guarded the entrance to the town. It was open to the public and a path led up to it. They decided to climb, despite the heat, as a cool breeze was blowing in from the sea. When they reached the castle, they were rewarded with a stunning view of the town and the coastline lying beneath them.

Sam took out his phone. 'Stay where you are. Don't move,' he commanded, as he fired off some shots of her posing beside the castle wall. He brought the phone to her and showed her the results: flattering photos of a tanned Sandy in a white dress, smiling for the camera, like some dark-haired Spanish beauty. 'Now I've got something to cheer me up when we're back in Dublin, staring out at the rain battering the window panes.' Sam grinned.

They started back towards the centre of the town. Sandy remembered she had planned to buy presents for her mother and aunt. She would get Patsy a bottle of perfume at the airport duty free shop. They came across a souvenir shop and she went inside, emerging some time later with two gift-wrapped packages. 'Let's go and get a drink. I'm parched,' she said.

Fifteen minutes later, they were in the old town that Sam had mentioned earlier. It was a collection of narrow little streets, with houses, small shops and restaurants. At the centre a square was dominated by a beautiful old church. There were palm trees and arrangements of the bright flowers that Sandy had already come to associate with this part of Spain.

The siesta was coming to an end and people were out strolling in the afternoon sun, whole families with children and grandmothers in black shawls. Groups of men sat on benches on the edge of the square, smoking and arguing animatedly. They found a café and sat outside, and soon the waiter came with their drinks.

Sandy let her eyes travel around the square. It was so restful here, so different from the hustle and bustle she was used to at home. She was beginning to regret that she hadn't agreed to stay longer. She turned to Sam. 'I love this place, I'll be sorry to leave.'

'We can stay longer if you like. I could book new plane tickets.'

'It wouldn't be fair to Patsy. I told her I'd only be gone for a week.'

He smiled. 'I knew you'd fall in love with Spain. We'll come again, Sandy.'

❋

That night, when they got back to the apartment, they packed their bags in preparation for the journey home. Their flight was at ten o'clock the following morning and they had to be at the airport in good time to return the car.

When the cases were ready, they went for a farewell drink at Ivy's. A melancholy mood had settled over Sandy. Their happy holiday was almost at an end.

'I'm going to miss this place when we get back to Dublin. I have so many good memories. Thanks for inviting me.'

'We'll come again soon,' Sam said, taking her hand. 'We can have the apartment anytime we want. All I have to do is ring my friend.'

The following morning their flight left on time and they were in Dublin at midday. Sam dropped her off at her apartment and promised to call later to take her for dinner. She opened the front door and gazed at her home. It was nothing compared with the beautiful apartment she had left behind in Spain.

She took out her phone and called Patsy to tell her she was back and would be in to the office shortly, then started to ring her mother but changed her mind. Instead, she would call and see her on her way into work. She unpacked her case and threw the dirty clothes into the laundry basket. Then she had a quick shower and got dressed in something more fitting for the Irish weather before setting off for Rathmines.

When she arrived, she found her mother in lively form. 'Back already?' she said, when she opened the door. 'It seems like only yesterday that you left. Did you have a good time?'

'Fantastic.'

They went to the conservatory.

'Let me make you a cup of tea.'

Sandy put out a hand to stop her. 'I haven't time to stay. I've got to go into work. I just called to see that you were okay.'

'Of course I am. Why don't you stop fussing over me, Sandy? There's nothing wrong with me. I'm as fit as a fiddle. Now tell me quickly about your holiday. I don't need to ask about the weather – you're a lovely colour.'

She told her mother about Club Atlantic, the trips they had taken and the places they'd seen. 'Here,' she said, riffling through her bag for the present she had bought. 'I got you something.'

'What is it?' Angela said, eyeing the package suspiciously.

'Just a little souvenir.'

Angela opened the package and withdrew a painting of a harbour with the boats at anchor and 'FUENGIROLA COSTA DEL SOL' written across the top. Immediately her face changed. She became agitated. 'Take it back,' she said, pushing the present away. 'I don't want it.'

'Why not?' Sandy was shocked by the force of her reaction.

'I've got enough knick-knacks around the house. They just clutter up the place. I don't need any more.'

CHAPTER 14

Sandy was fond of telling people that her business success was all down to her staff. There was some truth in this but it wasn't the whole story. She had worked tirelessly to grow the company. As a result, she had developed an excellent reputation among people in the entertainment industry and was highly respected, even by those who sometimes disagreed with her. They recognised her drive and stamina and admired the way she had taken the company from nowhere by hard work and determination.

While she had a tough, no-nonsense image, she also had a softer side. She went out of her way to give publicity to entertainers she felt needed a little push. And from time to time she had even been known to drop a good story because it threatened to ruin a struggling artist's career, something that was practically unheard of in an industry as cut-throat as hers.

But her staff had indeed played a significant part in the company's success. Ever since she had hired Patsy, Sandy had made a point of recruiting the best young reporters she could find and training them herself. Because they were a small operation, every staff member counted and there was no room for passengers. She worked her reporters hard and paid them well. Some went on to build successful careers in the mainstream media and always paid tribute to the grounding they had received at Music Inc.

She received regular enquiries about vacancies from aspiring young journalists keen to work for her. If they sounded promising, she would interview them and, if they impressed her and she had a job available, hire them. If not, she would file their details in a little book she kept in her desk and call them when a job became available.

Shortly after she returned from Spain she took a call from a reporter called Jack Rooney. He was not long out of college and had come to her attention early in his career. He was the showbiz writer on the *Gazette* and Sandy admired his snappy prose style and his nose for a good story. Now he said he had something important to talk about and suggested they have a drink at a quiet bar in Ringsend where they would be safe from the prying eyes of other reporters. Intrigued, she tried to find out more but he was reluctant to talk on the phone so she agreed to meet him.

In the bar she found him at a corner table, his dark hair falling across his face. She bought a beer and sat beside him. 'So what's it about?' she asked. 'You sounded like James Bond on the phone.'

He stared straight into her face. 'Are you hiring staff?'

'Why do you want to know?'

'I want to get out of the *Gazette*. I was wondering if you had any vacancies.'

As it happened, Sandy *was* thinking of boosting her writing team with another reporter. She wondered if he had been talking to someone at Music Inc, perhaps Patsy. 'Well, that depends. Tell me why you want to leave the *Gazette*.'

He gave a resigned shrug. 'My career is going nowhere. I work my butt off but I get no encouragement from my editor. There's never a word of praise. I'm just a cog in a wheel. I could come in with a story that Elvis Presley had been discovered driving a taxi in San Francisco and Pete Lavelle wouldn't even raise an eyebrow.'

She saw immediately what the problem was. Jack Rooney felt neglected and unloved. 'Have you mentioned this to Pete?'

'There's no point. I'd be wasting my time.'

'If you came to us, you'd still have to work pretty hard.'

'Work isn't the problem. I like what I do and I don't mind hard graft. But at least I'd be appreciated at Music Inc.'

'How much would you expect to be paid?'

'It's not about money. It's about working some place I enjoy. I'd be happy to take the going rate.'

'Okay,' Sandy said. 'Let me consider it and I'll get back to you.'

During the next few days, she turned the matter over in her mind. There was no doubt that Rooney would be an asset for Music Inc. She knew he was a hard worker with a record for digging up exclusive stories, and felt sure he would fit in smoothly with her present team. All he would require was a little care and attention.

But there was a problem. Jack's editor, Pete Lavelle, was one of Sandy's clients and regularly purchased stories from Music

Inc. She had known him all her career. She wondered how he would respond if she brought Jack Rooney on board.

A week later she rang Jack and offered him a job.

'I'm really grateful, Sandy.' He sounded delighted. 'You don't know what this means to me. I'm going to hand in my notice right away.'

'No,' she said quickly. 'Don't do that just yet. I'll get a contract drawn up. Read it carefully, and if you're happy with it, you can give notice.'

'I'll be happy, I know I will.'

'Just wait till you get the contract.'

He rang her after a few days to say he had received the contract and was happy with the terms. He had signed it and posted it back. 'I've also given notice. I've just told Lavelle.'

'How did he react?'

'Not too well.'

'Maybe he should have treated you better. Then he wouldn't have lost you.'

She didn't have long to wait before discovering the full extent of Pete Lavelle's wrath. A few minutes later, Patsy came into her office in a flap to tell her that a very irate Lavelle was on the line demanding to speak to her. 'Put him through.'

She picked up the phone. 'Hi, Pete,' she said.

'Don't try to soft-soap me, you snake. What the hell do you mean poaching my best writer? Jack Rooney has just told me he's leaving. Don't you have enough staff over there without stealing mine?'

'Stealing? What are you talking about? Do you think I kidnapped him? He came willingly.'

'You bribed him. Now I've got a hole in my entertainment

page and I've got to go out and find a replacement. And, as you well know, entertainment writers don't grow on trees.'

'People change jobs all the time, Pete. It's a fact of life. Anyway, he approached me first.'

'I thought you and I were friends.'

'We are.'

'Not any more we're not.'

'Calm down, Pete. It's not the end of the world. You'll easily find a replacement.'

But her words seemed to make him even angrier.

'Don't tell me to calm down. If you think I'm going to forget this, you've got another thing coming. Just wait. You'll be one sorry sucker before I'm finished.'

She heard a click and the phone went dead. She heaved a sigh. So Pete Lavelle was having a hissy fit. She'd put it out of her mind. He'd get over it in time.

❖

Sandy had come home from Spain reinvigorated and threw herself back into her job. Jack Rooney came to work at Music Inc and settled easily into the office routine. As she expected, he was an eager beaver who got on well with the rest of the staff. Soon he was using his contacts in the entertainment world to bring in important stories that boosted the company's profile, and Sandy was quick to show her appreciation of his worth.

It was a very happy time for her. Her romance with Sam was going from strength to strength. They saw each other practically every day and their evenings were spent in a round of parties, theatre visits, music events and intimate dinners at the interesting restaurants Sam had a knack of discovering. By now, there was no longer any doubt in her mind: she was madly in love with him.

She kept her promise and brought him to the office to meet the staff. He arrived with a large box of expensive chocolates and was at his charming best, making jokes and showering compliments like confetti. Within minutes, he had won everyone over. When he left, Patsy followed Sandy into her office and closed the door. 'What a gorgeous creature, what perfect manners, what charm and he's so good-looking. I didn't think God made men like that any more.'

'I'm glad you all liked him. But he's just a human being, like the rest of us, Patsy. He does have faults, you know.'

'I didn't see any. I hope you realise how lucky you are to have him.'

'He's lucky to have me too.'

'Well, make sure to hold onto him. Men like him are one in a hundred. When are you going to introduce me to his brother?'

'He doesn't have any brothers, I'm afraid. Only a sister.'

'Just my luck.' Patsy sighed. 'Does he have a cousin?'

'I'll ask him.' Sandy smiled. 'But don't hold your breath.'

She was delighted that the staff had reacted so positively to Sam but now she had another task to perform and hoped it would go as smoothly. She had to introduce him to her mother.

Angela had asked to meet Sam but Sandy had been put off taking him to see her because of her mother's ill health and erratic moods. Now that she appeared to have pulled herself together, Sandy decided the time was right. One evening when she was having a quiet drink with Sam after work, she raised the subject. 'You've heard me talk often enough about my mother.'

'Of course. How is she?'

'She seems to have got over her little setback, as she calls it, and is firmly back in her old routine.'

'That's good news.'

'I think it's time I introduced you to her.'

'That's even better news. I'd love to meet her. When?'

'As soon as I can arrange it.'

After giving the matter a lot of consideration, she decided to invite them both to lunch and to bring Aunt Betty along as well. The restaurant she chose was a nice middle-of-the-road place called The Skillet that served solid traditional food. It was in nearby Ranelagh. Her mother had been there before and liked it. Sandy arranged to pick her up, with Betty, and drive them there.

When she told her mother, she got all excited. 'I can't wait to see what he looks like. I suppose he must be handsome.'

'I'll let you be the judge of that.'

'Of course he is, Sandy. I know you too well. You wouldn't settle for anything less.'

The day finally arrived. The lunch was scheduled for one o'clock. Sandy left the office at midday and drove across to Rathmines where her mother and her aunt were waiting expectantly. She was pleased to see that her mother had got dressed up for the occasion and was wearing a smart jacket and skirt, with a white blouse. She had put on some makeup and had had her hair done specially for the occasion.

They settled into the car and set off. It was ten to one when they arrived at The Skillet and were shown to a quiet table that Sandy had reserved. They were given menus and offered drinks while they waited for Sam to arrive. The older women could barely conceal their excitement as the minutes ticked away. Then Sandy's phone rang and she heard Sam say he was on his way.

A few minutes later, he came in, wearing a neat grey suit and tie. The women's faces lit up. They couldn't take their eyes off the dashing young man who strode across the room and warmly shook their hands as Sandy made the introductions.

'I've been looking forward to this occasion for a long time,' Sam said, pulling out a chair and sitting down.

'So have we,' Betty replied.

'Sandy's told me all about you,' he continued. 'But she didn't say how elegant you were.'

Across the table, Sandy saw her mother's eyes sparkle with pleasure.

After that, the ice was broken. A babble of conversation broke out as the first course was served and Sam entertained them with a string of anecdotes and witty remarks. Sandy could only marvel at the way he flattered them with compliments and smiles, and joked playfully with them. He was the epitome of grace and good manners, all delivered effortlessly, as he held the two older women spellbound by his charm.

It was half past three when they finally left after Sam had settled the bill and given a handsome tip to the waiter, who bowed graciously as he showed them to the door.

'I haven't enjoyed myself so much in ages,' her mother said, as Sandy led her to the Porsche with Betty. 'We must do this again.'

'We certainly will,' Sam replied, kissing them affectionately on the cheeks. 'It's been a pleasure meeting you both.'

Sandy settled them comfortably on the back seat of the car and closed the door. She was thrilled at the way the lunch had gone.

Sam obviously was too. Before she got into the driving seat, he took her in his arms and kissed her goodbye. 'I think we can mark that up as a success,' he whispered.

It soon became clear that Sam's response to her mother had been genuine and not a show just to please Sandy. He told her so the next time they met. 'Your mother's an interesting woman and very lively,' he said. 'She's extremely well read.'

'She was a teacher,' Sandy explained.

'And your aunt struck me as a solid no-nonsense type. They're a good foil for each other.'

'I think Mum's a little bit afraid of Betty. She's her older sister. I relied on her heavily when Mum wasn't well.'

'Well, I didn't see anything wrong with her. She seemed very sharp and alert. She was chattering away like a jackdaw. I found her very entertaining. I hope we can meet again soon.'

Her mother's reaction was similar when she next called to see her. 'What a charming young man, Sandy. And what good manners he has. He was a perfect gentleman. Good manners are very important. But I'm afraid they're going out of fashion.'

'I'm glad you liked him. He liked you too.'

'I was very impressed and so was your aunt. You've got excellent taste in men, Sandy. And he's so handsome. You'd be proud to be seen anywhere with a man like Sam Ross. When will I meet him again?'

'Leave it with me,' she said. 'I'll come up with something.'

As it turned out, an opportunity presented itself a fortnight later when her mother announced that the church bring-and-buy sale was being held the following Saturday and Father Breen had asked her to help out at the book stall. This was something she was glad to do because she knew about books. Sandy welcomed it as an opportunity for Angela to get out of the house and start socialising again. She agreed to come along and give support. When she mentioned it to Sam he said he would come too.

Saturday was a beautiful autumn day with barely a hint of cloud in the sky. Sam arrived at her apartment at ten o'clock, dressed casually in a blazer, chinos and an open-necked shirt.

'I've been thinking,' he said. 'What time does your mum finish at the bring-and-buy?'

'Around lunchtime. Then someone else takes over. Why do you ask?'

'It's a lovely day. Why don't we take a spin down into Wicklow? We could invite your mum and stop off for tea in Greystones. I'm sure she would enjoy that.'

'Great idea. I'll tell her.'

It was midday when they arrived at the church hall to find the place packed with people hunting for bargains among the second-hand clothes and bric-à-brac. They pushed their way through the crowd till they arrived at the book stall where her mother was doing a lively trade. Her eyes brightened as soon as she saw Sam. 'What a lovely surprise,' she said.

'I couldn't resist the chance to see you again, Mrs D. It looks like you're busy.'

'We haven't stopped. There was a crowd of people waiting when the doors opened and they've been coming ever since.'

'That should bring in some money and keep Father Breen happy,' Sandy commented.

'I'm looking for something to read,' Sam said. 'Is there anything you can recommend?'

Angela started searching among the books that were neatly displayed on the stall. 'What do you like? Fiction, history, sport?'

'Oh, fiction, but I'm not fussy. You choose for me.'

After rummaging through the volumes, Angela withdrew a copy of *Captain Corelli's Mandolin* and handed it to him. 'Now there's a book you'll like. Once you start to read it you won't be able to put it down.'

'Sounds right up my alley,' Sam said, pressing a ten-euro note into her hand and refusing her offer of change.

'Sam and I are going for a drive down to Wicklow,' Sandy announced. 'We thought you might like to join us. We could stop somewhere and have tea.'

'I'd love that,' her mother replied. 'But I won't finish here for another half-hour.'

'That's okay,' Sandy said. 'We'll browse around and have a look at the other stalls till you're finished.'

❖

It was one o'clock before they got away after they had helped Angela count the takings and give them to Father Breen to lock away in the safe. They started south towards Wicklow, then drove up into the hills, Sandy and her mother sharing the back seat. It was a glorious afternoon, the sun slanting across the fields, the trees and woodlands bright with autumn colour.

'This is wonderful,' Angela remarked. 'It's been a long time since I was up here. I'd almost forgotten how beautiful it can be at this time of year.' She peered through the window at the sheep grazing in the fields and the mountains rising steeply before them. In the distance, they could see the ocean glinting like silver foil in the sun.

They passed through Enniskerry, then began the descent into Greystones.

The town was packed with day-trippers and there was a festive atmosphere, people sitting outside the pubs drinking beer in the sun. Sandy was delighted to see her mother enjoying herself so much. Sam drove a short distance to the outskirts of the town and turned into the grounds of a hotel. 'This place should do. What do you think, Mrs D?'

'Oh, yes,' she agreed. 'This looks just the ticket.'

As they were getting out of the car they noticed a garden at the back of the hotel with tables set out on the grass.

'Shall we sit outside or do you want to go indoors?'

'Why don't we sit in the sun?'

They were barely seated when a waitress appeared to serve them. 'Now,' Sam said. 'Has the fresh air given you an appetite? What would you like to eat?'

They ordered tea and sandwiches, scones and slices of lemon cake. Angela surveyed the neatly trimmed lawns and the flowerbeds with a glow of contentment on her face. 'This is a wonderful treat,' she said. 'Thank you very much for inviting me.'

'It's my pleasure, Mrs D,' Sam replied.

'And that's another thing. Now that we've been introduced, you must stop addressing me as Mrs D. You can call me Angela. That's my name.'

Sam smiled. 'If that's what you want, Angela, that's what I'll call you.'

She took a dainty bite from a slice of cake and addressed Sam again. 'This investment business you're involved in. Tell me exactly how it works. Is it very complicated?'

'Not really, provided you know what you're doing.'

'But there's risk involved, isn't there?'

'Of course, just like any business. But if you do your research carefully you can cut down the risk.'

'I'm not sure it would suit me. I have a friend who lost all her money when the banks collapsed. She had invested it in shares.'

'I'm sorry to hear that. Where do you put your money?'

Angela smiled coyly. 'What makes you think I have any?'

'Well, I'm assuming you have some savings.'

'I have a little nest egg set aside. But it's very small.'

'Where is it invested?'

'It's in the post office. I don't think that's likely to collapse, do you?'

'I sincerely hope not,' Sam replied. 'Otherwise we'll all be in trouble.'

They sat chatting in the hotel garden till five o'clock when the sun began to go down and the air grew cooler. Angela kept up an intensive conversation with Sam as if they had known each other all their lives. For Sandy, it was fascinating to see how well they got on together. She was delighted that the two most important people in her life had struck a chord.

Eventually, it came time to leave and they got back into the car to head for Dublin. When they finally arrived at Rathmines, Angela thanked them profusely for a marvellous trip. Before she got out of the car, she turned to Sandy. 'There's one thing intrigues me. With you and Sam living such busy lives, how do you manage to maintain a romance?'

Sandy laughed. 'Don't you know, Mum, that where there's a will, there's a way?'

CHAPTER 15

One morning Sandy woke up in Sam's bed to find him standing over her with a tray of hot coffee and toast. 'This is an unexpected treat,' she said, sitting up and brushing the hair from her face.

'I was up early,' Sam explained. 'I had some phone calls to make. I thought you'd like breakfast in bed.'

'Thank you very much.'

'Regard it as one of the advantages of domesticity.' He pulled over a chair and sat down at her side. 'In fact, I've been thinking. You and I have been seeing an awful lot of each other recently. We're always waking up in your bed or mine. We spend all our free time with each other. Why don't we move in together?'

She stopped with the coffee cup halfway to her mouth. 'You mean live with each other?'

'Yes – we're practically living together as it is.'

'This is a bit of a shock, Sam. I've never considered it before.'

'Why not? It seems to me like a natural progression.'

'There are so many things to consider. Whose home would we use?'

'It doesn't really matter. Yours or mine, it's all the same to me. The point is, we'd be together all the time. Just think how exciting that would be. And you know what people say . . .'

'Two can live as cheaply as one?'

'Exactly. We'd save a lot of money on utility bills for a start. But that's not the real reason. We'd be together all the time, Sandy, like a regular couple. It would almost be like getting married.'

'Do you mean we should do it right away?'

'That's up to you. But if you want time to think about it, that's fine. You can tell me whenever you're ready.'

Sandy finished her breakfast, got dressed and made her way to work. She had a meeting scheduled with Freddie Thornton, the firm's accountant, to finalise the company's annual tax return. He was waiting for her when she arrived with a gloomy look on his face. They went straight into her office where she received another shock.

'I'm sorry to have to tell you this but we owe the bloody Revenue two hundred and fifty thousand euro.'

'That much? Remind me what it was last year.'

'Two hundred thou. But profits are up. That's the good news. The bad news is that tax is up too.'

She looked him over. She thought he seemed tense today, not his peppy self.

'Is there any way we can reduce it?'

'I've used various tax reliefs to pare it to the bone,' the accountant replied. 'There's no way I can get it any lower.'

Sandy sighed. 'What was it Benjamin Franklin said? "Nothing

is certain in life but death and taxes." I suppose we'll just have to pay it.'

She signed an authorisation for Freddie to requisition the funds from the bank and he went off quickly without any of his usual small talk.

After he had gone she had a pile of mail and messages to deal with so it wasn't till lunchtime that she was able to focus on the main business of producing entertaining stories to sell to their media customers. By the time she got home around eight, she was exhausted.

She wasn't seeing Sam that night so she changed into some casual clothes and busied herself preparing a meal. When it was ready, she poured a glass of wine and sat down at the kitchen table to eat. Sam's suggestion about living together came swimming back into her mind. She realised it had been there all day. What was more, she discovered that she was uneasy about it.

It wasn't that she didn't love him. She was convinced he was the most attractive man she had ever met, and their recent holiday in Spain had cemented her love. Living together would mean she would sleep with him every night and wake each morning to find his handsome head on the pillow beside hers. They would spend most of their free time together. She would have him on permanent standby to confide in and give advice whenever she needed another opinion. She should have been jumping with joy at his suggestion. But she wasn't.

Sandy had been living on her own since she'd left the family home. In that time, she had grown used to having her own space and her own company. She loved her penthouse where she could close the door on the world and be alone. If she agreed to set up home with Sam, she would lose that freedom. Everywhere she turned, he would be there. Her private space would be gone.

But that wasn't all. They had been seeing each other for about three months. Sandy thought they knew each other pretty well by now. But living together would expose every personality quirk and defect. All their secret faults would be laid bare. Living together would mean there was no place to hide. It was a big step to take and she wasn't sure she was ready. A niggling voice warned her to be careful.

Another thought came into her head. If he wanted them to live together why hadn't he proposed marriage? Was he afraid of the commitment? Was he not as sure of their love as she was?

She tossed the situation back and forth, and it was past midnight when she finally went to bed. A new thought entered her head. How would Sam react if she said no? He was a tough businessman, used to getting his own way. Would he feel offended? Rejected? How would it affect their relationship? She finally drifted off to sleep, wishing he had never made the suggestion and their lives had continued as before.

When she woke the next morning, her mind was made up. She was going to turn him down. Her view might change with the passage of time but, right now, she wasn't ready. Agreeing to something just to please him was a recipe for trouble.

But she kept putting off the fateful moment for fear of Sam's reaction. The weeks slipped by and, thankfully, he didn't raise the subject. She began to think that he might have forgotten about it, although she knew that was a forlorn hope. Sam wasn't the type of man to forget something as important as this.

The moment came when they were having dinner one night at a new restaurant in Ballsbridge. Sam waited till they had ordered dessert before asking the question she dreaded. 'Have you thought any more about my suggestion?'

'Of course I have. I've thought of practically nothing else.'

He put down his wine glass and leaned forward with an expectant smile. 'And?'

Sandy took a deep breath. 'I can't do it, Sam, not yet.'

His face crumpled. She had never seen him so disappointed. He looked like a little boy who had been told to sit in the naughty chair.

'I agree it has a lot to recommend it,' she went on, quickly, 'and I'm truly flattered to be asked but I'm just not ready.'

'What does that mean?'

'I want things to continue as they are for the time being. Maybe in the future we might look at it again.'

'How much more time do you need? It's pretty straightforward. Will you live with me or not?'

'No.'

'Why not?'

'I've tried to explain, Sam. I'm not ready.'

'That's nonsense. You do love me, don't you?'

'Of course I love you.'

'So why won't you agree?' He was getting upset. She reached out to take his hand but he angrily drew it away. 'I must say, I'm very disappointed in you, Sandy. I thought you'd be happy to live with me. Now it turns out I made a big mistake.' He called for the bill, slapped some notes on the table, got up and stormed off, leaving Sandy sitting alone and the whole room staring at her.

CHAPTER 16

She asked the waiter for her coat and left the restaurant, her face burning with embarrassment and shame. She found a taxi outside that took her home. Once she was inside her apartment she threw herself down on the bed and cried her heart out.

It had been their first fight. She had never seen Sam so angry and realised she had hurt him deeply. She blamed herself for the fiasco. She had handled the situation badly and injured his pride. And she could see now that it was madness to have broken the news in a public place where so many people could witness her humiliation. She should have put him off and chosen a time when they were alone. But it was too late now. The damage had been done.

The following morning, she rang to apologise but her call went unanswered. She typed a quick text message: *Truly sorry for upsetting you. Please ring. Sandy xxx.*

She was still depressed as she made her way into Charlotte Quay but she welcomed the tumult of the clattering phones and the constant pressure of the busy office. She buried herself in work. At least it provided distraction from the unhappiness she was suffering.

Her colleagues clearly sensed her distress, for Patsy came into her office at lunchtime and suggested they go for coffee and a chat. But Sandy put on a brave face, forced herself to smile and politely turned her down. She wasn't about to let the staff know that she'd had a row with her boyfriend.

She worked through lunch dealing with queries, talking to contacts and keeping herself busy. At two, she took a short break and sent Stella to get a sandwich which she ate at her desk. By three, Sam still hadn't responded. By now she was convinced he was avoiding her. She left a further message on his phone and fired off another text: *Please contact me. We've got to sort this out. Love Sandy xxx.*

She was the last person to leave the office at nine o'clock. When she got to bed around midnight there had still been no response. Twenty-four hours had passed and she hadn't managed to make contact with Sam. The next day followed the same pattern. She rang, left messages and sent texts but he didn't reply. He was definitely freezing her out. Now her attitude began to change.

What had she done wrong that he should punish her like this? Nothing. She had turned down his suggestion that they should live together. But she hadn't rejected it completely. She had simply asked for more time. And how had he reacted? Like a spoiled child who hadn't got his way. He had shamed her in front of a restaurant full of people. No man had ever dared to treat her like that. And now he was refusing to take her calls.

Well, she had her pride too. If anyone was entitled to feel

aggrieved, she was. Sam's reaction had revealed a dark side of his personality that she had never glimpsed before. It simply reinforced her decision not to move in. Imagine if he was to behave like that while they were sharing the same roof. It would be intolerable. Perhaps she had had a lucky escape.

She made up her mind. She would make one final effort to contact him. If that didn't get a result, she would stop. She took out her phone and called his number. She listened to the ringing tone and was put through to his message minder. She took a deep breath. 'Sam, this is Sandy. I've made several attempts to contact you. This is the last time I'll call. If you don't respond, I'll assume you don't want to hear from me again.'

She closed her phone. The die was cast. The matter was now firmly in his hands.

The days dragged by and there was no response. Sandy was forced to accept that their beautiful relationship was over and she had to get on with her life without him. It wasn't easy. For the past three months they had seen each other practically every day and now there was a terrible void to fill.

Instead of glittering nights at the theatre or in some intimate restaurant filled with chatter and laughter, she returned each evening to the silence of her empty apartment. Instead of waking up with his warm body beside hers, she had to get used to her lonely bed. And that wasn't all. She had to put up with embarrassing queries from her mother about how Sam was and when they were going to have another jolly outing like the one to Greystones. She couldn't summon the courage to tell her the truth: that she would probably never see him again.

She had always known that falling in love meant taking a risk but it had happened to her almost without her realising it. And by falling in love, she had allowed him greater access to her than any man before. In Sam, she'd thought she had found the ideal companion to share her life. She had believed he was the man Fate had destined for her. She had trusted him totally and now this had happened.

Despite her best efforts, her mind kept revisiting happier times they had shared together: the Blur concert at Kilmainham Castle and the cosy supper afterwards at Paradiso beside the river, their first lunch together at Les Escargots when he had bowled her over with his charm. But mostly the memories were of the week they had spent in Spain.

That had been one of the happiest times of her life. She thought of the sun and the flowers, the strolls they had taken hand in hand along the promenade while the sea rose and fell against the shore, then watching the moon, like a yellow lantern, as they'd sat on the terrace at the apartment and listened to the chirping of the cicadas. There would be no more times like that. They were gone for good and would never return.

The first people to grasp that something was seriously wrong were Stella and Patsy. They were well tuned to her moods. One afternoon, Patsy persuaded her to go for a drink after work. Sandy was so downcast that she reluctantly agreed. They went to a quiet bar beside the river where they could talk. When they had their drinks before them, Patsy tentatively began, 'I know this is none of my business but I can't stand by and see you suffer like this. I can tell something's wrong and I thought you might want to talk.'

Patsy wasn't just Sandy's faithful deputy: she was also her best friend. If there was one person she could confide in, it was her. Suddenly she was overcome by a desperate need to spill out her heart. 'I've broken up with Sam.'

Patsy nodded. 'I guessed it might be something like that. How bad is it?'

'Pretty bad.'

'I'm sorry to hear that. I thought you guys really had it all. Do you want to tell me about it?'

For the next fifteen minutes, Sandy unburdened herself while Patsy listened patiently and didn't interrupt. When she had finished, she took Sandy's hand. 'I think you behaved admirably. You have nothing to blame yourself for. If you didn't want to live with him, he should have accepted your decision. As for the way he's treated you, it's disgraceful and I'm surprised at him. It certainly isn't the behaviour of the gentleman I thought he was.'

'I never wanted this to happen,' Sandy said. 'It was the very last thing I expected.'

'But you did nothing wrong. He is the one who's behaving badly. His pride has taken a knock but he'll get over it. And I'll bet he'll treat you with more consideration in the future.'

'I don't think there'll be any future.'

'Oh, c'mon, Sandy, every relationship has its ups and downs. He'll sulk for a while and then he'll realise the terrible mistake he's made and come running back to you, like a lost puppy.'

'I wouldn't bet on it.'

'We'll see. In the meantime, you should end this period of mourning. It doesn't suit you. There's a big wide world out there. Why don't you and I go and explore it?'

'What do you mean?'

'The Racket Boys are launching their new CD tomorrow

night at the Gardenia Club. We've been invited. It'll be a ball ... c'mon, Sandy, you'll enjoy it. Don't curl up and die because of some bloody man.'

Sandy felt her spirits lift. Talking to Patsy was doing her good. 'What time?'

'The party starts at nine. And I've already checked your diary. You have no appointments for the following morning. It means you can lie in bed till noon if you wish.'

The first smile for a long time forced itself onto Sandy's face. 'You should have been a psychiatrist.'

❀

The next day was relatively quiet, and by seven o'clock Sandy was able to escape from the office and go home to get ready for the evening. She was a little anxious about appearing in public without Sam Ross by her side in case it set tongues wagging but she agreed with Patsy that she needed to stop moping and let herself go a little.

She rustled through her wardrobe for something to wear and settled on a blue cocktail dress and heels. Next, she sat down at her dressing table and brushed out her long dark hair. It took another ten minutes to apply her makeup. By half past eight, she was ready to leave. She had agreed to meet Patsy at Doran's pub, which was close to the Gardenia Club. She called a cab and set off.

She found her friend already there. A couple of single men at the bar eyed her keenly as she walked across the floor and sat down beside her.

'You look like a million dollars,' Patsy said. 'That little blue number is perfect for you.'

'You don't look bad yourself.'

'Thank you, and now that we've finished admiring each other, what would you like to drink?'

'Glass of white wine, please.'

The waiter was hovering a few feet away. He came at once and took their order.

'How do you feel?' Patsy asked.

'A bit nervous.'

'What have you got to be nervous about? You're not breaking any law. You're entitled to go out and enjoy yourself.'

Sandy found herself smiling. Patsy's positive attitude was infectious. 'You're right.'

'Of course I am. Just go in there tonight and behave as if nothing has happened.'

It was ten o'clock when they left the pub and walked the short distance to the Gardenia Club. A crowd of photographers was lined up outside the door snapping everyone who went in. A bruiser in a dress suit examined their invitation before ushering them inside.

Immediately they were met by a wall of sound crashing out of the stereo system. The club was in semi-darkness and the only relief came from the flashing strobe lights sweeping along the walls and across the floor. It took the women a few moments to get their bearings and then they became aware of the mass of bodies lined up at the free bar and the handful of dancers gyrating to the music on the tiny dance floor.

Suddenly a loud voice sounded in their ears.

'Well, well, well, if it isn't Sandy and Patsy. It's great to see you, ladies. Come and join us at the bar.'

Sandy turned to find Alan Mansfield standing beside her. He was the manager of The Racket Boys, whose album was being launched tonight. He was a tall, attractive man in his early forties and was wearing a flashy white suit. He made a space for them at the counter. People stretched out their hands to greet them.

'You've got nothing to drink,' Mansfield declared. 'We can't have that. Not at my band's launch party.' He reached behind the bar for a couple of glasses, then delved into an ice bucket and withdrew a bottle of champagne.

'Have some champers,' he said, and shoved the glasses into their hands. Sandy took a sip and felt the bubbles tickle her throat.

Mansfield was continuing to talk: 'I must say, you ladies are looking very elegant tonight, unlike these dossers.' He nodded towards his companions at the bar, who grinned at his joke. 'I had to bribe the doorman to let them in. Have you heard the boys' new CD yet? It's going to be a winner. This is the album that will make their name.'

'I'll drink to that,' Sandy said, and took another sip of champagne. She was beginning to relax. She looked around the crowded room and recognised familiar faces. Many of their owners waved and blew air kisses.

At that moment a thin, dark-haired young man approached. He looked no older than twenty-five. Alan Mansfield drew him into the circle. 'Meet Johnny Sharp, the lead singer. Johnny, this is Sandy Devine and her friend is Patsy Maguire. They have a lot of influence in the entertainment media. And, lucky for you, they're big admirers of the band. So be nice to them.'

Johnny Sharp smiled modestly and shook their hands. He stood awkwardly for a moment as if the manager's words had left him awestruck. Then he turned to Sandy. 'I hope you like our new album, Ms Devine.'

'Oh, I'm sure I will.'

'Do you like blues music?'

'Very much.'

'We spent a lot of time putting the album together and it's got a lot of good stuff on it. It's getting a lot of air play.' He seemed to have run out of things to say.

There was another awkward silence.

Then he turned to Sandy again. 'I don't suppose you'd … er … like to dance, Ms Devine?'

Suddenly Sandy felt like a teenager again when she'd prowled the clubs and discos looking for gossip to sell to the papers. She put down her glass and took Johnny Sharp's extended hand. 'Why the hell not?'

❋

It was almost two o'clock when the two women got into the back of a cab and set off for home. Sandy rested her head on the soft leather seat. She had spent the night drinking champagne, chatting with acquaintances and kicking up her heels on the dance floor. Not once had she thought of Sam Ross.

'Glad you came?' Patsy asked.

Sandy closed her eyes. 'You bet. I had a ball.'

CHAPTER 17

Sandy was up at half past eight the following morning. Despite the champagne she had consumed she had a clear head and no hangover. She was in the kitchen drinking coffee when her phone rang. When she answered, she heard Patsy's voice. She sounded agitated.

'Are you sitting down?'

'Why do you ask?'

'Because I've got bad news. There's a story in the *Gazette* about you and Sam Ross and I don't think you're going to like it.'

Sandy's heart lurched. 'What are you talking about?' Already she was getting up from her chair.

'It's in the entertainment section. There's a photograph too. I'm only telling you because other people will see it and might call you. You should be prepared.'

'What does it say?'

'You should read it for yourself but it's not nice.'

'Okay,' Sandy said. 'Thanks for the warning. I'll get hold of the *Gazette* right away.'

She pulled on her tracksuit, locked up the penthouse and went straight down to the parking bay. Then she was driving towards the nearest filling station. By now, her imagination was inflamed. What had the *Gazette* printed that was so bad Patsy wouldn't tell her on the phone? It didn't take her long to find out.

There was a filling station nearby with a shop attached. She pulled into the forecourt, jumped out of her Porsche and made a dash for the entrance. There was a newspaper stand just inside the door. Sandy grabbed a copy of the *Gazette*, paid the attendant and returned to her car. She frantically turned the pages till she came to the entertainment section.

A photograph of Sam Ross was the first thing to hit her. He was sitting beside a dark-haired woman in a bar somewhere. They were smiling into each other's faces. She quickly scanned the accompanying story.

Investor Sam Ross doesn't believe in having one woman in his life when he can have two. Hunky Sam has recently been dating attractive Sandy Devine, the boss of the entertainment agency Music Inc. But a little bird tells us he has also been seeing former squeeze Claire DeLisle, the sultry actress best known for her role in the TV soap *Downtown Blues*. Could this turn into a case of handbags at dawn? Watch this space.

In shock, Sandy stared at the photo. This was going to make her the laughing stock of Dublin. Pete Lavelle hadn't forgotten his threat of revenge when she had given Jack Rooney that job. Here it was, right in front of her.

She drove straight back to the penthouse. By now her rage at Sam Ross was near boiling point. He had wasted no time in running back to the DeLisle woman. Not content with humiliating her at the restaurant, he was now making sure she would be an object of ridicule throughout Dublin. How was she going to show her face around town again?

She parked the car and rode up in the lift. As she was letting herself in, her phone started to ring. She clamped it to her ear, thinking it was Patsy calling to find out if she'd read the story yet. But it wasn't Patsy. It was a man's voice. She felt herself go cold as she heard Sam Ross.

'Sandy, I'm ringing to say if you've seen that picture in the *Gazette*, it's not what it appears.'

She gasped at his nerve. She couldn't believe this was happening.

'If you give me a few minutes,' he continued, 'I'll explain everything.'

She cut him dead. 'You've got a damned cheek calling me. Please don't do it again. As far as I'm concerned, everything is over between us.'

❖

The next few days were hell. Out of consideration for Sandy's feelings, few people in the office mentioned the *Gazette* story but of course everyone knew. Some of her friends rang to sympathise but they sounded awkward, as if they were discussing a death. Sandy was convinced that everyone in Dublin had seen the photograph and was busy chattering about it. She also knew that some would be taking a gleeful satisfaction in her plight. 'Now she's getting some of her own medicine,' they would say. 'Serves her right.'

Jack Rooney approached her one afternoon in a corner of the office. 'It was all my fault,' he said. 'If I hadn't asked you for a job, Lavelle would never have done this.'

'Don't blame yourself, Jack. You had nothing to do with it. There's a far bigger agenda at play here.'

'Well, I wanted you to know that I'm sorry about it.'

'Thanks, Jack. I appreciate it.'

But it wasn't just the public humiliation that hurt. She would get over that in time. Far worse was the knowledge that, once again, she had been proved wrong about Sam Ross. How had she allowed herself to be so completely taken in by him? It was his silken tongue, of course, his charm and smooth manners. He had swept her off her feet. She had thought he was different from the other men she had known while underneath he was no better than a guttersnipe.

She decided to find out more about Claire DeLisle, the woman in the *Gazette* photograph. The first time she had heard her name was when Minnie Dwyer told her that Sam Ross had been in a relationship with her. She wondered how long they had been together. In the privacy of her apartment, she sat down at her laptop and Googled Claire DeLisle.

A profile of a thin, dark, waif-like woman appeared. The information gave her age as thirty but, to Sandy's sharp eye, she looked much older. There were lines around her cheeks that the skilful application of makeup couldn't entirely hide. She certainly didn't rate the term 'sultry', which Lavelle had employed in his vindictive article.

As for her career, it had been anything but spectacular. She had appeared in a number of stage plays and television quiz shows. The pinnacle of her achievement appeared to be a small part as a barmaid in a television soap opera. At the moment she was 'resting', which meant she was out of work. Sandy was surprised. If Claire DeLisle had turned out to be a glamorous *femme fatale*, she might have understood Sam falling for her. But this poor starved-looking creature provided no competition at all. What on earth had he seen in her?

Now she set about cutting him entirely from her life. She bundled up the clothes he had left in her wardrobe and gave them to a charity shop, which was delighted to receive them since they were designer labels and almost new. She tore up his letters and notes and dumped them with the refuse. She gathered the various presents he had given her and donated them to another charity shop. When she had finished, not a trace remained to show that Sam Ross had ever crossed her doorstep.

She instructed Patsy that his phone calls were to be blocked, and if he turned up at the office he was to be refused admission. Under no circumstances was he to be allowed to see her. She could do little to prevent the text messages and calls that deluged her personal phone or the flowers he sent to her apartment, begging for a meeting. She hoped he would eventually grow tired and give up. But Sam Ross was not about to disappear so quickly.

One evening as she was leaving work, she heard someone call her name, and when she turned a figure emerged from the shadows. She froze when she saw him. He was dressed immaculately in a finely tailored suit and looked every inch the smooth, suave figure she had known. It took her a minute to overcome her shock.

'What are you doing here?'

'I've been waiting for you. I've been standing here for two hours.'

'I told you it was over between us,' she said coldly.

'But you were angry then. I hoped you might have calmed down by now.'

He approached but Sandy backed away.

'You never gave me a chance to explain. You won't take my phone calls. You won't reply to my texts. I've been turned away from your office. You've left me no option but to come out here and confront you.'

He stepped closer. 'That story in the *Gazette* is a tissue of lies. Why don't you give me a chance to tell you what really happened?'

'No,' she replied, and tried to walk past him, but he blocked her way.

'I'm not going to give up, Sandy. You're the only woman I care about. You're the only woman I love. This separation is breaking my heart.'

'Good. You brought it on yourself. This didn't start with Claire DeLisle. It started the night you walked out of that restaurant because I wouldn't agree to live with you.'

'That was a mistake. I know that now. Please let me give you my side of the story.'

She turned and looked into his face. He seemed so dejected and lonely that her resolve melted and, suddenly, she felt sorry for him. 'It would do no good, Sam. My mind is made up.'

'This will only take a few minutes. There's a bar across the road. Come and have a drink with me. Is that too much to ask?'

She wavered.

'Please. Once you've heard my side of the story, you'll see things in a different light.'

'All right,' she said. 'I'll give you fifteen minutes.'

There was only a handful of customers in the bar and they

found a table near the door. Sam took control of the situation. 'What would you like?'

'A glass of mineral water.'

He came back with the drinks and sat down. He heaved a sigh as he began.

'Okay, here's the real situation. I told you that *Gazette* story was a pack of lies but, like all such fabrications, it has a basis of truth. I *have* been seeing Claire.'

'So it's not lies, it's true.'

'I've been seeing her but not in any romantic way,' he went on. 'I'm not aware how much you already know but we were involved in a relationship for almost two years. It broke up shortly before I met you that evening at Minnie Dwyer's party. I won't go into the gory details. Let's just say I realised we were incompatible. Actresses are not easy people to live with and Claire was harder than most.

'About a month ago, she contacted me and asked for a meeting. She sounded desperate. When I saw her, she told me she was short of money. She was finding it difficult to get work and she had all the usual bills to pay, rent and living expenses and so on. I took pity on her and said I would help.'

Sandy listened quietly while he continued.

'I arranged for some money to be paid into her bank account. It was meant to be a loan but I don't expect to be paid back. The photograph that appeared in the *Gazette* must have been taken at one of our meetings. But the implication that we're involved in an affair is an outright lie. There is nothing between us. You're the only woman I love, Sandy.'

'How do I know you aren't lying to me?'

'Because I'm here now, begging you to take me back. Do I sound like a man who's carrying on an affair behind your back?'

'I said this started before that picture appeared. You refused to take my phone calls, remember? You cut me out.'

He hung his head. 'Yes, I did. And I want to apologise for that too. You hurt my pride when you said you weren't prepared to live with me. I overreacted. Please forgive me.' He reached out and took her hand. 'Can't we put this all behind us, Sandy? I've learned my lesson. I swear it won't happen again. Can't we wipe the slate clean and start all over?'

His excuse was plausible. He sounded contrite and he had apologised. But she stuck to her resolution. Too much had happened for her to take him back. 'It's not that simple, Sam. Things have changed between us. You hurt me badly and I still haven't recovered.'

'I'm sorry. What more can I say?'

She stood up. 'I have to go now.'

'Aren't you going to give me an answer?'

'No.'

'So how will I know if you've forgiven me?'

'When I ring and tell you.'

❖

Sam didn't contact her again. But, despite what he had done and the harm he had caused her, a corner of her heart remained open to him. She had seen his good side: his kindness, generosity and charm. And, of course, he was still the best-looking man she had ever met. But his behaviour that night in the restaurant had revealed a selfish arrogance that astonished her. Despite his apologies, she wasn't convinced that he could change.

Why hadn't he told her he was seeing Claire DeLisle before she found out through the *Gazette*'s nasty little story? On the face of it, what he had done was an act of charity – helping out a former lover who had fallen on hard times. But why had he kept it hidden if it was purely innocent? And why had he never mentioned Claire DeLisle's name in all the months they had been going out together?

Other thoughts occurred that made her shudder. She had trusted him completely and had never seen him so much as look at another woman. But he had disappeared frequently to London on business trips. What did he get up to when his meetings were over and a lonely evening stretched before him? He was an attractive man with no shortage of money and she knew that most women would find his blond, Nordic good looks appealing. Was it an exaggeration to think that he might be tempted? She began to recognise that there was a side to Sam Ross she knew nothing about.

She had forgiven him before when he had left her waiting for six weeks after promising to ring. This time she would not be so quick to forgive.

CHAPTER 18

As a news agency, Music Inc got an enormous volume of mail each morning. People who were looking for publicity would bombard the office with press releases or invitations to parties and events, hoping that Sandy or Patsy would favour them with a mention in their reports.

So, one of the first jobs that Stella had to do every morning was sift through the letters and divide them into three neat piles. One was junk mail and fliers that could be discarded. The second, and largest, was press releases and tip-off reports, which she passed on to Patsy. The last pile consisted of official letters, bills and invoices for payment, which she gave to Sandy.

The following morning, Sandy had barely settled at her desk with a cappuccino when there was a knock on her door and Stella entered. She had several letters in her hand, which she gave to her boss. One letter jumped out. It had the words 'OFFICE

OF THE REVENUE COMMISSIONERS' stamped in bold lettering across the front. She quickly tore it open and felt the blood drain from her face. She was holding a tax demand for three hundred and sixty thousand euro.

'Something wrong?' Stella asked. 'You look shocked.'

Sandy gulped. 'That's putting it mildly.'

'Is there anything I can do?'

'No, just leave it with me,' she said, waving her assistant away. 'I'll sort it out.' She continued to stare at the letter as the initial shock began to wear off. This had to be an administrative error. She read the letter again carefully. The sum sought by the Revenue officials was made up of a tax demand for two hundred and fifty thousand euro for the previous year, plus interest and penalties for not paying on time.

By now she was convinced there had been a mistake. Music Inc always paid its taxes when they fell due. And, besides, she distinctly remembered signing an authorisation for the company accountant, Freddie Thornton, to settle the tax bill. It was around the time Sam had made his ill-fated proposal that they set up home together. She picked up her phone and called Thornton.

The phone rang but there was no reply. Instead she heard a voice ask her to leave a message.

'Hi, Freddie,' she said. 'It's Sandy. Give me a ring as soon as you can. I've got a stupid tax demand from the Revenue that I need you to sort out.'

She turned off the phone and settled down to her morning's work.

❧

She was busy till midday, answering calls, logging tip-offs, checking reporters' copy and talking to her own private informants to keep abreast of the gossip swirling around town. By the time she decided to take a break and send Stella to the deli for a tuna roll, Freddie Thornton had not returned her call. She rang him again and got the same request to leave a message.

This time, she rang Freddie's secretary but again there was no reply. The earlier unease returned. Freddie was highly efficient and usually dealt with her enquiries promptly. She wondered if something was wrong. It took her a minute to come to a decision. When Stella returned from the deli, Sandy was waiting for her.

'Something's come up. I've got to nip out for half an hour. Just log any calls and I'll deal with them when I get back.'

She went down to the parking bay and settled into the driving seat of her Porsche. It took ten minutes to reach Freddie's office in Camden Street. On the way, she tried to remember the last time she had talked to him. It had been about three weeks earlier when he had called to check the details of the rent review she had agreed with the landlords of the Music Inc office suite. But when she arrived at Camden Street, she found the office closed and a pile of mail jamming the letterbox. Alarm bells rang in her head.

She got back into the car and drove out to Freddie's home in Blackrock. It was a renovated artisan's cottage near the DART station. She remembered attending a glitzy party there once. She parked, got out and pushed open the gate. The cottage had the same abandoned air as the office: the windows were covered with grime and the grass on the lawn was overgrown. She pressed the doorbell repeatedly but got no answer. Now it was clear that something was wrong.

She went back and sat in her car while she tried to figure out what to do next. She thought of Mark McIvor, the music promoter who had first introduced her to Freddie. He was a personal friend of the accountant and would surely know what was going on. But McIvor was just as bewildered as she was when he answered her call.

'When was the last time you spoke to him?' she asked.

'About three months ago. I ran into him in a restaurant.'

'And you haven't talked to him since?'

'No.'

'Isn't he still your accountant?'

'No,' McIvor replied. 'We parted company six months ago.'

'Oh? What happened?'

'We had a disagreement.'

'What about?'

'I wasn't happy with the service he was providing.'

'How do you mean?' Sandy probed.

There was a pause. 'If you must know, Sandy, I thought he was spending too much time at the poker clubs. I let him know and he didn't like it.'

'Poker clubs?' Sandy was astounded.

'Yes – didn't you know? Freddie has developed a gambling problem.'

She closed her phone and slumped back into the driving seat as a cold sweat broke across her forehead. Why the hell hadn't McIvor warned her? A terrible possibility began to sink in. She thought of the debonair Freddie, sharp, astute, always confident and amiable. He had managed the financial affairs of Music Inc for the past eight years and had never once given her cause for concern. Was it possible that he had embezzled the money to pay the tax and gambled it at the poker tables?

It was a nightmare. No, she thought, as she tried to drive the idea from her mind. I'm allowing my imagination to run riot. Freddie is a professional. He would never do something as terrible as that. But the thought would not go away. He could have run up gambling debts. He might have been desperate, and people in desperate situations sometimes did drastic things. She needed to get advice. She thought of Jenny Bickerstaff, the company lawyer. She was young, about the same age as Sandy, and Sandy had hired her when Music Inc was breaking into the big time. Her principal job was to check news reports for potential libel whenever Sandy had a tricky story on her hands that could get them into trouble. Jenny was solid and not easily given to panic. She would know exactly what to do.

Sandy took out her phone again and rang her. 'I need to talk to you,' she said, when Jenny answered.

'What is it?'

'It's something I don't want to discuss on the phone. When are you free?'

Clearly Jenny caught the note of anxiety in Sandy's voice. 'Have you got a problem?'

'I might have a very big problem.'

'In that case I'll drop what I'm doing. Come straight round. I'll be waiting.'

Sandy headed back into the city. All the way, her mind was imagining the worst. Was the Revenue demand the only irregularity or had Freddie run off with everything the company possessed? Were there other debts that she hadn't yet uncovered? Was she about to discover she was bankrupt? She was in a lather of panic by the time she arrived at Jenny's office in Mount Street.

'You need a cup of tea,' the lawyer said, as soon as Sandy was sitting down across the desk from her. 'As it happens, I've just boiled the kettle.'

She poured hot water into a silver teapot and produced two

cups and saucers. Once the tea was ready, she sat back in her chair. 'Now,' she said. 'You'd better start at the beginning and tell me what exactly has happened.'

It took Sandy a couple of minutes to run over the events of the day and her phone conversation with Mark McIvor.

'Okay,' Jenny said. 'First, you have to calm down. This could turn out to be a ghastly misunderstanding. I'll check with the Revenue at once, although I have to say they don't usually make mistakes. As for Freddie Thornton, he might simply have taken off on a holiday for all we know. Have you tried his secretary?'

'She wasn't there. His office is closed and his home looked deserted when I called. And then there's this business of his gambling.'

'Nevertheless all you have are suspicions. Why don't you go back to work and leave the matter with me? In the meantime, you can check that there are no more bills that haven't been paid. I'll call you when I get to the bottom of it.'

Sandy finished her tea. She felt slightly better after talking to Jenny. As soon as she got back to Charlotte Quay, she told Patsy she wasn't to be disturbed and began making phone calls. It took her thirty minutes to confirm that the rent on the office was up to date, as were the utility bills and other running expenses. That was a great relief.

It took another hour to stop all payments into Freddie Thornton's bank account and to set up new standing orders. If it turned out that the accountant *had* simply gone off on holiday, she would be left red-faced. But it was a risk she wasn't prepared to take.

She had just finished when her phone rang and she heard Jenny's voice once more. 'It's bad news, I'm afraid.'

'Tell me.'

'Your suspicions are correct. Freddie *has* skipped. He's left a trail of debt all over town.'

'What about the Revenue demand?'

'That wasn't a mistake. You owe them three hundred and sixty thousand euro.'

Sandy was devastated. She thought of the years of toil she had spent building up her business. This had the potential to destroy her. 'Is there anything I can do?' she pleaded. 'I've already paid the tax.'

'That's not technically correct,' Jenny pointed out. 'You authorised Freddie Thornton to pay it but the Revenue haven't received the money. As far as they're concerned, you still owe it.'

Sandy was almost in tears. 'But I haven't got it.'

'I'll talk to them and explain what's happened but I have to tell you that I don't hold out much hope of success.'

'Do your best,' Sandy begged. 'I'm desperate.'

It was several days before Jenny had anything to report although she rang Sandy several times to keep her abreast of the difficult negotiations she was conducting with the Revenue. In the meantime, Sandy went around like a ghost. She couldn't sleep properly for thinking of the enormous debt that was hanging over her. When she woke in the morning, it was the first thing to pop into her head. She lost her appetite. Even when she was caught up in a big news story, she would break off and stare into space when she thought of what was facing her.

Finally, Jenny called to say she had managed to persuade the woman she was dealing with in the Revenue office to drop the penalties. 'It was like pulling teeth, I can tell you. I pointed out that you hadn't deliberately withheld payment. I told her how desperate you were and she finally took pity on you. However, they're insisting that you must pay the original tax and interest. That comes to three hundred thousand euro.'

It was still an enormous amount for Sandy to pay on top of the money Freddie Thornton had embezzled. To cover it, she was forced to raid the nest eggs she had set aside as her personal savings. Thankfully, she had no mortgage to pay on her home. But it meant that after the years of hard work, all she had to show was the penthouse and her red Porsche.

She had a meeting with Jenny to discuss what to do next. 'Can I sue Freddie Thornton?'

A grim smile crossed the lawyer's lips. 'Of course you can. But first you have to find him.'

'Does nobody know where he's gone?'

'I'm afraid not. He's vanished into thin air. I understand the police are already searching for him. I didn't tell you this but you weren't Freddie's only victim. He appears to have embezzled a number of his clients. From what I hear on the grapevine some of them lost a lot more than you.'

'That's not much comfort.'

'I know.'

'I should have been more careful. Mark McIvor got rid of Freddie because he didn't like him gambling. He could see the danger.'

'But how were you to know? He always performed his work efficiently, didn't he?'

'Yes.'

'So, you had no reason to be suspicious. Don't blame yourself, Sandy. It's time to move on. You'll have to get another accountant, of course. Why don't you use one of the big firms?'

'I'm not sure I'd like that. I'd miss the personal touch. What I liked about Freddie was that I could call him at any time and he'd deal with me at once.'

'In that case, I can recommend a small firm. It's run by a long-established accountant called Patrick Smith. He's real old-school and straight as a die.'

'Why can you recommend him?'

'He's my husband's uncle.'

'So if he takes off with my money, I can blame you?' Sandy said, with a touch of gallows humour.

'If Patrick Smith takes off with your money, we may all emigrate,' Jenny replied.

❋

It took Sandy a long time to get over the shock of what had happened. It wasn't just the money she had lost, hard as that was: it was also that she had allowed herself to be duped. She had trusted Freddie Thornton too much with the firm's money, which made her feel stupid. She vowed to be more vigilant in future.

She kept the bad news from the staff and carried on as if nothing had happened. She spent a couple of months feeling glum and hard done by and then, slowly, she managed to pull herself together and buckled down to work.

But the loss of her savings was reflected in other ways. She had to cut back on many of the little luxuries she had enjoyed. She spent less on clothes, fashion accessories and fine dining. She even considered trading in her Porsche for a cheaper car.

She set about making economies at Music Inc, trimming costs and eliminating waste to make the business slimmer and more efficient. Eventually she emerged from the catastrophe. But little did she know that another was waiting round the corner.

CHAPTER 19

One morning in November Patsy put her head around the door. There was an anxious look on her face. 'There's a woman on the phone, says she's your mum's next-door neighbour. She wants to talk to you urgently.'

'Put her through straight away.' She picked up the phone.

'It's Sheila Malone,' a voice said. 'I'm sorry to bother you but your mum's had an accident. I'm with her now.'

Sandy's heart stopped. 'How bad?'

'It's hard to tell. She had a fall and there's a gash on her forehead. She's conscious but there's a lot of blood.'

'I'll come immediately,' she said.

She called Patsy into her office and told her what had happened.

'My God, is she badly hurt?'

'I don't know, but I must go to her at once. You'll have to take over.'

'Of course. I'll take care of everything.'

Sandy hurried down to the parking bay and got into her car. Thank God she had Patsy to fall back on. She had recently raised her salary but she was worth every cent.

The rush-hour traffic had receded and she made it to Primrose Gardens in fifteen minutes. All the way, she kept praying that her mother wasn't seriously injured, that it might be something that a bandage or a sticking plaster would sort out. But it was the fact that she'd had the accident at all that really alarmed her. How had it happened? What had she been doing?

She locked the car and started immediately up the path to the house. Sheila Malone saw her coming and held the front door open. 'She's in the kitchen. She's still bleeding. I wouldn't have known anything about it except I heard her banging on the wall. When I went in, I found her lying on the floor. I had to get her into a chair.'

At least her mother had had the presence of mind to raise the alarm, Sandy thought. That was something positive. 'I don't know how to thank you, Sheila.'

'Oh, it was nothing. I'm just glad I was here to help.'

Sandy rushed along the hall and into the kitchen. Her mother was sitting at the table with a towel around her head. There was blood all over her face and nightdress. She looked at Sandy with a dazed expression as she came into the room.

'What have you done to yourself?' Sandy asked, in a voice she might use with a child who had grazed her knee.

'I came in to make breakfast and I must have had a dizzy spell. I think I hit my head on the table.'

'Let me have a look at it.'

Sandy carefully unwound the towel to reveal a nasty-looking wound above the eye. It was still seeping blood. It took her just a second to decide this was more than the local GP could handle. She had to take her mother to hospital. She pulled out her phone, rang the emergency services and asked for an ambulance. Then she sat down beside her.

'I'm not going to the hospital,' Angela protested. 'All I need is a rest in bed with a couple of aspirins and I'll be fine.'

'Don't argue with me,' Sandy said firmly. 'That wound needs to be stitched.'

'But who'll look after the house?'

'The house will look after itself. Sheila will keep an eye on things.'

'Don't worry, Mrs Devine,' the neighbour said. 'Just do what Sandy says. That cut seems pretty deep. You need a doctor to look at it.'

Tears welled in her mother's eyes and slowly rolled down her cheeks. 'I hate hospitals. I hate doctors. I know what they're like. They'll just prod me and poke at me like I was a piece of meat. They use people like me to practise on.'

'Don't be silly,' Sandy said. 'You're going whether you like it or not. Now, I don't want to hear another word about it.'

While they waited for the ambulance, Sandy rang her aunt. 'Mum's had an accident. I've called an ambulance. I'm taking her to hospital.'

'What?' her aunt exclaimed. 'Is it serious?'

'I hope not. She fell and cut her head pretty badly. She needs to have a doctor examine her. And the wound will have to be stitched.'

'I'll meet you at the hospital.'

'There's no need. I can handle it myself.'

'No,' Betty insisted. 'You have enough on your plate. At times like this, you can do with all the support you can get.'

'Okay, I'm grateful.'

She was finishing the call when she heard the bell ring. Sheila was already halfway down the hall to open the door.

Two fit-looking ambulance attendants came bustling in. 'Okay,' one said. 'Where's the patient?'

Her mother was put onto a stretcher and carried out to the waiting ambulance. Sandy climbed in beside her and held her hand. She could pick up her car later. It was a short ride to the hospital and the Accident and Emergency Unit.

When they got there, the ambulance staff spoke briefly to a secretary at the admissions desk, then disappeared with the stretcher down a corridor and through a couple of doors marked 'PRIVATE: NO UNAUTHORISED ENTRY'. Sandy was left to deal with the secretary.

'Can you provide the patient's personal details, please?'

She answered the young woman's questions and was then asked to take a seat and wait. Fifteen minutes later, Betty appeared through the entrance doors. She came across to Sandy and sat down beside her. 'This is a big shock,' she said. 'Where is she?'

'They've taken her off somewhere.'

'You were right to call the ambulance.'

'She didn't want to come. I practically had to force her.'

Betty sighed. 'Your mother can be very stubborn. She's always had a fear of hospitals and doctors since she was a little girl. She fell off her bicycle one time and had to have stitches. She never got over it. Now tell me exactly what happened.'

'I don't know. She thinks she had a dizzy spell in the kitchen when she was making breakfast. But she wasn't very coherent.'

'She was probably a bit stunned.'

'Sheila Malone, who lives next door, said she heard Mum banging on the wall. She has a key and when she went in she found her lying on the kitchen floor.'

'Good job she was at home.'

'Exactly my thought. What if Sheila hadn't been there? What if Mum had been unconscious? She could have been lying there for hours before she was found.'

She turned and looked into her aunt's face. 'She might have bled to death.'

Betty gave Sandy's hand a gentle squeeze. 'Don't think like that. The point is, she *was* found.'

'I can't help it. I'm her only child and I feel responsible for her.'

'And you're a good daughter,' Betty said soothingly. 'Now, just chase those gloomy thoughts away. She's in the right place. She'll get all the attention she needs.'

The two women sat talking as the time ticked away. When Sandy glanced at the large clock above the entrance desk, three-quarters of an hour had passed. She looked around the waiting room. All about her were people on crutches, with their arms in slings or their heads bandaged. There were women with bawling infants. Despite the hospital's attempts to make the waiting room cheerful, with fresh paint and potted plants, it was still a depressing place among all this pain and misery.

'What's keeping her?' Betty wondered.

Sandy got up and walked to the secretary's desk. 'Have you any idea what's happening to my mother?'

The secretary looked stressed. 'Afraid not. When she's ready, the doctor will come and tell you.'

'Is there some place we could get a cup of tea?'

'There's a refectory on the next floor. If you want to go there, I can page you when there's any news of Mrs Devine.'

'Thank you,' Sandy said. 'We'll do that.'

They took the lift to the next floor and found a bright café decorated in soft pastel shades. It was in stark contrast to the waiting room.

'What will you have?' Sandy asked her aunt, gazing at the array of cakes and sandwiches on display.

'Tea will be fine.'

'Want a currant scone with it?'

'Yes, that would be nice.'

'Go and get a table. I'll be with you in a moment.'

Betty found one beside the window looking out over the hospital grounds. Sandy joined her a few minutes later with the tea and scones. 'I've been afraid of something like this happening ever since Dad died.'

'They were very close,' her aunt agreed. 'I don't think I've ever seen a more devoted couple. When your father died suddenly, it was a terrible blow to her. He was a fit man. She depended on him a lot.'

Sandy took a sip of tea. 'Where did they meet? Mum never told me about those early days. Any time I asked, she just brushed me off.'

'It was one Sunday at Mass.'

'Really?'

'Yes, your father was very involved with the local church. He did the book-keeping for old Father Dolan and organised the church finances. He lived with his elderly parents in Primrose Gardens. Your mother and I were renting a flat nearby at the time. They used to walk home from Mass on Sunday mornings.

That's how they first got to know each other. Your father must have been ten years older but it was a whirlwind romance. Within a few weeks they were married and moved in with Tom's parents. Then his parents died and they had the house all to themselves.'

Sandy shook her head. 'I never knew any of this.'

'Your mother didn't like to talk about it. Despite the gap in their ages, it was a very good marriage. Tom Devine was a wonderful husband. He would have done anything for her. I never saw a happier couple, and when you came along, it was just the most perfect little family.'

Sandy wished she had talked to her aunt sooner. She might have provided answers to a question that had always bothered her. 'Why did they never have any more children?'

Her aunt took a deep breath before replying. 'It wasn't for want of trying, I can tell you that. Your mother would have loved a bigger family. She had several pregnancies but they all miscarried. Maybe if it had happened today, things might have been different.' At these words, Sandy felt a twinge of sadness. So she had guessed right. All those times when she had pestered her mother for a little brother or sister, Angela had probably been grieving for another lost child.

Betty cut her scone and spread butter and jam on it. 'I'd prefer you to keep this conversation to yourself, Sandy. Your mother is very touchy. I wouldn't want her to think we were gossiping behind her back.'

'Of course. I won't say a thing.'

They finished their tea and Sandy rang Patsy at work. 'I'm at the hospital. We had to call an ambulance.'

'Is it serious?'

'I hope not. The doctors are still treating her.'

'She'll be fine. In the meantime, don't be worrying about the office. Everything is under control.'

'Thanks, Patsy. I'll get in as soon as I can.'

She cancelled the call and heard a voice announce her name over the address system. 'Ms Devine, come at once to the admissions desk.'

The two women hurried back downstairs where they found a nurse and a doctor waiting for them. The doctor was a large man of about forty with a thick mane of dark hair. The name tag on his jacket read: Dr James McClean. He turned to Sandy.

'Are you Ms Devine?'

'Yes.'

'Your mother is fine. That was quite a nasty cut she sustained to her forehead but we've cleaned it and stitched her up and she'll be right as rain in no time.'

'That's great news. Can we take her home now?'

He shook his head. 'Not immediately. Her speech is slurred and she sounds a little incoherent. She may have suffered some concussion from the fall. We're going to keep her in for a few days and carry out some tests.'

Sandy's face fell.

'There's nothing to be concerned about, Ms Devine. This is purely routine procedure. Now, tell me something. Has she been eating properly?'

'Why do you ask?'

'She's slightly underweight for her age and height.'

'There was a period a few months ago when she seemed to go off her food,' Sandy said.

'Why was that?'

'It was just a phase she went through. But recently she'd got her appetite back.'

'Okay, we'll check her out. And we'll do our best to make sure she gets plenty of nourishing food while she's with us. Now, she's demanding to see you so you'd better go to her at once. Nurse O'Neill will show you to her room.'

CHAPTER 20

They found Angela in a private room on the second floor with a window looking over the road. There was a television fixed by a bracket to the wall, playing one of her favourite soaps. She was sitting up in bed in a hospital gown with a plaster covering the gash on her head. Sandy could tell at once that she was in a belligerent mood. 'What did I tell you?' she said, as soon as Sandy and Betty appeared. 'Didn't I say they wouldn't let me go once they got their claws into me? Now they'll use me for the student doctors to practise on. I know what they get up to. I've read articles about it in the papers.'

Sandy was so happy to see her looking better that she found herself laughing.

'They just want to carry out some tests on you.'

'Tests? You mean experiments, don't you? They're going to

use me as a guinea pig. Well, I'm not staying a day longer than necessary. I'll sign myself out if I have to.'

'Calm down,' Betty said sternly. 'What are you complaining about? It's like the Shelbourne Hotel in here. You press a button by your bed and the little nurse comes running in to see what you want. You get three square meals a day. And a private room. There are people on waiting lists just to get a bed in here, never mind a room of their own.'

'They can have this one any time they want.'

'You should count yourself lucky. Now, how are you feeling?'

Her mother shrugged. 'I've been telling you all along there's nothing wrong with me. But nobody's listening.'

'Let the doctors decide that,' Betty said. 'They're the experts.'

Her sister rolled her eyes.

'How long were you lying on the kitchen floor?' Sandy asked.

Angela puckered her brow and tried to concentrate. 'Probably a couple of minutes before Sheila came in. She got me into the chair.'

'Can you remember exactly how it happened?'

'I went into the kitchen to make breakfast. I was at the sink to fill the kettle and the next thing I knew I was on the floor and there was blood everywhere. I think I must have tripped.'

'You said it was a dizzy turn.'

'Maybe it was. I can't remember.'

'Have you had dizzy spells before?'

'Not really. Sometimes I feel tired and I might doze off for a minute or two. It happens at night when I'm watching television. But everybody does that.'

Sandy exchanged a quick glance with her aunt. 'You don't doze off during the day?'

'Never.'

'Make sure to tell the doctors all this. They'll want to know. You've got to tell them everything.'

Her mother looked indignant. 'You're not suggesting I would lie to them, are you?'

'No, but it's important that you don't conceal anything. I'll be back this evening with your nightie, dressing gown and slippers, Is there anything else you need – books, anything like that?'

'How long am I going to be here?'

'No longer than necessary. They'll let you out again as soon as you're ready. Would you like me to bring a couple of television magazines so you can check your favourite shows?'

'That's a good idea.'

'What about a cake or some biscuits?'

'No, thank you.'

'Okay. There's a phone by the bed. If you need to talk to me about anything, you've got my number.' She bent and kissed her mother's cheek and held her hand. 'Do me a favour, will you?'

'What?'

'Don't be fighting with the staff. They have a difficult job. Don't make it any harder.'

Sandy and Betty made their way downstairs to find a taxi. 'I don't like this talk of dizzy spells and dozing off,' Sandy said to her aunt.

'Oh, for God's sake, you've being trying for months to get her to see a doctor. Now she'll have all the doctors you could wish for. They'll give her a thorough check-up and probably let her out in a day or two. If you ask me, she's fine. She's complaining and that's always a good sign.'

The taxi dropped Betty, then drove the short distance to

Rathmines and Sandy's waiting Porsche. When she got there, she decided to go into the house and check it over. There were some bloodstains on the kitchen floor, which she mopped up, and a few cups and plates in the sink waiting to be washed. She opened the fridge and found it stocked with provisions. She tidied up, then went round the house to make sure that everything was in order.

The garden was in good shape. She checked the window ledges and found they had all been dusted. On a table beside the television, she came across a copy of a novel with a bookmark inserted between the pages.

She went into her mother's bedroom and found a pile of recently laundered clothes waiting to be put away. All of this reassured her. It meant that her mother was alert and attending to her household chores. But the dizzy spell still concerned her. Sandy had a nightmarish horror of something similar happening again and this time no assistance being to hand. The consequences were too terrible to contemplate.

Satisfied that all was well, she locked up, got into her car and drove across town to work. Patsy was waiting for her. They went into Sandy's office and closed the door.

'Well?' her deputy began. 'How is she?'

'They've treated the gash on her head but they're keeping her in for a few days. They want to carry out some tests.'

'That's good. It's no harm to have a thorough health check every once in a while, particularly at her age.'

It was exactly what Betty had said but Sandy wasn't sure. She thought of the worrying signs she had noticed in her mother: the memory loss, listlessness and the mood swings Angela had experienced. What if the tests revealed something serious? She chased the thought from her mind. Betty was right. Her mother would get a few days' rest and nourishing food. She'd be discharged a new woman. It was really a blessing in disguise.

'It gave me a scare, Patsy. It was sheer good fortune that the next-door neighbour was there and able to help her.'

'She'll be fine, you'll see. Now let me bring you up to date on what's going on.'

Afterwards Sandy told Patsy to take her lunch break, then took off her jacket and for the next four hours worked solidly at her desk. It was six o'clock before she finished. She left Patsy to put the operation to bed, then set off once more for the hospital. On the way, she stopped at a newsagent's and picked up a couple of glossy television magazines. She knew her mother would get hours of pleasure from them.

She found her finishing her evening meal. 'What did you have for supper?' she asked cheerfully, picking up the menu card and studying it.

'Poached eggs on toast, chicken salad, grilled pork chop. Betty was right. This place *is* like the Shelbourne Hotel.'

She glanced at her mother's plate. 'So you had the chicken. Was it nice?'

'It was very nice,' her mother replied. 'And I had a lovely piece of poached cod for lunch with boiled potatoes and green beans. I'll give them full marks for their cuisine.'

This remark brought a smile to Sandy's face. 'So, you're settling in nicely. This isn't such a terrible place after all.'

'I never said it was terrible. Everyone has been very kind to me. But it's not my home, Sandy.'

'Well, it's only for a few more days and then we'll have you out of here.'

She handed over the slippers, dressing gown and nightdress,

then the magazines. 'Here, I brought you some reading material. I take it you can get all your favourite channels on the television?'

'Oh, yes.'

'Is there anything else you need?'

'I think I've got everything. There's one thing bothering me. Who is looking after the cat?'

In all the confusion, Sandy had forgotten her mother's cat. 'I'll take care of it. You just concentrate on getting better.'

'Good. I wouldn't like the poor animal to go hungry because of me.'

They sat chatting for almost an hour before Sandy stood up. 'I have to go now but I'll drop by again in the morning. I'll ask the nurse about the best time to visit.' She bent to kiss her mother's cheek and felt a tug at her heartstrings. How often had her mother looked after her when she was a child, bathing a scratched knee or a bruised elbow? Now their roles had been reversed. 'Okay,' she said, standing up and straightening her skirt. 'Sleep well tonight. Ring if you need me – and remember what I said about co-operating with the doctors.'

At the door she turned to wave goodbye and then she was gone.

On her way back, she nipped into a supermarket, bought some cat food and a microwave meal, then drove on to Rathmines. As she opened the gate, the cat emerged from under a bush in the front garden and rubbed her back against Sandy's leg. 'You're hungry, aren't you? C'mon, I'll feed you.'

The bowl was on the back step. Sandy rinsed it, then opened one of the tins, filled the bowl with food and another with fresh water. The cat began to purr contentedly as she started to eat.

Sandy made a quick check of the house, then locked up. She went next door and brought Sheila Malone up to date with her mother's situation.

'How long will she be in hospital?'

'A few days. Do you mind keeping an eye on the house for me?'

'Not at all. I'll be happy to.'

Sandy thanked her and drove home. She got undressed, pulled on a dressing gown, then poured a glass of wine and ate her supper at the window while she watched the moon shining on the river. It had been an eventful day and now she felt tired. Eventually she washed up, got undressed and slipped between the sheets. Please, God, let Mum be all right, she prayed, as she drifted off to sleep.

❖

The hospital stay turned out to be longer than expected. Three days went past and there was still no indication of when Angela would be discharged. By now, she was beginning to get argumentative.

On the fourth morning when she went to visit, Sandy found a young nurse changing the sheets on the bed while her mother sat in a chair. She took the girl aside. 'Have you any idea when my mother will be allowed home? She's been here for three days. Can I take it that the wound on her head is healing all right?'

'Oh, yes. It's coming along very well.'

'She's very anxious to get home. She's beginning to get restless.'

'I'm afraid I can't help you, Ms Devine. They're still carrying out tests. You'd need to ask Dr McClean.'

'When can I speak to him?'

'He's busy right now. I'll tell him you asked.'

'Thank you. It's just so I can put my mother's mind at ease.'

'I understand. Once the tests are completed, he'll probably want to talk to you.'

The nurse helped her mother back into bed and left. Sandy sat down beside her. Angela started to complain. 'You told me I'd only be in here for a short while. Now it's nearly a week.'

'It's three days.'

'Four counting today. I warned you what would happen once they got their hands on me but you wouldn't believe me. I feel like a prisoner in here.'

'I'll talk to Dr McClean as soon as I can. Now, tell me how you've been getting on.'

'I'm bored to death, if you want to know. Do you know what they had me doing yesterday? Memory tests, like I was a schoolchild.'

'Memory tests?'

'They asked me all these silly questions like what day of the week it was and what the date was and what the President's name is. Then they gave me these sums to do, addition and subtraction. Imagine, me, who was a teacher, being asked to subtract nine from thirty-three as if I was a child. It's a complete waste of time and money, if you ask me. No wonder the health service is in trouble.'

Sandy felt a chill along her spine. 'Well, they must have a good reason for asking those questions. I'm sure you gave them the correct answers.'

'Of course I did. Then they read out these sentences and got me to repeat them. Now can you explain to me what on earth that's got to do with me cutting my head?'

'They've got all these new tests in hospitals now. It's not like the old days.'

'You can say that again. Is somebody feeding the cat? I'm worried about her.'

Sandy gave her mother's arm a comforting squeeze. 'The cat is fine. I feed her every day, best-quality cat food. You won't recognise her when you get home. She's putting on weight.'

Her mother laughed. 'Well, I'm glad some poor creature is happy even if it's only the cat.'

Eventually Sandy left her and went out to the car, where she was inside it, she took out her phone and rang her aunt. 'I'm worried,' she said.

'Where are you?'

'At the hospital. Mum's just told me something that scared me. She said they had her doing memory tests yesterday.'

'What are they?'

'They asked her what day of the week it was and what month of the year.'

'What's so scary about that?'

'Can't you see? They must be checking her brain.'

'Of course they're checking her brain! She had a fall and hit her head. Didn't Dr McClean say she might have got concussion? I expect they do that in every case like this.'

'But memory tests? That looks like something more serious.'

'You're beginning to sound like your mother, Sandy. You're making a mountain out of a molehill.'

'You think so?'

'Of course I do. Relax, why don't you? Everything is going to be fine.'

But Sandy couldn't relax, no matter how hard she tried. She was convinced that something was wrong. Another day passed and there was still no word from Dr McClean and no sign of a discharge date. When she went to visit her mother the following evening she found her very angry.

'You won't believe what they did today. They had me hooked up to monitors, checking my heart. They've already taken blood and urine samples. And as if that wasn't enough, they've started taking X-rays of my brain.'

'They did what?'

'Took a scan of my brain. I keep telling you, they're using me as a guinea pig. Well, I've had enough. They can't detain me against my will. If they don't let me out of here, I'll bring them to court and sue the pants off them.'

Sandy made a decision. She held her mother's hand and gently caressed it. 'Don't get agitated. I'll get to the bottom of this, I promise.'

On her way out she stopped at the nurses' station. 'Is Dr McClean available to see me?'

'I'm afraid not. He's finished for the day.'

'Would you tell him I need to speak to him urgently? I'm Mrs Devine's daughter and I need to know what's happening to her.'

'Of course. I'll make sure he gets that message first thing in the morning.'

'Thank you,' Sandy said.

●

She didn't sleep well that night. Since her conversation with her mother, she had been consumed by worry. Something was going on at the hospital that she hadn't been told about and she was determined to find out what it was.

The following morning she was up early and ready to go to work. With her frequent absences from the office, the paperwork was piling up. She had a quick breakfast of coffee and toast and set off, planning to make a dent in the stacks that were cluttering her desk.

It was eight o'clock when she slid her car into its reserved space at Charlotte Quay. The sky was grey and overcast and a wintry wind was blowing up off the river. She picked up a latte and made her way up to her office. She had barely sat down when her phone rang.

'Yes?' she answered.

'This is Dr McClean's secretary. You wanted to speak to him?'

'That's right.'

'Dr McClean can see you in his office at eleven thirty. Does that suit?'

'That's perfect. I'll be there. Thank you very much.'

At last, she thought. We're going to get some answers. She worked steadily till ten past eleven then set off to drive the short distance to the hospital.

Dr McClean was waiting in his office. He looked up as she came in and gave her a pleasant smile. 'Please sit down, Ms Devine. I'm sorry if I've appeared evasive these last few days but I wanted to be absolutely certain before I spoke to you.'

'Yes?'

'It's not good news, I'm afraid.'

Sandy felt a chill at the back of her neck. This was what she had secretly dreaded and had pushed to the furthest recesses of her mind. 'I knew it,' she said. 'She's got Alzheimer's, hasn't she?'

CHAPTER 21

The doctor looked at her with surprise. 'What made you say that?'

'All the memory tests you've been carrying out. You were checking her brain, weren't you?'

'Yes, we were. We were trying to find the cause of your mother's confusion and memory loss. But we didn't find Alzheimer's.'

'No?'

'Ms Devine, your mother is suffering from a rare condition called pernicious anaemia. The symptoms are similar to Alzheimer's but fortunately it isn't fatal. Mrs Devine is fifty-two. In patients of her age, it can cause confusion, irritability, tiredness and lack of balance. The dizzy spell she had is typical of the disease.'

Sandy bit her lip. 'Can it be treated?'

'Yes, it can. It's caused by low levels of vitamin B12. Sufferers are unable to absorb the vitamin from food and this affects the production of healthy red blood cells. But we can give them B12 injections.'

'Will she recover?'

'She will always suffer from the condition but it can be managed.'

Suddenly Sandy was overcome with emotion. Despite her best efforts, she felt her chest heave and then the tears were flowing down her cheeks. 'Forgive me,' she muttered.

Dr McClean took a box of tissues from his desk and gave it to her. 'Here,' he said. 'Dry your eyes. Take your time. I know this is difficult for you.'

After a few minutes she managed to regain her composure. She blew her nose and dried her eyes again. 'So what happens now?'

'That depends on family circumstances. I understand your mother lives alone.'

'That's right.'

'Is she able to look after herself?'

'Oh, yes. Until recently she did everything, cooking, cleaning, shopping.'

'The accident she had, she can't remember how it happened. Thankfully, it wasn't too serious but she might have more.'

'What are you suggesting?'

'She shouldn't be left alone She should have someone to look after her, at least till her condition stabilises. If you can't do it yourself perhaps you might want to consider a full-time carer to look after her.'

'I don't think she'd like that. She's a very independent woman.'

'You're her only living relative?'

'There's her sister, my aunt.'

'Look, Ms Devine, you don't have to make a decision right

away. I suggest you have a talk with your aunt and come to the best arrangement. In the meantime, I'm going to prescribe a course of vitamin B12 shots. She's had one here in the hospital already but will need to have one every week. Her local GP can administer them. I'll be in touch with her and she can also monitor her progress. I'd also like to see her again in a month's time.'

He wrote down the appointment time and date on a little card and gave it to her. 'I know this is a shock for you but you shouldn't be too despondent. Depending on how she responds to treatment and changes her lifestyle, your mother could have many years of life ahead of her.'

'Thank you. Is she ready to be discharged now?'

'Not quite.' He checked his watch. 'She'll be having lunch in an hour and afterwards we plan to remove the stitches from her head wound. Why don't you come back again at about three and you can take her home?'

She thanked him, shook hands and stood up. She was still in a state of shock and her legs felt unsteady. When she reached the door, she turned back. 'Should I tell her or will you?'

'It's my responsibility to tell her, Ms Devine.'

'When will you do it?'

'This afternoon. I plan to have a little talk with her. Don't worry. I'll break the news very gently.'

'Is it all right if I go and see her for a few moments?'

'Of course. She's been asking for you.'

Sandy left the doctor's office in a daze. Outside her mother's room, she paused for a second. Then she forced a smile on her face, rapped sharply on the door and went in.

Angela was sitting up in bed watching television.

'I've got good news,' Sandy announced. 'They're letting you go home today.'

'When?'

'At three o'clock. They're going to take out your stitches and then you'll be discharged.'

Sandy watched as joy flashed across her mother's face at the prospect of getting back to her own house. 'How do you feel?' she asked.

'On top of the world now that I'm getting out. I've been telling everyone who will listen that there's nothing wrong with me apart from the cut on my head.'

'Do you want me to help you pack your things?'

'Sure I have only a few bits and pieces. The nurse can put them in a bag.'

'In that case, I'll go. I'll be back again at three to take you home.' She bent down and kissed her mother's cheek. 'See you later,' she said, and hurried from the room.

Outside, the grey skies had turned to rain. Sandy ran to her car and sat for a few moments to pull herself together. She felt as if her chest had been punctured and all the breath drained out of her. There was so much to do, so many things to plan that she didn't know where to begin.

She drove straight to her aunt's house. When she opened the front door, her aunt's face dropped. 'What's the matter? You look like you've seen a ghost.'

'I've just come from the hospital. I've got some bad news. Mum has something called pernicious anaemia.'

'What is it?'

'It has to do with her red blood cells. I don't understand it all but it's what caused her memory loss and mood swings. And the dizzy spell in the kitchen.'

'Come in,' Betty said, and led her into the neat modern

kitchen at the back of the house. 'Before you say any more, let me make a strong pot of tea.'

Sandy flopped into a chair while Betty got busy with the kettle and teapot. A few minutes later, she was pouring two cups.

'You don't look well.'

'I'm in a state of shock.'

'I'm not surprised. Tell me what the doctor said.'

Sandy recounted her conversation with Dr McClean. When she had finished, her aunt put down her cup. 'I suspected something was wrong with her. I didn't tell you because I didn't want you to get alarmed.'

'I did, too, but I didn't want to believe it. The doctor said she shouldn't be left alone until her condition stabilises. He suggested she might need a carer to live with her.'

Betty shook her head. 'Let's not run away with ourselves. Before we go there, we should examine the options. You can't look after her. You've got your business to run. It would make more sense if she came and stayed with me.'

Sandy looked up quickly. 'But you've got Uncle Henry to think about. It wouldn't be fair on either of you.'

'Henry wouldn't mind. We've got a spare bedroom now that the kids are all gone. She is my sister, after all.'

'No,' Sandy said. Already she could see the problems that would arise. Her mother was a strong-willed woman. She would never consent to live with someone else.

'It wouldn't work. It has to be her own house. That's the only place she'll settle.'

'Then you'll need to get a nurse – maybe even two nurses, one for the daytime and another for night. It'll cost a fortune.'

'I don't mind paying,' Sandy said.

'And your mother is going to hate having strangers in her house. This is not going to be easy, Sandy.'

'I know, but if that's what has to happen she'll have to learn to put up with it. Maybe I could move in and stay nights with her.'

'I don't see how that could work either. Your job involves all sorts of crazy hours.'

'I could do some of my work from home. That's how the business started in the first place.'

Betty paused to consider. 'When is she being discharged?'

'This afternoon at three.'

'I'll stay with her tonight.'

'Are you sure?'

'Yes. I'll pack a bag, then go with you to the hospital.'

'Okay.'

'Let's not try to do everything at once,' Betty said, giving Sandy's arm a squeeze. 'The priority is to get her home. Later we can decide how we're going to handle this long term.'

❖

Eventually they got into the car and drove back to the hospital. On the way, Sandy called into Primrose Gardens and picked up some clothes for her mother. She made another stop at a supermarket for provisions. Her mother had been in hospital for five days and would need fresh groceries. When they arrived, they found her sitting in a chair in her room, in her dressing gown.

By now, Dr McClean would have broken the news to her. Sandy wondered how she was going to react. But she didn't mention the doctor at all. She demanded to be told what had kept them. 'I've been waiting here for ages,' she complained. 'You know how much I want to get home.'

'We had to get you some fresh clothes.' She opened a carrier bag and took out her mother's best skirt and blouse and a new pair of tights. 'Have you had a shower yet?'

'Just this morning.'

'Okay, stand up and I'll help you.'

'I'm not an invalid, you know. I'm well able to dress myself, thank you very much,' her mother said, taking the skirt and struggling into it.

She turned and smiled. 'I'm sorry for barking at you. I don't know what came over me. It's just that everything's been topsy-turvy for the past week. Now, let's get out of here. I can't wait to be at home and back to my old routine.'

'Don't you want to thank the nurses for looking after you so well?'

'I've done it already.'

❀

Her mother sat in the back of the car with Betty while Sandy drove. All the way to Rathmines, she babbled like an excited schoolgirl. Her attitude had changed completely in the course of a few minutes.

Her mood brightened further when she saw her house. Once they were inside, Betty took over. 'Let's all go into the conservatory,' she said. 'You can put the television on.'

Angela sat down in her favourite chair with a sigh of contentment. Sandy sat on one side of her and her aunt on the other.

'There's something I want to tell you,' Betty said. 'I'm going to stay with you tonight.'

'There's no need for that,' Angela replied. 'What will Henry say?'

'Henry won't mind. Besides, I want to do it. I've missed you since you went into hospital. We can sit and talk about the old days.'

'What a lovely idea. I'd like that.' She turned to Sandy and grasped her hand. 'It's so good to be back in my own house. Promise me something,' she said. 'Promise you'll never leave me. Promise you'll never send me to that hospital again.'

Sandy pressed her lips against her mother's warm cheek. She felt like weeping again but she fought back the tears.

CHAPTER 22

She woke the next morning with her mind made up. Overnight she had come to a decision. Her mother had pernicious anaemia, but it could be treated and Dr McClean had said she could have many years of life ahead of her. With the help of her aunt she would face the situation head on and deal with it. In the meantime, she would take some leave from work and give her mother her full attention.

She went into the kitchen, put coffee on to brew, then pulled out her phone and rang Patsy.

'Any news about your mum?' Patsy asked.

'Yes, she's been diagnosed with a condition called pernicious anaemia. It causes tiredness and confusion.'

'I'm sorry to hear that, Sandy. Is there anything I can do?'

'Yes. I need to take some leave to sort things out. Can you hold the fort at Music Inc? It may be for some time.'

'Of course. Is there anything else?'

'No, that's it. I'll ring every day to keep in touch.'

'Don't worry about anything. Just concentrate on your mother. I'm sorry, Sandy. I really am. Tell her I was asking for her.'

'I'll do that. You're a gem, Patsy. I'm truly grateful.'

Next she rang Betty. 'Are you able to speak?'

'Sure. I'm sitting in the conservatory.'

'Where's Mum?'

'In the kitchen cooking breakfast for us.'

'Really?'

'Yes. She insisted so I decided to let her go ahead. It's her house. I don't want to appear like I'm taking over the place.'

'So everything went okay?'

'It went perfectly. After you left, we sat chatting for a long time. I think it did her good to talk. Then I made some scrambled eggs for supper. We were in bed by eleven.'

'Did she say anything about her interview with Dr McClean? He was going to break the news to her.'

'She didn't mention him at all. She just seemed pleased to be home.'

'I'm amazed. It sounds like you've done a great job.'

'It's not work, Sandy.'

'Nevertheless, you'll want to get back to Henry. I'll relieve you tonight. What time do you want me to drop by?'

'Some time this afternoon, say two o'clock?'

'That's perfect. You've been wonderful this past week. I don't know how I would have managed without you.'

'You would have coped, Sandy. We're a family and that's what families do. They look after each other. See you at two.'

Sandy finished the call, relieved that her mother was reacting so well to the news. She made some more phone calls and at midday she had some lunch.

❖

At a quarter past one, she packed an overnight bag, locked up and set off for Primrose Gardens. On the way, she stopped at a florist's to buy some roses and a card. There was a bakery next door where she purchased a cake. It was ten to two when she pulled up outside her mother's house.

Angela came to the door with a wide grin on her face. 'Who are the flowers for?'

'Who do you think? And I also got you a welcome-home card and a cake. So you can put the kettle on and we'll have a nice cup of tea before Betty goes home.'

'I'll do it right away. But first let me get a vase for the roses. They're beautiful, Sandy.' She buried her nose in the bouquet and inhaled the fragrant scent. 'You're a good daughter, so thoughtful.'

Sandy kissed her cheek. 'You're worth it, Mum.'

Her mother didn't waste any time hurrying into the kitchen with the gifts that Sandy had brought. Next minute water was splashing into the kettle. Sandy walked into the conservatory and found her aunt watching television. 'Have you time for some tea and cake?'

'Sure,' Betty replied.

Sandy sat down beside her and lowered her voice. 'I'm amazed how well she's reacting. I don't mind telling you I was a little edgy.'

'There's no need. Everything went like a dream.'

'No arguments?'

Betty frowned. 'She knows better than to argue with me. I've also let her know you're staying tonight and she seems quite happy with the idea.'

'She doesn't think we're imposing on her?'

'Not at all.'

'Well, that's a relief. Is there enough food in the house? Is there anything she needs?'

'There's plenty of food, including the roast chicken you bought yesterday. It's in the fridge.'

At that moment, her mother returned from the kitchen with the teapot, cups and forks for the cake. 'Well, this is nice and cosy,' she declared. 'It reminds me of when Sandy was a little girl and we used to have birthday parties. You know what I missed most in that hospital?'

'Tell us.'

'A proper cup of tea. They didn't know tea from a hole in the road.'

Afterwards Sandy called a taxi to take Betty home.

'Phone me if there are any problems,' her aunt said, as she was getting into the car. 'Not that I expect any. If I don't hear from you, I'll assume that everything is okay.'

When Sandy returned to the house, she found her mother had wrapped up and taken herself into the garden. Yesterday's rain had passed and a weak sun was struggling through the clouds. It was peaceful there and the traffic sounds seemed muted and far away. She went over to join Angela. 'How do you feel?' she asked her mother.

'Marvellous.'

'Your wound's more or less healed.' She peered at her mother's forehead. There was only a slight red mark to show where the stitches had been. 'They did a good job. You won't even have a scar.'

'So they managed to get something right. Tell me something,' her mother asked. 'Why are you fussing over me?'

'You're recuperating from an injury. You need tender loving care.'

Her mother shook her head. 'You don't fool me, Sandy. That's not the real reason.'

'All right, if you must know, I feel guilty. I've been neglecting you since Dad died.'

'Not at all,' her mother scolded. 'You ring me every day. You call in several times a week. And, besides, you have a very busy life with your company to run. Who is looking after it?'

'Patsy.'

'She'll be glad when you go back to work.'

'I won't be going in for a while. I'm going to spend more time with you.'

'But there's absolutely no need. I'm fine.'

'I want to. I got a fright when you fell and injured yourself. I want to make sure you're safe.'

Her mother turned to look at her. 'So Dr McClean told you?'

'Yes.'

'He says there's something wrong with my blood cells and I have to get vitamin injections.'

'Yes, every week. Dr Hanley will do it.'

'But this doesn't mean I've gone senile, Sandy.'

'Of course not.'

'So I'm not like one of those old ladies who has to be waited on hand and foot. I'm still a young woman. I've still got all my faculties, thank God. And, what's more, I've got every intention of beating this anaemia thing. I've no intention of throwing in the towel.'

'Of course not, Mum. That's the kind of fighting spirit I like to hear.'

'Damned right,' Angela said.

Sandy decided to drop the subject. 'I've got an idea,' she said. 'Betty left a roast chicken in the fridge. Why don't we have a little dinner party, just you and me? I'll cook some vegetables and open a bottle of wine. We'll light some candles. You'd like that, wouldn't you?'

'I'd love it.'

They returned to the house and Sandy went into the kitchen to start the dinner.

'Can I help you set the table or anything?' her mother asked.

'Don't you want to watch television?'

'I can do that anytime. Besides, it will only take a couple of minutes.'

'Okay, we'll eat in the dining room, if that's okay with you. It will feel more like a proper dinner party.'

'It's a long time since I've been to one,' her mother said, excitedly. 'I'm going to enjoy this. Should I get dressed up?'

Sandy laughed. 'There's only you and me. But if you want to get dressed up, who am I to stop you?'

It took Sandy a mere half-hour to prepare dinner. When she brought the food into the dining room, she found Angela already seated expectantly at the table wearing a dress Sandy hadn't seen before. She drew the cork out of the wine bottle and poured two glasses.

'To us,' she said. 'Long life and happiness.'

'We should do this more often,' her mother said, and took a large sip from her glass.

✿

It was almost midnight when they went to bed. Sandy went off to her old room and got undressed. The day had gone very well, much better than she had expected. Her mother had been perfectly agreeable and hadn't once argued. In fact, it had been a pleasure to be with her. For the first time since she had been given her mother's diagnosis, Sandy felt her heart lift a little.

The days slipped past. She would call Patsy at work each morning to keep abreast of events at Music Inc. Around midday Betty would phone and chat with her sister for a while, then have a brief conversation with Sandy.

In the afternoons, they went out for a drive to a nearby park or to the beach where Sandy made sure her mother got out of the car and walked for a while to get exercise. On the way home, they would stop off at a café for afternoon tea, which Angela regarded as a treat.

Gradually, Sandy began to relax. Looking after her mother was proving to be a much less difficult task than she had expected. Then came the time to visit the GP, Dr Hanley, which Angela had resisted for months.

CHAPTER 23

Dr Claire Hanley was in her mid-forties and small, with a cheerful face and a reassuring bedside manner. Her surgery was ten minutes away on Rathmines Road. Sandy had phoned in advance to make an appointment and was informed that Dr McClean had been in touch and they were expecting her mother. Once they were seated in her consulting room, Dr Hanley smiled and took Angela's hand. 'Now, Mrs Devine, what's this I've heard about you? You've been in a scrape and ended up in hospital. Bend your head a little and let me see that wound.' She pressed her glasses tight against her face and drew closer. 'Mm, they did a neat job. It's healed very nicely. I hope they treated you well in there?'

Angela shrugged. 'I've got no complaints.'

'Good. Now, do you mind if I check your pulse and take your blood pressure?'

'They did all that in the hospital,' her mother said.

'I know, but these are for my own records.'

Sandy noticed that a firm tone had crept into the doctor's voice. She wasn't going to stand for any nonsense. Her mother sat quietly while Dr Hanley measured her blood pressure and pulse, listened to her chest, then shone a torch into her eyes and throat. She completed her examination and made a few notes.

'Now, Mrs Devine, I understand while you were in hospital, they discovered something else wrong with you. Dr McClean has informed me that you've got pernicious anaemia. Can I take it that he has already explained it to you?'

'Yes.'

'You know it's caused by low levels of vitamin B12 so you've got to have vitamin injections to make you better.'

'He told me all that.'

'Good, so if you'll just roll up your sleeve.'

Claire Hanley had pulled on a pair of plastic gloves and was preparing a syringe while Angela bared her arm. The doctor skilfully inserted the syringe then wiped Angela's arm with a cotton swab and placed a sticking plaster over the puncture mark. 'That's it. Nothing to it. Now, Mrs Devine, I want to ask you a few questions for my records. Let's begin with your daily routine. Take me through your day. What time do you get up in the morning?'

'That depends on how well I sleep.'

'Take an average day – yesterday, for example.'

The doctor took notes while Angela relayed the things she had done from the moment she'd got up until she'd gone to bed.

'What about food? Do you eat regularly, breakfast, lunch and dinner?'

'Yes.'

'How well do you sleep at night?'

'Pretty well. Some nights I'm not tired.'

'What about exercise?'

'I clean the house and do the gardening. That's exercise, isn't it?'

'Of course. Do you ever go for a walk?'

Angela glanced at Sandy. 'Sometimes. My daughter's taken me for a lot of walks recently.'

'That's good. Make a conscious effort to get regular exercise. It's good for your heart, your lungs and your general sense of well-being. It will also stimulate your appetite and help you to sleep better. Now, I'm going to give you a diet plan. We need a good balance of different types of food, particularly fresh fruit and vegetables. Will you promise to follow it?'

Angela nodded.

'Your general health is fine. Now, what about your social life?'

'What about it?'

'Do you get out much?'

'Not really. I prefer my own company.'

'Well, I think that should change,' the doctor said. 'You should develop more social contacts, join a club, see your friends. You're still a relatively young woman. It's not good to be on your own too much.' Dr Hanley opened a drawer and drew out a sheet of paper. 'That's the diet plan. You can read it when you get home. Now, I want you to stay in regular contact with me. I'm making an appointment for you to see me again. Let's say the same time next Thursday.' She scribbled the date on a card and gave it to her. She stood up and shook hands. The reassuring smile was back on her face. 'You're going to be grand, Mrs Devine. Just do what I suggest and everything will be just fine.'

❖

Angela waited till they were in a café on Rathmines Road to vent her frustration. 'You witnessed that performance. What was she getting at, treating me like a schoolchild?'

Sandy took her hand. 'Why don't you just do what she tells you? Are you going to follow her advice?'

Angela scowled. 'It looks like I don't have much choice, doesn't it?'

They finished their coffee and Sandy drove her home. When they got out of the car, they stood for a moment looking at the garden.

Her mother took a few steps forward. 'I can see a few weeds sprouting up.' She went into the house. A few minutes later, she reappeared, wearing her wellingtons and gardening gloves, with a trowel in her hand.

Sandy stood aside to let her pass. Her mother went straight over to the rose bed and began digging out weeds by the roots and putting them into a plastic bin bag.

'They're the very devil, you know. If you don't keep them under control, they'll take over the entire garden in jig time.'

❖

The days passed. Sandy moved a desk into her bedroom and had an internet cable installed. Now she was able to work from her mother's house and take some of the pressure off Patsy. Working also helped take her mind off the one issue that was now dominating her thoughts: how soon her mother's condition would have stabilised.

Angela continued to behave perfectly normally. She took care of her appearance, dressing each day in a clean blouse and skirt or a nice dress from the collection in her wardrobe. She ate properly and went for a walk every afternoon with Sandy.

She did the housework and kept the garden neat. She kept her appointment with Dr McClean, who declared himself satisfied with her progress. She saw Claire Hanley regularly. She even got involved in a local book club and Sandy drove her there once a week, then returned to pick her up. When she got home she would talk animatedly about the new friends she was making.

By now, she seemed to have accepted Sandy's presence in the house – indeed, Sandy was convinced that her mother enjoyed her company. But she knew this was only a temporary arrangement. She hadn't forgotten Dr McClean's warning that Angela was not to be left alone. Sooner or later, a long-term solution would have to be found.

One evening after dinner, Sandy tried to raise the subject. 'You do know I can't stay here for ever? I'll have to go back to work.'

'Of course – you've got your business to run.'

'So what are we going to do?'

'How do you mean?'

'Dr McClean thinks you need someone to look after you. He says you shouldn't be left alone.'

'What would he know?' Angela snorted. 'I had a dizzy spell and cut my head, that's all.'

'And what if you have another?'

'That's not going to happen.'

'Listen, Mum, what would you say if I got a nurse to live with you? She'd look after you and help you around the house. She'd be company for you. You could choose her yourself if you like.'

Angela gave her a withering look. 'I won't have strangers in my house, Sandy, poking around in my private business. I won't stand for it.'

'So how do we solve this problem?'

There was an embarrassed silence as her mother stared at her over her reading glasses. 'Did I hear you right? What problem are you talking about? I don't see any problem.'

Sandy let the matter drop. There was no point in upsetting her.

CHAPTER 24

Christmas came. By now, Sandy had noticed a marked improvement in her mother. She looked healthier and more alert. She had more energy and kept herself busy in household tasks. She threw herself into the book club. The mood swings seemed to have disappeared and now Angela was almost back to where she had been before her husband had died.

The week before Christmas was spent in shopping and decorating the house. Angela insisted that they get a tree and retrieved a box of decorations from the attic. She took great trouble over her cards and presents. She seemed to be thoroughly enjoying life again.

Betty invited them to spend Christmas Day at her house and Angela was quick to agree. 'What's the point of cooking a turkey just for two of us?' she said to Sandy. 'Besides, Christmas is a family time. I'll enjoy seeing all my nephews and nieces.'

On Christmas morning they attended Mass at the local church before driving across to Betty's house. There were about fifteen people for lunch, including children. Angela immediately took off her coat, slipped on an apron and went into the kitchen to help with the cooking.

❖

It was after ten o'clock when Sandy and Angela eventually arrived back at Primrose Gardens.

'What a wonderful day,' Angela said, as she prepared for bed. 'You know, Dr Hanley was right. I should get out of the house more.'

❖

One dark evening in January as Sandy was driving her mother back from the book club, Angela announced that they had a new member. She was a widow called Emily Sutherland and had been brought along by one of the regulars.

'How many members have you got now?'

'Ten. That's about the limit. Any more and no one would get a chance to say anything.'

'Did Emily enjoy it?'

'She seemed to.'

As the weeks wore on, Sandy heard more and more about Emily Sutherland. It turned out she had worked as a librarian and knew her books. Angela and she had become quite friendly.

'You should have heard her talk about Edna O'Brien tonight. She's really very good. It was a joy to listen to her.'

'Is she a local lady?' Sandy asked. 'Where does she live?'

'Some place called Sunnylands.'

'What is it?' Sandy asked.

'A retirement village.'

'Does she like it there?'

'She loves it. Listening to her, you'd think it was the Ritz Hotel.'

'Where is it?'

'Rathfarnham.'

'Hm,' Sandy said.

She decided to find out more about Sunnylands. One evening after her mother had gone to bed, she sat down at her computer. She discovered Sunnylands was a small development of flats for single retired people, with a community centre and a clinic attached. The director was a Dr John Hyland and she decided to give him a call.

Two days later, she drove Angela to spend the afternoon with Betty while she went to view Sunnylands and talk to Dr Hyland.

The retirement village was built on the site of a former preparatory school and was set in private grounds with neatly trimmed lawns and gardens. Well away from the main road, it was surrounded by walls and gates. Sandy was immediately impressed by what she saw.

She was met by the director, a thin man in his late forties, who took her on a tour of inspection of the facility and the residential area. The flats comprised a bedroom, bathroom, kitchen area and sitting room. Sandy noted the large television set in the corner. Everywhere she looked, she saw shining surfaces, gleaming paintwork and well-scrubbed floors. It was obvious that hygiene was a high priority.

The inspection tour ended in Dr Hyland's office.

'I'm interested for my mother,' Sandy explained. 'She's been diagnosed with pernicious anaemia.'

'What age is she?'

'Fifty-two.'

'That's quite young. I'm sorry.'

'She copes very well. Indeed, most of the time you wouldn't know there was anything wrong with her. But a few months ago, she had an episode of confusion at home when she fell and cut her head. She had to be hospitalised. I've been told she mustn't be left alone.'

'Then Sunnylands would be ideal for her. Your mother would be secure here. There would always be someone to keep an eye on her day and night. There is a bell in each flat which she can use if she needs attention. On the other hand she would be free to receive visitors and organise her time to suit herself.'

'Really?'

'Yes. We have a wide range of recreational facilities and there are plenty of other people for her to spend time with. I can assure you she would be very well cared for. We aim to create a community at Sunnylands. If she comes to live with us, we'll make every effort to ensure she feels comfortable and safe.'

The meeting ended with a discussion of the fees. As Sandy suspected, they were huge. Sunnylands had to pay a lot of staff, and there were the usual overheads, plus insurance, food and medical care. She told Dr Hyland she would contact him again and left with a growing conviction that if Angela could be persuaded to settle anywhere it would be there.

In the days that followed, she turned the situation over in her mind. She would willingly pay her mother's fees. The big difficulty would be in encouraging Angela to go.

She knew one thing for certain. Her mother would never agree to anything against her will. If she was to make the move, Angela would have to be convinced it was her own idea, not

Sandy's. She decided the first step must be to get her to visit Sunnylands and see it for herself. The opportunity presented itself the following week.

One night as they were driving home from the book club, her mother announced that Emily Sutherland had invited her to her birthday party.

'That's nice. When is it?'

'Next Saturday afternoon.'

'How old is she?'

'Tsk,' Angela said. 'You never ask a lady a question like that. I'm surprised at you.' She chuckled. 'She's fifty-five. But you didn't hear that from me.'

'And where is the party being held?'

'Where she lives. At Sunnylands.'

Sandy could barely believe her luck. Here it was, the opening she had been looking for, and Angela had presented it herself. Her voice shook slightly as she asked the next question: 'Will you be going?'

'I haven't decided.'

'Who will be there?'

'Some of her friends – and her children, of course. She has two adult sons. Did I tell you that?'

'No.'

'Well, she has. Emily could have lived with them when her husband died but she wanted her independence. That was why she opted for Sunnylands.'

This was amazing. Instead of regarding Sunnylands as some form of concentration camp, as Sandy might have expected, her mother was presenting it almost as a sanctuary from the stresses of the world. 'Well, if you decide to go, you'd better let me know in advance. I might have other plans.'

'Don't worry, I'll give you plenty of notice.'

Sandy was now in a state of nervous anticipation but she had to wait till Friday before her mother announced her intention. 'I've decided to go. She was kind enough to invite me and it would be bad manners to refuse.'

'As you wish.'

'But what am I going to wear?'

'You've got plenty of clothes. I'll help you choose. That's all part of the fun.'

Saturday arrived. The party was scheduled for three o'clock. In the meantime, they had picked a smart two-piece suit that her mother seldom wore. With the addition of a white blouse, good shoes and some jewellery, she looked very fetching. 'I should have got my hair done,' Angela announced, as she got in beside Sandy and fastened her seatbelt.

'Your hair is fine. Indeed, you look very glamorous.'

'Really? It's a long time since anyone said that.'

'Yes. You should dress up more often. You're an attractive woman, you know.'

'Now you're pulling my leg,' Angela replied, with a grin. 'But perhaps I'll take your advice.'

Sandy fired the engine and they set off. It took twenty minutes to reach their destination. Sandy watched her mother as she took in the surroundings of Sunnylands – the impeccable lawns, the gardens and the smart, well-kept buildings. She could tell she was impressed.

A small, plump lady was waiting to welcome Angela when she got out of the car. They both waved to Sandy, who watched till they had disappeared inside before driving away.

She had arranged for her mother to ring her when she wanted to be picked up and Sandy spent the remainder of the afternoon catching up with some personal business. It wasn't till ten past seven that she received the call. In the background, she could hear laughter and merrymaking.

'I'm ready to leave,' Angela said.

'Sounds like you've had a good time.'

'I've had a ball. I can't wait to tell you all about it.'

❀

After that, events moved quickly. Angela enthused about the wonderful party and the nice friends to whom Emily had introduced her, the lovely facilities at Sunnylands and how friendly the staff had been. The following week, she announced that Emily had invited her out again, this time to have afternoon tea. Before long, she was visiting almost every week and, each time she returned, she raved about the retirement village.

Sandy waited patiently, wondering when her mother was going to take the decision she fervently believed would be in everyone's best interest.

It came one evening as they were getting ready for dinner. Angela waited till the meal was served before making her announcement. 'I've been thinking,' she said.

'Yes?' Sandy replied, catching her breath.

'Living with me puts a big strain on you. You've hardly any time for yourself.'

'Oh, Mum. You know I don't mind.'

'Now, please don't argue. I appreciate what you're doing and I'm very grateful. But it's not fair. You're a young woman and you have your own life to live too. I think I've been rather selfish expecting you to give up your time like this.'

'I do it willingly.'

'Nevertheless, it's not right. You said yourself that it couldn't continue indefinitely. I've come to a decision.'

Sandy was sure she could hear her heart thumping in her breast.

'I think I should move into Sunnylands.'

CHAPTER 25

Sandy held her breath, almost afraid to speak in case she might say something that would cause Angela to change her mind. She had taken the plunge. 'Are you absolutely sure?'

'Yes. It would be perfect for me. I'd have Emily and my new friends. I'd enjoy the company. We're even thinking of starting our own book club.'

'So you've discussed this with Emily?'

'Yes. She thinks it's a great idea. There's only one difficulty. Emily says the fees are quite steep. But I've got some money put away.'

'Don't worry about the fees. I'll look after them.'

'I couldn't allow you to do that, Sandy.'

'I insist. If this is what you want, we'll do it.'

'It *is* what I want.'

'Okay, I'll ring tomorrow and check if they have space for you.'

'They have,' Angela said quickly.

'How do you know?

'Emily told me. She knows everything that goes on in there.'

❀

At the first opportunity, Sandy called her aunt to tell her.

'That's a stroke of luck,' Betty said. 'What made her come to that decision?'

'She's got a friend at Sunnylands who's convinced her. I've seen it for myself and it's really very good. She'll have lots of company. There are loads of things to do and the residents have plenty of freedom. There's even a clinic where she can get her vitamin shots and any other medical attention when required. Anyway, it was entirely her own idea. I didn't put any pressure on her.'

'Let's hope she settles. When is she going?'

'Nothing's been arranged. I have to talk to the director.'

'Let me know when she goes in and I'll come with you.'

'Okay.'

She rang Dr Hyland and told him of her mother's decision.

'Would you like her to have a tour of our facilities?'

'She has already been several times. She has a friend who is a resident.'

'Would that be Mrs Sutherland?'

'That's right.'

'She mentioned that she knew a lady who was interested. Your mother would be starting with an advantage. But it might be no harm for her to see everything for herself. It helps to avoid difficulties later on. And you're comfortable with our fees? They may appear steep but we have a lot of expenses here at Sunnylands.'

'I understand. The fees are acceptable.'

She made an appointment to visit with her mother the following weekend. Betty came with them and Dr Hyland proudly showed them round the living quarters, the new dining room and the recreation rooms, where a group of men and women were playing bridge.

'It's very impressive,' Betty said, when the tour was finished and they were having tea. She turned to Angela. 'Do you think you'll be happy here?'

'I think I'll be *very* happy.'

It was agreed that she would move in on the following Friday morning. Sandy helped her mother to pack the clothes and personal items she would be taking with her. She took her favourite books and a picture of Sandy, as a little girl, with her husband, Tom, to place at her bedside.

There was a poignant moment when it finally came time to leave 43 Primrose Gardens. It had been Angela's home since she was married. It was where Sandy had grown up and where she had started her business. Angela had many happy memories of the life she had spent here. Her eyes filled with tears as she went through each room, silently saying goodbye.

'What's going to happen to the cat?' she asked, when they were outside and the front door had been firmly closed.

'Don't worry about her. I'll take good care of her.'

'Don't forget to feed her every day. You know the type of food she likes. And you'll make sure the garden is maintained?'

'Everything will be taken care of.'

At last she got into the car where Betty was waiting to go with them again.

❀

They were met at the entrance by Dr Hyland, who showed them to the flat Angela had been allocated. He gave her an information pack and smiled. 'You're very welcome to Sunnylands. I hope you'll be very happy here as a member of our little community.'

He showed her where all the switches were and how to operate the utilities, and then he left. He was barely gone when there was a knock at the door and Emily Sutherland came bouncing in with a posy of flowers. The two of them went into a conspiratorial huddle.

'You're going to love it here,' Sandy heard Emily say. 'Oh, the times we're going to have.'

❀

Sandy drove Betty home then returned to Rathmines, fed the cat and packed her clothes. She felt tremendous relief that at last a solution had been found that suited everyone, especially Angela. Now she was looking forward to getting back to her apartment and picking up the threads of her life again. For the past few months, she had spent every night at Primrose Gardens.

She left the Porsche in the parking bay and took the lift to the penthouse. There was a pile of mail in her letterbox. When she opened the door, she saw the spring sunlight streaming through the window and her spirits rose. She unpacked her belongings and put them away, then went into the kitchen and poured a glass of wine. She sat down at the table and opened her mail. It was mainly bills and charity appeals. Next, she took out her phone and called Patsy. 'Guess who?'

'Sandy! How are you?'

'I'm fine, thank you very much. I trust you haven't run the company into the ground while I've been away?'

She heard Patsy laughing. 'Not quite but I'm working on it.' Suddenly she became serious. 'How's your mum, Sandy?'

'She's coming along quite well, and has decided to move into this wonderful retirement village we found. I've just left her there.'

'That sounds fantastic.'

'It is. I'm calling to tell you that I'm coming back to work. I'll be in around three. We can have a coffee and you can bring me up to speed.'

'That sounds good. We've all missed you, Sandy.'

'Well, now I'm back.'

She ended the call and went to stand by the window. Below, the city was buzzing with activity. She was looking forward to rolling up her sleeves and getting back to work. She'd missed the clamour, the excitement and the mad adrenalin rush of Music Inc. It would be good to return to it.

The staff were waiting for her when she came through the doors at five past three. Someone had gone out and bought a cake with 'WELCOME BACK' written across it in pink icing. They crowded round to shake her hand. Half an hour had elapsed before she was able to separate Patsy from the mêlée and go down to the plaza for coffee.

'Anything I should know?' Sandy began, when they were seated at a table in the sun.

'Nothing major. There's a list of items I've set aside for your attention but it's not urgent. You can deal with it when you get a chance.'

'I want to thank you most sincerely for giving me support at a difficult time,' Sandy said. 'I couldn't have managed without you.'

'There's no need to thank me. It's my job, Sandy. Besides, I know you would have done the same for me had it been the other way round.'

'Nevertheless, I'm so grateful. As a token of my appreciation, I've decided to promote you. It's something I've been thinking about for some time. I'm going to make you executive editor. We'll get the carpenters to knock up an office for you beside mine. And there'll be an immediate increase in salary.'

Patsy gasped. 'What will it mean?'

'It means you'll oversee the day-to-day running of the Music Inc operation. It's what you've been doing while I've been away. It'll free me up to get out and about a bit more, develop new customers and contacts.'

Patsy's face lit with joy. 'I don't know what to say.'

'Don't say anything. Now, you've been working very hard while I was away. Why don't you take some leave?'

'I'd love to, if you're sure you can spare me.'

'Of course I can. Why don't you check the net and see if there are any last-minute holiday bargains?'

CHAPTER 26

Patsy went off on a ten-day holiday to Tenerife and came back with a host of stories about all the wonderful men she had met. 'Did you know that they don't have any winter over there? I mean real winter like we get here. I got talking to the barman in a club one night and he told me it just gets a bit cooler and it rains a little more.'

'I'm sure you didn't spend all your time talking about the weather,' Sandy joked.

'That would be telling.' Patsy laughed.

'Are you planning to go again?'

'You bet. First chance I get.'

Sandy was pleased to have her back. Much as she was enjoying the hectic pace of work at Music Inc, she had missed her friend and was glad of her company when they took a night off and went to a record party. It was also good to have someone in charge when she visited her mother. Thankfully, Angela had settled in well at Sunnylands and was busy gathering a bunch of cronies around her.

One morning as she was discussing the daily news schedule with Patsy, she was surprised to find an item concerning Platform Two, the rock band that Sam Ross had invested in. 'Why's this item on the schedule?' she asked.

'They're playing three concerts in the O2 in a fortnight's time.'

'But what's the news value of the story? It looks like a promo piece to me.'

Patsy gave her a look. 'You've lost touch since you've been away, Sandy. They've gone very big in the UK. They've got a number-one hit in the charts.'

'Really?' Sandy replied, feeling slightly put out.

'Yes. This piece is an interview that Jack Rooney got with the lead singer, Oggi Simpson. He talks about all sorts of stuff: politics, global warming and world hunger. It's really just the usual predicable platitudes but all their fans will want to read it.'

'I hadn't realised.'

Patsy smiled. 'Well, you've been under a lot of pressure recently. Your mind has been on other things, with your mother's illness and all. It's understandable.'

Sandy felt annoyed with herself. Once upon a time she would have known every single record in the music charts and every detail about the artists. She had taken her eye off the ball and now she needed to get focused again – quickly. But she was also piqued because it looked as if Sam Ross's judgement had proved better than hers. He had seen the possibilities in Platform Two and she hadn't. And Sandy didn't like to be wrong.

The news about the Platform Two concerts had another result. It made her realise with a start that it was a long time since she had thought about Sam Ross. She had been distracted by so many problems that she had almost forgotten about him. Now she couldn't help wondering how his life was working out without her.

Was he making lots of money? Had he found another girlfriend? With his good looks and charm, it wouldn't be too much trouble for him. She sighed as she remembered the pain and embarrassment he had put her through. It was a pity he had proved to be such a deceitful man. If he had been more honest and less arrogant, they might have had a good relationship together.

She put Sam Ross out of her mind and concentrated on her work. But a few nights later as she was getting ready for bed, she was surprised to find herself thinking of him again. She remembered the happy evenings she had enjoyed in his company and the nights they had spent together in her bed. It crossed her mind that she might have been too hard on him.

Had she been too quick to send him away that time he had asked her to take him back? Had she cut off her nose to spite her face? It came as a shock to realise that she missed him. Eventually she fell asleep with images of Sam still on her mind. And they were there in the morning when she woke.

This will have to stop, she said to herself. My romance with Sam is over and it won't be put together again. She made a decision as she ate a quick breakfast in the kitchen. Every time a thought of Sam Ross comes into my head, I'll nip it in the bud. Otherwise, I'm storing up trouble for myself.

But it wasn't so simple. A week later, an envelope arrived for her in the morning post. When she opened it, she found two tickets for the opening Platform Two concert at the 02 arena, with a handwritten note from Sam.

> Hi Sandy, Hope you are keeping well. I thought you might like to attend this concert – it may change your mind about the band. Kind regards, Sam.

She read it again, searching for some hidden personal meaning. But it was just a plain, businesslike note. He had probably sent out similar letters and tickets to all the media journalists in the city. She put it aside and concentrated on her work. An hour later Patsy came in and spotted the tickets on her desk. 'You've got an invitation to the gig. Are you going?'

'I haven't decided.'

'You have to go. This is a major event. The concerts have sold out. The tickets are already changing hands for five times the original price.'

Sandy's jaw dropped. 'You're not serious.'

'I am. This is going to be mega, Sandy. If you don't want them, I'd be delighted to take them.'

'I'll let you know later.'

As the day wore on, Sandy's curiosity began to grow. The Platform Two that Sam had taken her to see had been mediocre at best. What had happened in the meantime that everyone wanted to get to their concert? She had to find out. As they were finishing up at eight o'clock, she said to Patsy, 'I'm going to take your advice. I'll go to the concert. Would you like to come with me?'

'I'd bite your hand off for one of those tickets.'

'There's no need to go to that extreme. We've got a date.'

As the day of the concert drew closer, her interest continued to grow till she ended up just as excited as Patsy. The concert was at eight o'clock. Thankfully, it was a fairly quiet day and Sandy was able to get away at six. She dashed home to get ready, chose one of her best outfits, then took a taxi to the O2. Patsy had changed at work and was already waiting when Sandy turned up.

A special guest area had been set up for people with invitations and a crowd was milling around. When they passed through the barrier, they were immediately approached by a waiter bearing a tray of champagne and they each took a glass.

'Only way to see a concert.' Patsy laughed. 'With VIP tickets and champers. Proper order, I say.' She drained her glass and took another. Meanwhile Sandy was scanning the faces, expecting to see Sam. There was no sign of him although she recognised many other faces. Patsy had been right. This *was* a mega event. It looked like most of the local music industry had turned out.

She chatted to several people she knew and then, at a quarter to eight, they began to drift into the auditorium to their seats. The two women finished their drinks and joined them. They were pleasantly surprised to find themselves in the first row of the hall right in front of the stage. Sandy looked around at the audience. The bulk were young but not exclusively. She noticed quite a few older people as well.

A few minutes later, the lights dimmed and the warm-up act came on. They played for half an hour, then left the stage to muted applause. A man in a tuxedo walked to the microphone. 'Thank you all for coming tonight. I think you're in for a really spectacular experience. Let me introduce you to the band that is already taking the rock world by storm. I give you ... Platform Two!'

A loud cheer went up as the musicians walked onto the stage where the drum kit and sound system had already been set up. They were in their early to mid-twenties. But someone had given them a makeover. Sandy remembered a bunch of gangly young men who looked like overgrown schoolboys. Now they oozed confidence and swagger in their leather jackets and torn jeans. Without further ado, the lead singer, Oggi Simpson, grabbed the microphone and the band launched straight into their first song, a raucous bluesy number that quickly had the audience tapping their feet. Sandy settled down to enjoy the show.

They played for two solid hours without a break, and when they finally left the stage after giving three encores, people were on their feet calling for more. Sandy was astounded. She had just sat through a performance that had blown her away. It was the most electrifying concert she had attended in a very long time. This was not the band she had seen a year ago. They were much more polished and professional, and their repertoire had developed a sophisticated edge. Sam's investment had obviously been put to good use.

As they made their way out, she ran into more people she knew. They were all talking excitedly about the show, how fantastic it had been and how they couldn't wait to hear the band again. Tomorrow the press would be raving about Platform Two. As they settled into a taxi to take them home, she turned to Patsy. She could rely on her for a realistic opinion. 'Did they live up to your expectations?'

'And some. I thought they were brilliant. What about you?'

'"Brilliant" is the only word to describe them.'

◆

The following morning when she was coming out of the bathroom, she heard her phone ringing. She gave a start when she recognised Sam Ross's number, and clamped it to her ear.

'I hope I didn't wake you up.'

'Sam?'

'You haven't forgotten me, then?'

'That would be difficult.'

She heard him laugh.

'I'm calling to ask how you enjoyed the concert last night.'

'How did you know I was there?'

'I have my spies just like you.' He was the old confident Sam from the days when they were lovers.

'But *you* weren't there. Or, at least, I didn't see you.'

'I didn't go. I can't stand the fuss of opening nights. Besides, I've sat through so many rehearsals with Platform Two that I know every chord and drumbeat off by heart. But the concert was a huge success.'

'Congratulations. I enjoyed myself immensely.'

'Well, that's the important thing. What did you think of the band? They're a bit different from what you remember, aren't they?'

'They were fantastic, Sam. How did you do it?'

'I'll tell you all about it when I see you. In fact, that's one of the reasons why I'm ringing. Are you free to have dinner with me tonight?'

She caught her breath. She had tried to put Sam Ross out of her life and now he was back again. 'I'm not sure, Sam. We have a lot of issues, you and me.'

'Oh, c'mon,' he coaxed. 'You're still not upset with me after all this time? Surely we can be friends.'

'Of course we can. But I'm not sure it extends to having dinner with you.'

'Why not? I won't bite you.'

'Well, for one thing, I'm not sure I'm free. I'd need to check my diary when I get into the office. Can I ring you later?' She knew it sounded like a feeble excuse and that he would see through it right away but it was the best she could think of.

'Okay, do that. I've got something important to tell you and lots of juicy gossip that I know you'll enjoy. So you can regard the dinner as work if it makes you feel any better.'

Her head was still in a spin as she put down the phone and began to get ready for the office. The call had been totally unexpected but she was surprised to discover that she'd been pleased to hear his voice again. And she was keen to see him and learn how he had worked the miracle of turning a mediocre group of musicians into rock superstars. Besides, he had something important to tell her. She wondered what it might be.

By the time she got into work, her mind was made up. She would accept his invitation. She knew she would enjoy the gossip and might even pick up some stories for Music Inc to develop. There was only one doubt. How could she keep this dinner on a strictly professional level and not allow it to wander off into something more personal? She'd have to play that by ear.

She waited till lunchtime before ringing him just so she wouldn't seem too keen. But when she picked up the phone, she found his number engaged. She tried again fifteen minutes later and it was still engaged. Sam was obviously a very busy man now that he had a big success on his hands. Everybody would want to talk to him. After one more attempt, she left a message asking him to call her.

A few minutes later, her phone rang and it was him.

'I'm free this evening,' she said. 'Where do you want to meet?'

'That's the best news I've heard all morning,' he said, with genuine pleasure in his voice. 'There's a wine bar called Rapello in Chatham Street. Can you meet me there at seven thirty? In the meantime I'll book a table somewhere nice for dinner. I'm really looking forward to seeing you again, Sandy.'

CHAPTER 27

At seven fifteen, she stepped into a cab to drive the short distance to the city centre and Chatham Street. She was wearing her dark business suit and a white blouse. She wished she had gone home to change but she hadn't had time. Instead she'd had to make do with a trip to the bathroom at Music Inc where she quickly brushed her hair and applied a little mascara and lipstick before setting off. It was her own fault. If she had accepted Sam's invitation this morning she could have planned her day better.

Rapello was a chic bar that had been squeezed between a row of offices and shops. She paid the taxi fare and struggled to make her way through the crowds jamming the entrance. Sam waved when he saw her and stood up to guide her to the seat he had kept for her in the corner.

As it turned out, he hadn't got dressed up either. He was wearing chinos with an open-necked sports shirt and had a woollen pullover tied around his waist. There was a warm smile on his handsome face.

'Where's this recession everyone's talking about?' Sandy said, as she sat down beside him and he kissed her cheek. 'I've never seen a bar so packed since the Irish rugby squad won the Triple Crown.'

Sam laughed. 'It's mainly people who work nearby,' he explained. 'They'll all be gone by eight. Maybe I should have suggested somewhere quieter.'

'This is fine.'

He looked into her eyes. 'It's great to see you, Sandy. You're as beautiful as ever.'

She blushed. Sam had lost none of his charm in the months since she had seen him. 'Thank you, but I don't feel it. I had to rush here straight from work.'

'Let me get you a drink. What are you having?'

'A glass of red would be nice.'

'Coming up.'

He turned to look for a waiter and Sandy used the opportunity to take in her surroundings. Rapello was designed in a classy modern style with smart furniture and art-nouveau prints on the walls. Most of the clientele appeared to be young professionals.

'One glass of red wine,' Sam said, as the waiter appeared and put it on the table beside her.

She thought he sounded tired. 'Busy day?'

'That doesn't even begin to describe it. I've been fielding phone calls since seven this morning. Now that the band are a success, everybody wants a slice of the action. But I'll talk about that later. How has your life been since the last time I saw you?'

'Do you want the good news or the bad?'

A look of concern crossed his face. 'Is there bad news?'

'Unfortunately, but I'll start with the good. Despite the downturn in the economy and a financial setback, which I won't go into, Music Inc is surviving. We're set to make a small profit this year. Our receipts are holding firm and I've managed to trim costs a little.'

'So people haven't lost their taste for scandal?'

'Some things never change.'

'And the bad news?'

'My mother had a fall recently and had to be hospitalised. While she was there, they discovered she has pernicious anaemia.'

He looked puzzled. 'What is it?'

'It's a rare condition that affects the blood cells. It can leave the patient confused and irritable. The symptoms can be similar to Alzheimer's.'

'Good Lord.' He reached out and took her hand. 'I'm really sorry, Sandy. Why didn't you call me? I would have been happy to help.'

'It all happened very quickly. My aunt stepped in and together we coped. But Mum can't be left on her own so she's moved into a retirement village called Sunnylands. It has marvellous facilities and she receives constant attention. She's very happy there.'

'That must cost a pretty penny.'

'It's expensive but I can manage.'

'Your mother seemed fine on the occasions when I met her. She was lively as a cricket. It sounds like you've had a run of bad luck, Sandy. What was the financial setback you mentioned?'

She wondered if she should tell him and decided to plough ahead. 'My accountant robbed me of three hundred thousand euros in a tax swindle.'

'*What?* How did he manage that?'

'I trusted him too much.'

'Why don't you sue him?'

'He's fled the country. The police are searching for him. I'm told I'm not the only one.'

He laid a comforting arm round her shoulders. 'You really have had a rough time.'

'That's putting it mildly.'

'But you seem to have come through it. You're a survivor, aren't you?'

'You tell me.'

'You don't give in easily. That's one of the things I admire about you.'

Sandy decided to change the subject. 'Let's talk about something more cheerful,' she said. 'I'm dying to find out how you managed to whip Platform Two into shape. When I saw them first, they didn't look at all like a band that would make the big time.'

'Do you remember the last time we talked about them?'

'It was in Marbella.'

'And you were a bit miffed.'

'I was afraid you were going to lose your investment. You put two hundred grand into the band, didn't you?'

'That's right. Would it surprise you to learn that I've already got back my investment? From now on everything I make is profit.'

'You still haven't told me how you did it.'

'I took your advice,' he said.

'But my advice was not to invest.'

'Yes, but you also told me they needed to work harder on their material and presentation. You said they would never make the big time in the raw shape they were in. So I staggered the investment. I sat down with their manager, Tommy Wright, and told him they needed to come up with better songs, change their image and, above all, keep rehearsing till they were ready to go back in front of a live audience. I set targets for them and released the cash in stages when I was satisfied they were making progress. I worked them hard till they became the polished act you saw last night. My investment in that band was one of the best decisions I ever made, Sandy. I'm set to make a lot of money from Platform Two.'

'I was wrong,' she said. 'And you were right. You saw something I missed.'

'But you had a hand in it too.'

'Now you're just being kind.'

'No, it's true.'

'So what's the next step?'

'I've spent all day talking to concert promoters in the UK and Europe. They're lining up to book the band. And we've already cut a deal for their first album.'

Sandy's ears pricked. 'Do you mind if I use that information for Music Inc?'

'Give me another week to sign contracts and I'll let you have the full story. You can have the exclusive.' He sipped his drink. 'This is a win-win situation for all involved. The members of the band stand to make a fortune from their work. But it wouldn't have been possible if I hadn't taken the decision to risk my money on them.'

'And if you hadn't decided to ignore my advice.'

'Sandy, don't put yourself down. It was your advice that got them where they are.'

It was after eight when they left the bar. Sam said he had heard good reports of a new fish restaurant out in Howth and had booked a table there. 'You like fish, don't you? You told me that the second time I saw you.'

'So you remembered.'

'Sandy, I was under your spell from the first time we met.'

•

Sam had left his Audi at home so they took a cab and drove north along the bay. It was a lovely spring evening and the air was fresh and warm. Sam was at his most charming. He was triumphant after his success last night with Platform Two but didn't gloat. He had been generous with his compliments and they hadn't been lost on her. Already she could feel the old bond that had existed between them stir into life.

The restaurant was on the West Pier in Howth where the fishing trawlers were tied up. Outside, the seagulls were screeching and diving for fish scraps. People were sitting at tables outside the pubs along the seafront enjoying the balmy evening air.

They were quickly shown to a place beside the window where they could look out at the sea. Sam called for wine and picked up the menu. Around the walls of the restaurant, nets and lobster pots jostled for space beside oars and fishing tackle to create a quaint maritime atmosphere.

'This place is cute,' Sandy remarked.

'And I hear the food is superb. But we'll soon find out about that. Have you decided what you want to eat?'

She had had a light lunch and now she was ravenous. 'Steamed mussels to begin, then monkfish.'

A young waitress took their order – Sam opted for fish soup and grilled lobster. While they waited for the first course, they gazed out at the sun as it began to sink into the ocean. For

Sandy, the scene brought back memories of the holiday when their romance was at its height.

The conversation turned again to Sam's business.

'I'm glad of your success,' she said. 'You really are very shrewd.'

He shrugged modestly. 'I've made some bad investments that lost me money. I don't mind admitting that.'

'But this one has come good in bucketfuls. You're going to be very busy.'

'But not too busy for other things, Sandy. Tommy Wright gets paid to look after the day-to-day affairs of the band, organising accommodation on tours, liaising with the concert promoters and the record company. I intend to concentrate on strategic development.'

'I know the business,' Sandy said. 'Believe me when I say it won't be easy.'

'Let's see.'

The mussels and fish soup arrived, and Sam ordered more wine. He was in a relaxed mood tonight, determined to enjoy himself, and as he wasn't driving he could let his hair down. It didn't escape her that he had chosen to celebrate his success with her, just the two of them in a lovely little restaurant when he could have been carousing at a music party in town.

She felt any lingering doubts evaporate as the evening wore on. Sam was at his witty best, telling jokes and sharing gossip. She was captivated once more by his easy manner, his attention and courtesy. Her thoughts went back to the very first meal they had shared together in Les Escargots when she had fallen for him. But as the dinner came to an end, the conversation turned once more to Platform Two.

'You said you had something important to tell me,' she reminded him, as he summoned the waitress for the bill.

'Yes, I have. I've kept the best news to the last.' He reached into his jacket pocket and withdrew an envelope. 'I'm not the only one who will benefit from the band's success.'

'How do you mean?'

'I put in fifty thousand euro for you. You own five per cent of their profits, Sandy. Open that envelope. It's a copy of the investment agreement.'

CHAPTER 28

She sat back in amazement. Was this real? If it was, it would spell the end of her financial problems. So long as Platform Two continued to be successful, she would be a wealthy woman. But another thought rushed into her mind. Was it a bribe? Was Sam attempting to buy his way back into her heart?

'Go on,' he urged. 'Open the envelope.'

Her fingers trembled slightly as she withdrew a sheet of paper. It was a legal document, signed and witnessed with an official stamp at the bottom. It stated that in consideration of €50,000 invested in Platform Two, Alexandra Devine was to receive five per cent of the band's earnings from concerts and the sale of recordings in perpetuity.

She looked up to find him waiting expectantly. 'Why did you do this?'

'Why not, for Heaven's sake? We were a couple at the time. I was in love with you. I thought you deserved a slice of the profits if the band were a success.'

She pushed the document back across the table. 'It's very kind, Sam, but I can't accept it.'

'You don't understand, Sandy. It's not a question of accepting or rejecting. You own a share of the band's earnings. It's yours by right.'

'I wish you hadn't done this, Sam. You should have consulted me first.'

'You would have had a fit if I'd told you. You were annoyed that I was putting money in. You'd have blown a gasket if I said I was investing for you too.'

'Then let me pay you back the fifty thousand.'

'No. It was a gift, Sandy. Can't you just accept it in the spirit in which it was intended? I thought you would be pleased.'

They were heading for an argument, which was the last thing she wanted. She didn't want to ruin the evening with another fight. 'Okay,' she said. 'Thank you. You've been very generous.'

He brightened at once. 'That's more like it. You'll enjoy a steady stream of income. And it will last for years. The band are only on the threshold of their career. You can pay your mother's bills and restore the money your accountant stole. You're going to be rich, Sandy.'

She forced herself to smile. 'You're right. I suppose I am.'

'Put that document in a safe place where it won't be lost. It's your ticket to financial security. Now, let's get you home. I've got another early start in the morning.'

He beckoned the waitress once more and asked her to order a cab. Twenty minutes later, it was dropping Sandy off outside her apartment block. She said goodnight and hurried inside to the sanctuary of her penthouse. She was still recovering from the shock of Sam's announcement.

She got into bed and lay for a long time staring at the ceiling. The more she thought about the events of the evening, the more her feelings began to change till in the end she felt embarrassed by her behaviour. What had come over her? And what must Sam think of her reaction? That she was a spoiled, ungrateful brat. Anyone else would have been overwhelmed by his generosity. Only a mad woman like her would have attempted to throw it back in his face.

Another thought occurred and made her feel worse. Sam had invested the money for her long before they had fallen out. It had been done when their romance was at its height. He had only revealed it tonight when it had turned out to be successful. She had misjudged him. The investment couldn't possibly have been a bribe.

As she lay in her lonely bed, she realised how much she missed him. She thought of the passionate nights they had spent together, the meals, the outings, the trips to the theatre. She needed Sam Ross. She needed his company and his reassuring presence. She thought of the months when she had struggled with her mother's illness. How much easier it would have been if he had been around to support her.

She had handled the situation disastrously tonight. In the morning, she would ring him to apologise, and this time she would accept his gift with good grace for the generous gesture it was.

◆

It was almost nine o'clock when she opened her eyes to see the morning light streaming in through the curtains. She got up, dressed and drank a cup of coffee. When she rang Sam's number, she found herself once more being invited to leave a message. 'Hi, Sam,' she said. 'I'm just ringing to thank you for a wonderful evening. Give me a call when you're free.'

Next she called her mother. She found her in a cheerful mood, eager to gossip. They spoke for a few minutes and Sandy promised to visit that evening. Then she went down to the parking area, got into the Porsche and headed into work.

Patsy was already there and briefed her on the news stories they were pursuing.

'I must say, you've settled in to your new job very fast,' Sandy remarked.

'Thank you.'

'Enjoying it?'

'What do you think? You trained me, Sandy. Music Inc is Paradise for a news junkie like me. No normal person would put up with the insanity around here. Of course I enjoy it. I love it.'

Just then Sandy's phone rang. When she answered, she heard Sam's voice. She waited till Patsy was gone, then closed the door. 'I want to apologise,' she began.

'Whatever for?'

'For the way I behaved last night. It was disgraceful. You gave me a most generous gift and I refused it. I don't know what to say except that I wish I could turn the clock back.'

'But you accepted it in the end. There's no need to apologise. I understood how you felt. You're an independent woman. You don't like to be beholden to people.'

'There's a difference between independence and bad manners.'

'Well, there's no need to feel bad about it. Why don't we put it behind us?'

'You're very gallant, Sam.'

'Now you're making me blush. Let's not mention it again. As for this evening, I should be free around seven. I was hoping you might help me unwind.'

'I'd love to but I've promised to visit my mother.'

'Then I'll come with you.'

'Are you sure?'

'I'd like to see her again. I can pick you up if you like and afterwards we might go somewhere nice to eat.'

'I'd love that. See you at my place.'

'That's settled, then. We've got a date.'

❖

Sandy sailed through the afternoon in a light-hearted mood. She couldn't wait for seven o'clock to come so she could see Sam's handsome face again. She busied herself with administrative chores, and before she knew it, it was five o'clock. She cleared her desk and told Patsy she was leaving. She drove straight home. She wasn't going to repeat the mistake of yesterday. This time, she was going to prepare properly for her date.

She ran a bath and luxuriated in the scented water for half an hour. Then she went into her bedroom and took out the same black cocktail dress she had worn on their first official date when they had met at La Belle Époque. It had knocked his socks off then. Hopefully, it would do the same tonight.

She was putting the finishing touches to her ensemble when she heard her phone ring.

It was Sam. 'I'll be leaving soon. Does seven thirty suit?'

'Seven thirty is fine.'

'I'll pick you up outside the complex.'

This time he was dressed in a smart suit, shirt and tie. The tiredness was gone from his face and he looked delighted to see her. He kissed her as she got into the car. 'Okay, where are we going?'

'Rathfarnham. I'll give you directions when we get there.'

Sam started the car and they set off. He turned to her with an admiring glance. 'You look stunning.'

She felt herself tingle with pleasure. 'Thank you, Sam. You look quite fetching too.'

He laughed. 'So the Mutual Admiration Society is back in business.'

They found Angela in the dining room, playing cards with Emily Sutherland and some of her friends. Her eyes lit up when she saw Sam. 'This is my daughter's young man,' she announced, as she introduced him to the group. 'He's an investor.'

Sam shook hands as the ladies examined him with interest. 'I thought I'd pay you a little visit Mrs D,' he said. 'I brought you a present.' He pressed a paper gift bag into her hand.

'What is it?' she asked, peering in.

'It's a lemon cake. You had it that day we went to Greystones.'

'I remember the occasion well. It was a wonderful afternoon. You're very thoughtful. Now why don't I take you on a quick tour of inspection and then we can go back to my flat and have a nice cup of tea?'

She said goodbye to her friends and they set off, Angela leading the way. Ten minutes later they arrived at her accommodation. She ushered them into the sitting room while she busied herself in the kitchen, and soon after she reappeared with a tray bearing cups and plates and the cake cut into slices. She sat down beside Sam. 'You're looking very smart, if I may say so. How are your investments going? I hope you're making plenty of money.'

'I can't complain, Mrs D.'

'There you go again. Didn't I tell you before to call me Angela?'

'You did. I'm sorry.'

'Where have you been these last few months? I meant to ask Sandy. She never talks about you at all.'

'Well, I've been very busy. I've been back and forward to London. I've invested in a rock band and I'm pleased to say they're very successful.'

'Ah,' she said, sitting forward as if she had just arrived at some momentous conclusion. 'That's what drew you and Sandy together. You're both involved in the music business.'

He smiled. 'You've got it in one. I met Sandy when I was looking for advice about my new band.'

'And was she able to help you?'

'Oh, yes, enormously,' he said, with a sideways glance at Sandy.

'That's what makes the world go round, people helping each other. But, then, you know that. That's why you're such a successful businessman.'

'How have you been keeping?' he asked.

'Very well, thank you. I had a little setback and had to go into hospital – I fell and cut my head. But I'm fully recovered, thank God.' She lowered her voice. 'Now I've moved here.'

'It's a beautiful place. Do you like it?'

'Oh, yes. I've made lots of friends here. Sunnylands suits me just fine.'

They stayed for an hour, Sam and Angela chatting like long-lost friends who had just been reunited. When it came time to leave, she insisted that Sandy bring him again. 'I enjoy conversation with intelligent people,' she announced. 'I find it very stimulating. Unfortunately most people just talk nonsense.'

'There's not much wrong with your mother's mind,' Sam remarked, as they got into the car and prepared to drive away.

'Let's hope it lasts.'

They went for supper to a quiet restaurant in Portobello. Sandy tucked into a plate of grilled chops while Sam regaled her with gory details of his negotiations with the concert promoters. As the candles cast shadows around the room, her thoughts went back to similar occasions when their romance had been in full bloom. 'So everything is coming good for you. You must be very happy.'

He stopped eating and put down his knife and fork. 'Not quite. If you must know the truth, Sandy, I haven't been happy since the day you left me.' He reached out and took her hand. 'I've missed you terribly. You and I were good together. Everyone said so. Why don't we give it another chance?'

She lowered her eyes. 'You hurt me badly, Sam.'

'I know, and I'm ashamed. Why don't we put the past behind us and start again?'

'You'd have to change.'

'I will.'

'And how will I know?'

'You'll see the evidence in my behaviour. I'm not a fool, Sandy. You're the only woman I've ever loved. I'm not about to lose you again.'

Later Sam drove the short distance to her address. He pulled up and turned off the ignition.

'Thank you for a wonderful evening,' Sandy said.

'My pleasure,' he replied.

There was an awkward pause and then his arm went slowly around her shoulders and he drew her close. Their lips met and in an instant her body was aflame. She clawed at him, pulling his shirt aside while her hands frantically explored his body.

'Slow down,' he whispered. 'We'll get arrested. Let's wait till we're inside.'

CHAPTER 29

Sam and Sandy had made their peace. Suddenly her life had turned around once more. Her finances had been restored, Music Inc continued to flourish and her mother was happily installed in Sunnylands. Everything was right in Sandy's world.

Sam never again suggested living together but it happened anyway without any formal decision being made. When he was in Dublin, they saw each other almost every day and invariably they ended up in Sam's house or Sandy's apartment. Gradually she began to move clothes and other personal items into his house and he did the same.

She discovered that living together had none of the drawbacks she had feared. She still had her personal space because Sam's growing involvement with the band meant regular trips to London to talk with recording companies and television executives. And she also had Music Inc to go to if she felt the need to escape.

But as time passed, she found herself wanting to be with him more and more, and missing him when he was not around. Sam had kept his promise to turn over a new leaf. He had become less demanding. He never questioned her. He had become what she had always hoped – the perfect partner, a rock of common sense and decency, the handsome Nordic god she had seen the first time she clapped eyes on him at Minnie Dwyer's party.

She realised she was back where she had been before they had had their falling out. She was madly in love with him again, only this time their love was stronger and more secure. She no longer feared potential rivals like Claire DeLisle or worried about what he might be getting up to on his trips away. She knew that Sam had learned his lesson. As a result, she trusted him without reservation.

Her new-found happiness didn't escape the attention of her colleagues. One morning Patsy said, 'I see the gleam is back in your eyes.'

'Really? You're very attentive.'

'You're in love. I know the signs.'

There was no point denying it. 'I'm back with Sam.'

'So you've forgiven him?'

'Yes, and this time it's for good.'

A few weeks after their reconciliation, Sam threw a party for the boys in the band and their manager, Tommy Wright. It was held at his house in Sandymount and Sandy was invited along to meet them. Contrary to their wild-boy image, she found them polite and almost reverential towards her. They seemed to be under the impression that she had persuaded Sam to invest in them and thus provide them with the opportunity to develop into the successful act they had become.

They gathered around her and bombarded her with questions about Music Inc and music journalism.

'How do you get hold of all those stories?' Oggi Simpson wanted to know.

'People tip me off.'

'Why do they do that?'

'Because I pay them well.' She laughed. 'Some celebrities even tip me off themselves.'

'Really?'

'Sure. Others are so desperate for publicity that they'll do almost anything to get a mention in the papers.'

'Well I never.' Oggi looked astonished.

'Let me give you some advice,' Sandy went on. 'You guys are getting quite big and, if Sam has his way, you'll get even bigger. When you're relaxing, try to stay out of trouble. Keep your private lives to yourselves. You never know who'll pick up the phone and talk to the tabloids.'

'We don't have to worry about that,' the drummer, Ger Bates, said. 'Tommy's hired an agent to handle our publicity.'

'That's for good publicity,' Sandy replied. 'But it's bad publicity that sells newspapers. Don't do anything you wouldn't want your mothers to know about.'

Afterwards, when the party had broken up and they were alone, Sandy said, 'They're a lovely bunch of guys. But they're as naïve as babes in arms. I tried to warn them about staying out of trouble. Maybe you'd have a word with Tommy Wright.'

'I'll make sure of it,' Sam said.

With every week that passed, her mother seemed more content with her new life at Sunnylands. Besides Emily Sutherland, she had made several new friends and had started attending the book club she had mentioned. It met every Wednesday afternoon. She had enrolled in bridge classes and even took part in exercise sessions several mornings a week. It was a long time since Sandy had seen her so happy.

But her move had left Sandy with several chores to take care of at the house in Primrose Gardens. First, she went every morning to feed the cat. Then there was the garden. It needed regular attention if it wasn't to run wild.

Eventually, she employed a gardener to trim the lawns once a week and weed the flowerbeds, and a window cleaner to call every fortnight. She also struck a deal with Sheila Malone, her mother's next-door neighbour, to look after the cat. But she knew that a longer-term solution would have to be found.

It was Sam who brought up the subject one evening when they were sitting in front of the television in Sandy's apartment. 'I've been meaning to ask you,' he said. 'Now that your mum has settled in Sunnylands what are you going to do about the house?'

'Nothing's been decided.'

'Have you discussed it with her?'

'No.'

'You could sell it,' he said. 'Unless you want to live in it yourself.'

'But I'm perfectly happy living here. Anyway, it's not mine to sell. That would have to be my mother's decision.'

'So what are you going to do?'

'I'll leave it for a while. My mother might change her mind about Sunnylands. Before we make a final decision about the house, I want to be absolutely sure that she's going to stay there.'

'You know there's been a rash of break-ins recently in that area? I don't want to frighten you but the house is a sitting target.'

He was right. Even with the windows being cleaned and the gardens cared for, the house had a lonely, unlived-in character now. It wouldn't take any half-intelligent burglar very long to figure out that it was empty.

'There is one other possibility you haven't considered.'

'What's that?'

'If you don't want to sell it, you could always rent it to someone. You should have no difficulty finding a tenant. The house would be occupied and it would also bring in some revenue. It would help offset the fees you're paying for Sunnylands.'

What Sam was saying made sense. One day when she went to visit, she raised the subject with Angela. They were sitting in the garden when Sandy said, 'You've settled in so well here.'

'Oh, yes,' Angela replied. 'I'm very happy.'

'I was wondering what we should do about the house.'

'How do you mean?'

'It's sitting there empty. I'm afraid it might get burgled.'

A look of horror crossed Angela's face. 'Really?'

'There's been a spate of break-ins recently. Sam thinks we should rent it to someone, maybe a young couple who would take care of it.'

'He's right,' Angela said. 'I've lived in that house all my married life. I hate the thought of it being vandalised. Why don't we do that?'

'You're sure?'

'Do it at once.'

✤

But before the house could be rented, it would first have to be tidied up, decorated, her mother's old furniture put in storage and new modern furniture bought. The following weekend, Sam hired a van and they set off for Primrose Gardens to begin the work.

Sandy had brought a large trunk to store the personal belongings that Angela had not taken with her to Sunnylands, and while Sam began the heavy task of shifting the furniture, she went into her mother's bedroom and started clearing it out. She began with Angela's books and ornaments, covered now with a light coating of dust. She placed them in the trunk.

Then she started on the wardrobe. It was mostly clothes that Angela hadn't worn for years. When she had finished, she turned to the dressing table, working her way through each drawer till she came to the bottom one. When she pulled it out, she discovered it was empty, except for a small metal box. She tried to open it and found it locked.

She shook the box and heard something rattle inside. What could it be? Perhaps it was jewellery, although her mother wasn't a great fan of brooches and other trinkets. She bent again to the drawer and carefully ran her fingers round the sides till she came upon something taped to the back. When she removed the tape, she found a key.

By now her curiosity was aroused. She inserted the key and pulled back the lid. Inside were several old black and white photographs and a letter. She studied the photographs. They showed a tall, dark-haired man standing beside a fountain in a square. In the background there was a brightly decorated church, its elaborate spires reaching for the sky.

She picked up the letter and examined the envelope. There were two addresses, one where the letter had been originally sent – 3 Calle Cervantes, Fuengirola, Spain – and the second an address in Dublin to which it had been returned. Across the top something was written in Spanish.

She hesitated, but, again, curiosity got the better of her. She opened the envelope and drew out the letter. It was dated 12 November 1980 in her mother's handwriting.

Dear Alejandro,

I have good news for you. You are going to become a father. Today my doctor confirmed that I am ten weeks pregnant. I am so happy. I am coming back to Spain so we can be together for ever. Please write and tell me when I should come.

Your loving Angela.

CHAPTER 30

Sandy stared at the letter as the blood drained from her face. She felt her skin grow cold and her heart begin to thump. She stood frozen to the spot as her eyes fastened on the date: 12 November 1980. A terrible reality came crashing in on her. If what the letter said was true, it could mean only one thing.

She called to Sam and he came hurrying into the room.

'What's the matter?' he asked. 'You look like you've seen a ghost.'

'What does this say?' she asked, her fingers trembling as she gave him the envelope and pointed to the words written in Spanish along the top.

'"Not Known at This Address. Return to Sender." What is this, Sandy? What's going on?'

'I found this letter in Mum's drawer. Here,' she said. 'Read it for yourself.'

His eyes quickly scanned the letter then looked at her again. 'What does it mean? I don't understand.'

'Look at the date, November the twelfth, 1980. I was born six months later on May the twenty-eighth, 1981. When that letter was written, Angela was almost three months pregnant. The dates tally perfectly. If this is true, Tom Devine was not my father. This man Alejandro was.' She was trembling with shock.

'You'd better sit down,' Sam said. 'I'll get you some water.' He went to the kitchen, returned with a glass and stood over her while she drank. 'Feeling better?'

'A little.'

'Before you rush to conclusions, let's consider this calmly. Are you sure this is your mother's handwriting?'

'It looks like it, although the letter was written over thirty years ago. Oh, Sam, I feel like the ground's just opened up beneath me.'

'We've no proof it's genuine.'

'It appears genuine. And look at the official Spanish postmark. November the sixteenth, 1980.' A sudden thought occurred to her. 'What's the English equivalent of Alejandro?'

'Alexander.'

Her heart continued to hammer in her breast. 'My name is Alexandra. Now, don't tell me that's a coincidence. Then there are these.' She gave him the photographs. 'They were with the letter. Look at the man in the pictures. He's tall and dark, like me. Angela is smaller. Don't you see that all the pieces fit together, Sam?'

He put his arms around her to comfort her. 'I have to admit it's pretty convincing. But it's still not conclusive. What are you going to do?'

'Mum is the only person who can tell me for certain. I'm going to confront her.'

'Don't do that, Sandy.'

'Why not?'

'Something like this could send her off the deep end. You're in shock right now. Do nothing till you've thought out all the consequences.'

❖

It was impossible to continue working so they decided to call it a day. They packed the furniture and clothes into the van and Sam drove Sandy home to the penthouse. Most of the journey was conducted in silence as she struggled with the enormity of what she had found. In the space of a heartbeat her world had been turned upside-down. Much of what she had taken for granted all her life was turning out to have been built on sand.

Sam pulled up the van at the gates to her complex. 'Do you want me to stay with you tonight and keep you company?'

'Thanks, Sam but I'd prefer to be on my own.'

'Then take my advice and get an early night. Things might look different in the morning. And don't do anything till I call you. Will you promise?'

'Yes.'

Sandy went up to her apartment, made a mug of milky chocolate and swallowed some paracetamol. Then she got undressed and slid into bed. She found it impossible to sleep. Her mind was still fevered as she mulled over the shocking discovery she had made. By now, she had convinced herself that the letter was genuine and she began to feel angry that Angela had kept the truth from her for so long.

Why had she allowed Sandy to believe a lie? Surely she had

the right to know who her real father was. To keep her only child in ignorance of her parentage was unforgivable.

Her mind turned to Tom Devine, the man she had always known as her father, and the many happy memories she had of him: the Sunday walks, the presents he had bought her, the holidays in Connemara, the time they had gone to London and seen Buckingham Palace. She thought of how devastated she had been when he had died and how much she still missed him. She remembered his kind, smiling face, his comforting words when she was worried or in trouble, the way he had always looked out for her, insisting that she complete her Leaving Certificate exams when she had wanted to become a rock star. He had been everything a father should be and no girl could have wished for better. Except he wasn't her father, he was an imposter. And he had been a willing conspirator in the plot to keep the truth from her.

Why had he done that? Why hadn't he explained the situation to her? Why had he never told her? She felt anger surge again in her breast.

Her thoughts jumped to Alejandro. She had often wondered how a brown-haired mother and a red-headed father could have produced a dark-haired daughter. Now she knew. The address on the envelope had revealed Alejandro's surname as Romero and he had lived in Fuengirola. She remembered the pretty little town with its squares and churches from when she had visited it with Sam. She wondered what Alejandro was like and if he had been as handsome as the photos suggested. How had he and Angela met? Had they been in love? And then another thought struck her. Was he still alive somewhere in Spain, married, with other children, which would mean she had brothers and sisters?

No sooner had she thought of him than the anger flared

again. He had rejected her too. He had sent back Angela's letter. Why had he done that? And how had Angela reacted when she had discovered that she was pregnant and alone with no one to turn to? Why had she kept the letter and the photographs? Why hadn't she destroyed them?

There was so much to consider and it had come out of the blue. Sandy could no longer think straight. Finally, she drifted off to sleep, her mind still wrestling with dozens of unanswered questions.

When she woke, the shock had passed and she could think more clearly. But the questions had not been resolved. She went into the kitchen and made scrambled eggs, toast and coffee. While she ate, she examined her options. She could destroy the letter and the photographs and continue her life as if nothing had happened. Maybe in time the letter would slip from her mind and the questions would disappear. But she knew she couldn't do that. She wouldn't be at peace till she got answers. She wouldn't be able to look Angela in the eye again till she had the truth.

There was one person who might be able to help. Betty had told her a little bit about how Tom Devine and Angela had met and got married. She might know about Alejandro and the letter. She would go to her at once and ask her to tell her all she knew. But before she did that she would talk again with Sam as she had promised.

He answered at the first ring, as if he had been waiting for her call.

'Sleep all right?'

'Not really,' she replied. 'But I'm calm and I've decided what I'm going to do. I'm going to ask my aunt what she knows.'

'Are you sure?'

'Yes.'

'What makes you think she knows any more than you?'

'Because she's Angela's only sibling. If there's anyone she would have confided in, it's Betty.'

'Be careful, Sandy. You're getting into some serious stuff.'

'Yes, but it's my stuff too. I think I have a right to know.'

'Good luck. I'll call and see you around six. You can let me know how you get on.'

She checked the time. It was half past nine. Betty's husband, Henry, would have left for his part-time job at a local warehouse and she would be alone at home. She lifted the phone and rang.

'Hi, Betty,' she said. 'It's me. I'm driving over to your house. I should be there in half an hour. You and I have to sit down and have a serious talk.'

'What about?'

'I'll tell you when I get there.'

❖

Betty's house was shining in the morning sun when Sandy got there, the paintwork gleaming, the lawns trimmed and the flowers blooming in the window boxes. Sandy was about to disturb the tranquillity of the peaceful house but she felt she had no other choice.

Betty brought her into the kitchen. An apple cake sat on a plate in the middle of the table. 'Before we do anything, let's have a cup of tea,' her aunt said, moving immediately to fill the kettle. 'How have you and Sam been keeping? Well, I hope.'

'We're both fine. I told you he has invested in a band. They've been very successful. It keeps him busy.'

'Busy can be good,' Betty replied. 'It stops people thinking too much and brooding. But there's a limit.'

The kettle whistled as it came to the boil and her aunt poured water into the teapot.

'Let it draw for a moment,' she said. She cut two slices of cake, then poured the tea and finally sat down opposite Sandy. There was an apprehensive look on her face, as if she scented trouble. 'So, you wanted to talk.'

'I've been concerned about Mum's house now that she's settled down in Sunnylands. It's sitting idle and I'm worried about burglars.'

'You're right to be worried. There's been a plague of break-ins recently.'

'I convinced her we should rent it out to tenants.'

'Oh?' Betty said. 'She didn't object?'

'She seemed very happy with the idea. Yesterday Sam and I went over there to clear out the furniture and stuff. I came across this.' She opened her bag and took out the letter. 'I found it in a drawer in her bedroom.' She passed it to Betty, who glanced at the envelope and the colour left her face. 'Read it,' Sandy said.

Betty recoiled. 'I don't need to. I know what it'll say.'

'Nevertheless, I think you should look at it.'

Betty took out the letter and the photographs. She put on her reading glasses and studied them. When she was finished, her eyes looked sad. 'This brings back a lot of bad memories. Your mother hoped you would never find out about this.'

'But I have. And now I'm here. I want you to tell me all about it.'

Betty was becoming agitated. 'I can't do that, Sandy. Angela made me promise.'

'But the promise isn't binding. I've learned about it on my own. And, anyway, I have a right to know.' She took her aunt's hand and looked directly into her eyes. 'Tom Devine wasn't my father, was he?'

Betty bit her lip. 'No.'

'Alejandro was?'

Betty nodded slowly. 'Yes.'

CHAPTER 31

'I need more tea,' Betty said. 'I'm finding this really difficult.'
She lifted the pot and poured another cup. 'What are you going
to do about it?'

'I haven't decided yet.'

'I'll tell you what I know but on one strict condition. You
must never mention it to your mother.'

'She doesn't have to know that I got it from you.'

Betty shook her head and a firm tone entered her voice.
'Where else could it have come from? She's not stupid. If Angela
knew you had found out it could kill her. Her one concern was
that you should be protected. Now either you agree to my terms
or you can leave.'

Sandy could see there was no point arguing. Her aunt was
not going to change her mind. 'All right.'

Betty drank some tea and steadied herself. 'Your mother and

I grew up in Arklow, County Wicklow, where our parents ran a country pub. They died when you were just a little girl so you probably don't remember much about them.'

'No, I don't,' Sandy said.

'There were two sisters, me and Angela. I was the older one but Angela had the brains. She was very clever with books and languages. She passed her Leaving Cert with flying colours and got a place at UCD so that meant she had to move to Dublin. I decided to move with her and we shared a flat. I got a job and Angela started her studies at university.

'I don't have to tell you, Sandy, we had a ball. Dublin was such an exciting place compared to Arklow. It was like Paris or New York to us. I was the wild one. I fell in with a bunch of girls from work and we'd be out dancing every night. Angela came with us sometimes but more often she was studying, her head stuck in books. She was very determined to pass her exams and become a teacher.

'She finished her exams in the summer of 1980, then had a long wait to get the results. She was at a bit of a loose end till one day she spotted an advert in one of the papers looking for an au pair to teach English to two Spanish children who lived in Fuengirola on the Costa del Sol. She applied for the job. I remember she was very excited at the prospect of working down there with the lovely weather and the sun and everything.'

'I can imagine,' Sandy said.

'She had to get references, of course – they weren't going to give this job to just anyone. They were a well-to-do family called Gomez. I think the father was a doctor. But in the heel of the hunt, they came to Dublin to interview Angela and offered her the job. They said they would send her a plane ticket.

'She couldn't believe her luck. That was a very happy time,

what with all the preparations and the packing and everything. Once she left, Angela was very good at keeping in touch. She wrote to me every week to tell me how she was getting on. She loved the job but it wasn't all work. She had free time in the evening so she was able to get out and explore Fuengirola and make new friends.

'One day, she told me she had discovered a little Irish bar called the Emerald Isle and it was very popular with Irish tourists. She used to go there a lot to talk to Irish people. I suppose she was a bit homesick, although she never said so. The man who ran the bar was a Spaniard called Alejandro Romero.'

At the mention of the name, Sandy jumped but Betty pressed on. 'According to Angela, he was very handsome, with dark features and flashing eyes. What was more, he was quite taken with her. She said he used to make a fuss of her and give her free drinks and so on. The next thing he was taking her out to restaurants and for drives in his car to visit out-of-the-way places. He introduced her to his friends and they fussed over her too. Of course, she was completely bowled over. What young girl wouldn't have been – a handsome man paying her attention like that?'

'Did she say how old he was?'

'He was maybe four or five years older than her. That was part of the attraction, don't you see? Alejandro was a sophisticated man of the world. Anyway, her summer job came to an end and she had to return home. I thought she was a bit down in the dumps at leaving Spain and Alejandro behind.

'But she continued to keep in touch with him. It was all done on the phone. Of course, back then, very few people had their own phones so each week she went down to the public phone box at the end of the street and rang Alejandro at the Emerald Isle.

'She was always happy after those phone calls although I

could see the difficulties involved in conducting a long-distance romance. But it didn't seem to bother her. Meanwhile she got her exam results. She had passed with distinction and now she started applying for teaching posts. Of course, with such a good degree, it wasn't long before she landed a job – at St Gabriel's School in Rathgar, which was perfect because it was nearby.

'But she wasn't happy for long. I began to notice that a sort of blanket of gloom had settled over her. She seemed worried and depressed all the time but I put it down to the stress of teaching those children. Then one day I came in from work and found her weeping in the kitchen.'

Betty paused and took another sip of tea. 'I asked her what was wrong and she said she had missed her period. Well, that happens sometimes, as you know, so I told her not to worry. But then she said it was the second one she had missed and I knew there could be only one explanation. I sat her down and asked her bluntly if she might be pregnant.

'I questioned her about Alejandro Romero and she told me she had made love with him on the night before she left Spain. It was the first and only occasion. Now we were faced with a terrible dilemma. Angela was on a temporary contract and it was due for review in six months. That was a very different time in Ireland, Sandy. We both knew that she could lose her job.

'I urged her to see a doctor at once but she refused. I think she was in denial and didn't want to face the truth. She said she would wait for one more month and then she would go. In the meantime I told her to contact Alejandro and tell him, but when she rang the Emerald Isle she couldn't get through. She called several more times but couldn't contact him.

'She missed her period the next month and now there was no doubt at all. She saw the doctor and he confirmed that she was ten weeks pregnant. That's when she decided to write the letter you found. But when it was returned, her world fell apart. God help her, I never saw a creature so desperate. She didn't know where to turn.'

'What did she do next?'

'There was a school break coming up and she decided to go down to Spain and find Alejandro. She said he loved her and was a decent man and would stand by her once he knew. She had this idea that they could get married and everything would turn out all right. But she came back after a week, and the moment I saw her, I knew that it had gone wrong. She said the bar was closed and boarded up. Alejandro had left Fuengirola and nobody knew where he had gone.'

Betty paused. She was choked with emotion. She took out a handkerchief and blew her nose. Sandy sat still, her heart filled with sympathy for Angela, and wonder at how this story was going to finish. 'Well, it looked like the end of the road. Here she was, a single girl and pregnant, the father disappeared. There was no way she could hold on to her teaching job. So how were she and her baby going to survive?

'Poor Angela was at her wits' end. Of course, an abortion was out of the question. It wasn't available here for one thing and, anyway, her conscience wouldn't let her even contemplate it. She said she was determined to have her baby, come what may.

'And that was where Tom Devine entered the picture. I already told you that Angela and Tom had become friendly through the church and they used to walk back together after Sunday Mass. He was a lot older than her but he was a lovely, kind man. One Sunday afternoon, Angela came home and said the problem was solved. Tom had agreed to marry her.

'I was surprised to say the least and, of course, I was delighted for her. But I asked if Tom knew all the circumstances. I could see it might cause big problems if she was marrying him under false pretences. But she said, yes, she had told him she was pregnant and Tom had said he didn't mind. I suppose he must have been in love with her. He said he would marry her and rear the baby as his own. And that's exactly what he did.

'It was a very happy marriage – I don't need to tell you that. I don't think they ever had an argument in all the years they lived together. And he loved you as if you were his own child. But Angela never got over that experience. She never mentioned Alejandro again. She didn't even like anyone to mention Spain because it brought back all those sad memories she had.

'And then Tom died suddenly, and you know what happened next. She never got over the shock. She was never the same again and, sadly, it was all downhill after that.'

Betty stopped and blew her nose again. 'You've heard it all now. I've told you everything I know.'

Sandy stared at her. She had been mesmerised by what her aunt had told her and now she could see her mother in an entirely different light. She wasn't the selfish woman she had suspected. She had endured a terrible experience and survived. She had been a good mother who had loved Sandy.

As for Tom Devine, he had done something that few men would. He had reared her as his own child, given her his name and loved her unconditionally. She could no longer be angry with him: she forgave him for the part he had played in concealing her true identity.

'I have one more question. Why was Angela determined to keep all this from me?'

'Isn't it obvious?' Betty replied. 'She thought you wouldn't love her if you knew.'

CHAPTER 32

Betty seemed relieved that the conversation had finally come to an end. She stood up to wash the cups and plates. 'Remember your promise,' she said. 'Angela must never know we had this conversation.'

But for Sandy that was only the beginning. The story had left her emotionally drained. She had got important information about her paternity but it had only raised new questions. Why had Angela named her after her lover, Alejandro, despite all that had happened? And the other big issue: why had she kept the letter and the photographs? But those were questions that only Angela herself could answer.

She thanked her aunt and left the house. As soon as she got into her car, she had a sudden urge to visit her mother in Sunnylands.

She found her sitting in a quiet corner of the lounge with Emily

Sutherland. They had sheets of writing paper before them. 'We're deciding on our next read for the book club,' Emily announced. 'We've got to steer a middle course, you see. Some of them want low-brow stuff and others want books that are so dense no one can understand them. It's not easy keeping everybody happy.'

Angela smiled at her daughter, clearly glad to see her. 'How are you, my dear?' She looked happy and content in that peaceful corner. How differently she must have felt when that letter had come back unread from Alejandro.

'I'm fine.'

'And how is Sam? Still poking about with his investments?'

'He's fine too. Busy as usual.'

'You look tired,' her mother continued. 'Have you been sleeping properly?'

Sandy avoided the question. How could she tell her that she had spent half the night tossing and turning and still hadn't fully recovered from her conversation with Betty? 'I've just called in to bring you up to date about the house.'

'What house?' Emily asked.

'Mine,' Angela explained. 'I'm putting it up for rent.'

'Really? Are you happy to have strangers living in it?'

'I don't mind. It's better than leaving it sitting there waiting to be robbed. There's been an outbreak of burglaries recently.'

Emily shivered with distaste. 'That's awful. What are the police doing about it?'

'Trying to catch the thieves, I hope.'

'Anyway,' Sandy continued, steering the conversation back on course, 'we've decided to put your furniture into storage and buy new stuff, something hard-wearing and inexpensive. Then we'll probably get the decorators in to give it a make-over.'

'How are you going to find tenants?' Angela asked.

'We'll hire a letting agent to do that.'

'Have you spoken to one?'

'Not yet. We'll wait till we've finished. Then the agent will have a better idea of how much rent to charge.'

'It sounds very complicated,' Emily put in.

'Not really,' Sandy replied. 'Once we hand it over we'll have nothing more to do with it. We'll just leave everything to the agent. She'll vet the tenants and check their references and make sure the rent is paid, of course.'

'You're very good doing all this work for your mother.'

Sandy glanced at Angela. She looked so content, blissfully unaware of the turmoil that was swirling round her daughter. 'I don't mind. I just want Mum to be happy. Now she'll have one less thing to worry about. So tell me about the book club. Is it going well?'

'It's taken off like a rocket,' Angela said. 'They all want to join. But we have to limit the numbers so we've drawn up a waiting list.'

'Who are "we"?' Sandy asked.

'Emily and me. We're the committee. It was our idea to start it so it's only fair we should run it.'

'Some of the applicants aren't really suitable,' Emily said, lowering her voice. 'Some of them don't even read books. They just think if they don't join, they might be missing something.'

'And what book have you chosen for next week?'

'Maeve Binchy's *Tara Road*,' Angela said. 'Maeve is very accessible and she writes wonderful stories, all those marvellous characters. I think good characters are what make a book. Readers want to feel involved.'

'I'm with you on that,' said Sandy. 'I can see the book club is in good hands with you two ladies running things.'

Emily smiled modestly. 'Well, your mother and I are avid readers. I think you can say we've got good taste.'

Sandy sat chatting for half an hour, then took her leave. By the sound of things, Angela and Emily would have hours of enjoyment running the club and plotting who to let in and who to leave out.

She drove back to her apartment, sat by the window and drank a glass of wine while she turned everything over in her mind. She couldn't wait to see Sam and tell him what she had learned from Betty.

He turned up at six and sat in silence as she related the story of her mother's love affair with Alejandro, how she had gone looking for him and found he had disappeared.

'That's terrible. Your poor mother. It helps explain her behaviour, don't you think?'

'Yes, but what I can't understand is why she kept the letter and the photographs. And then when I was born, she named me after him. It doesn't make sense when you consider all that he did to her.'

'But you have only part of the story, remember. You don't know what really went on between your mother and Alejandro. They are the only ones who can tell you that.'

'I can't talk to my mother. She made Betty promise that she would never tell me. Betty said it would kill her if she knew I had found out.'

'Then you'll have to be satisfied with what you've learned, Sandy. You've done your best. If I was you, I'd put it out of my mind and move on.'

❧

Over the next few days, Sam and Sandy finished clearing out her mother's house, then got in a firm of decorators that had been highly recommended by one of Sam's friends. They installed the new furniture, put up curtains and hung some modern prints on the walls. When they had finished, the house had been transformed. Now it looked bright, airy and full of space. The next task was to find a letting agent. There was a firm in Ranelagh Sandy had been told was very good. She called in one day and was met by a confident, bustling young woman called Caroline O'Neill.

'When can I see it?' she asked, once Sandy had explained her mission.

'I can take you now if you like.'

They got into Sandy's Porsche and drove the short distance to Primrose Gardens. The moment she saw the house, Caroline's eyes lit up. When Sandy had taken her on a tour of inspection, she said, 'It's perfect. I love the décor and the size. And you have gardens front and rear. Good properties in this area don't come on the market very often and this one is excellent.'

'What sort of rent could we expect?'

'Around two thousand a month, I'd say.'

'And you're sure you can find tenants?'

'Absolutely. This is in a prime location. It's well served by schools and amenities and close to the city centre. I'm thinking of a corporate letting, some business executive who's been relocated to Dublin. We deal with a lot of people like that. They usually turn out to be excellent clients and there's the added bonus that the company pays the rent so there are rarely any problems in that regard.'

'Put it on your books and let me know when you get someone.'

A week later, Caroline rang to say she had found a family who wanted the house. The father was an electronics engineer with a multinational company and had been transferred to Dublin for three years. He had a wife and two small boys. What was more, they were willing to pay €2,500 a month, which would go a long way to cover Angela's fees at Sunnylands.

'I deal with families quite a lot and they're always good tenants. They treat the house as their own home. It's very rare to have trouble with a family.'

'Well, if you're confident, go ahead and sign them up.'

A few days later, a leasing contract arrived and Sandy took it out to Sunnylands for Angela's signature. She was delighted to learn that people were prepared to pay such a large sum to rent her house and proudly relayed the information to her friends. After that, everything clicked along like clockwork. The first month's rent and the deposit were lodged in Sandy's bank account, minus the letting agent's fee. She gave a sigh of relief. One more problem had been solved. Now she could turn her attention to other matters.

Promoting Patsy to executive editor of Music Inc had been an inspired decision. Patsy was a good boss who worked hard and led by example. The staff liked her and, as a result, the operation ticked over smoothly. But now that her mother was happily settled in Sunnylands, Sandy found time hanging on her hands.

She took to going into the office at Charlotte Quay for a couple of hours each morning where she would look after bills and invoices and chase up some of her contacts. She made a point of not interfering in Patsy's work, staying too long or doing anything that might undermine her friend. Sandy knew she wouldn't like it if someone did any of that to her.

As the days passed, she grew increasingly restless. It wasn't simply that she no longer had the constant pressure of Music Inc to occupy her time and energy: something deeper was gnawing at her peace of mind. Sam noticed it too but put it down to the shock discovery of the letter and the conversation with Betty.

One evening as they were having dinner, he announced that he was going to London to deal with some business involving Platform Two and suggested that she might like to come with him. 'The change of scenery will do you good. And now that spring has arrived, London will be looking its best.'

'Won't you be tied up in meetings all day?'

'Unfortunately, I will.'

'So what would I do?'

'You could go sightseeing. I'll be free in the evenings. In fact I've just had a better idea. The meetings will take a couple of days. Why don't we go for a week and have a nice little break?'

The idea was appealing. It might lift her out of the boredom that had settled over her. Besides, she felt she was due a break after the stress of recent weeks. 'Okay,' she said. 'I'll come.'

'So it's agreed. I'll organise everything. I know a nice little hotel in Kensington that will be ideal. It's close to everything. There are lots of places to visit and loads of really first-rate restaurants.' He was making it sound very attractive.

'When are we going?' Sandy asked.

'Two days' time. You can start packing.'

The thought of the holiday perked Sandy up. It was years since she had been to London. Indeed, the most vivid memory she had of the city was the time she had gone there as a little girl with her parents. The following morning, when Sam had left her apartment, she sat down at her laptop and began trawling for tourist information.

Kensington was smack in the centre of the best part of the city. It was near the West End and close to the chic areas of Knightsbridge and Belgravia. On the doorstep were Kensington Gardens and Hyde Park. Close by were the Royal Albert Hall and Kensington Palace and smart shops like Harrods. There was a wealth of museums and art galleries all within walking distance. Next she checked the weather forecast. It was going to be bright and sunny. Sandy got out her cases and began to fill them with clothes.

The flight was leaving at nine o'clock so they were up early and ready for the taxi that had been booked to take them to the airport. Then it was a short hop till they were putting down at London Heathrow. There was the usual airport hassle, then another taxi ride until they were deposited at midday outside the Paramount Hotel, a small boutique establishment in the shadow of Kensington Gardens.

Sandy was in need of a change of clothes. A porter in a striped waistcoat helped carry their luggage to their room. Sam tipped him, then departed for a series of meetings with Platform Two's manager, Tommy Wright, accountants and concert promoters. He promised to be back by six to have dinner at a nearby restaurant.

Sandy lay down on the bed and felt her eyelids droop. All the rushing about had drained her. Soon she pulled herself together, put on jeans, runners and a light jacket, stuck a tourist map in her bag and adjusted her shades before setting off into the afternoon sunshine. She headed off towards the green expanse of Hyde Park.

When she got there, it was quiet and provided a respite from the honking traffic of central London. Most of the strollers appeared to be tourists like her, clutching bottles of water and guide books. Occasionally a posse of riders cantered by on their sleek ponies. She kept walking for about half an hour, then sat on a bench beside the Serpentine to watch some children feeding breadcrumbs to the ducks.

She felt a wonderful sense of liberation settle over her. The quiet and the wide green open spaces were balm to her senses. She had a whole afternoon to wander as she pleased without ticking deadlines or ringing phones. By two o'clock she was hungry so she set off in search of something to eat and came across a delicatessen with tables outside. She sat down and ordered coffee, with a ham baguette. While she ate, she took out her map and plotted her route back to the Victoria and Albert Museum.

The museum was more crowded than the park but she spent a pleasant time strolling from room to room, viewing the extensive collection of ceramics and silverware. She was so engrossed in the exhibits that it was half past five before she got back to the Paramount Hotel. She had just finished dressing when Sam arrived, looking thoroughly disgruntled.

'You look worn out,' she remarked.

'I *am* worn out. I hate these bloody meetings with accountants. They seem to get a perverse pleasure out of making the simplest things appear complicated. But I had a good day. I got my way in the end.'

'Have a shower and get dressed. You'll feel better when you have a nice plate of food in front of you and a glass of wine in your hand.'

'How did you get on?' he asked. 'Manage all right without me?'

'I had a lovely day strolling through the park. I'll tell you all about it at dinner. Now hurry up and get ready before they give our table away to someone else.'

❖

The restaurant was dim and intimate with lamps on the tables and a guitarist sitting in a corner playing soulful love songs. Sam was obviously starving because he ordered a steak while Sandy contented herself with grilled trout. They drank glasses of brandy before heading back to their hotel.

Sandy was in a romantic mood but she was to be disappointed. Sam got undressed immediately while she nipped into the bathroom to change into a lacy nightie she had brought specially. She slipped in beside him and cuddled against his warm body. She was rewarded with a loud snore. Sam was already fast asleep.

❖

The following nights were more exciting. Once Sam had got over his initial exhaustion, he proved to be an energetic lover. The days slipped away and the weather stayed fine. He completed his business and devoted himself to her. They went shopping, visited various must-see tourist attractions, took in a concert and went to a West End show.

But as the holiday drew to a close Sandy felt the earlier restlessness return. Some unfinished business demanded her attention and, try as she would, she could not shake it off. She began to realise that she would not be satisfied till she had resolved it.

On their last evening, Sam had arranged for them to eat in a French restaurant in Chelsea that had attracted a host of five-star reviews. They had a superb meal accompanied by an excellent bottle of burgundy. As the desserts were being served, she reached out and took his hand. 'I have a question to ask you, Sam, about a matter that is very important to me. There is something I have to do. It's been bothering me for some time.'

'What is it?'

'I need to know more about my background. Angela and Alejandro are the only people who can tell me. But I can't talk to Angela. That leaves Alejandro. You speak good Spanish. Will you come to Spain with me and help me find him?'

CHAPTER 33

He stared across the table at her. 'Sandy, I thought you were going to put all this behind you?'

'I can't, Sam. Believe me, I've tried but it keeps coming back. I won't be able to rest till I've at least made an effort to find him.'

'But you don't know if he's still alive, for God's sake. Besides, Spain is a vast country. It would be like looking for a needle in a haystack.'

'I have the address where the letter was sent to in Fuengirola. We visited it – remember? That pretty little town along the coast from Marbella? We could start there.'

'But it happened over thirty years ago. Why would anyone remember?'

'They might.'

'You're deluding yourself, Sandy. You're asking me to go on a wild-goose chase. If Alejandro is still alive, he could be living anywhere. And what makes you think he'd want to see you? He might have married and have a family. Why would he welcome you suddenly turning up on his doorstep?'

'Because I'm his daughter. If he's still alive, I want to meet him. I want to talk to him. I want to know exactly what happened between him and Angela. It must have been something strong to make her keep that letter and name me after him.'

Sam heaved a heavy sigh. 'Once you get your teeth into something, you don't give up, do you?'

'No, Sam, not something as important as this.'

❖

The flight back to Dublin left on time and it was one o'clock when the plane put down. The taxi dropped Sandy at her apartment, then travelled on with Sam to Sandymount where he wanted to collect his mail and make some phone calls. He promised to ring her later in the afternoon.

Sandy took the lift to her penthouse and unpacked her cases. She called Patsy to make sure that everything was under control at Music Inc, then Sunnylands to check on her mother. When she had finished, she made a cup of tea and sat down at the kitchen table. Since her talk with Sam last night, her desire to look for Alejandro had grown stronger. Now she was determined to go. If Sam wouldn't accompany her, she would do it on her own.

She hadn't much to go on. She knew very little about Alejandro apart from his name and possibly his age. Betty had said that he was four or five years older than Angela, which would make him fifty-six or -seven. She had the photographs to show what he had looked like as a young man but he would have changed over the last thirty years.

She suddenly saw the difficulty of the task she had set herself.

Sam was quite right. It would be like looking for a needle in a haystack. But she was determined. She had made her decision and she was going to stick to it. If she didn't try to find him she would regret it till the end of her days.

It occurred to her that Betty might have more information about him, maybe something she had hidden or forgotten. But she was afraid to ring her aunt. She had been so reluctant to talk that it had been an ordeal to extract the information she had managed to get. If she went back again she would only upset her further. She would have to go with what little she had.

She sat at the kitchen table making her plans as the afternoon wore away. She would need somewhere as a base in Fuengirola while she made her enquiries. But that wouldn't be difficult: it was a tourist town and there were bound to be plenty of hotels. She would need money, maybe a lot of money. She could use her credit cards to begin with, perhaps open an account with a Spanish bank and transfer funds into it as necessary.

The language would be a major problem. She had only a few words of Spanish. She would have to hire an interpreter. She got out a sheet of paper and made a list of things to do. As it grew longer, her spirits sagged but she pressed on.

Her thoughts were disturbed by the ringing of her phone.

'Brooding about Alejandro?' asked Sam.

'You read my mind.'

'That's not difficult. So you're still hell bent on looking for him?'

'I'm more determined than ever.'

'And nothing will persuade you to drop this crazy idea?'

'No.'

'Then I'll come with you. I'd never forgive myself if I let you go alone.'

Immediately she felt as if a burden had been lifted from her shoulders. Having Sam with her would be a tremendous advantage. He spoke the language and had some experience of how things worked in Spain. 'I'm truly grateful, Sam. You don't know how much this means to me.'

'I think I do. That's why I've agreed to come. I'm on my way over to you now.'

Twenty minutes later, she heard the security buzzer sound to tell her Sam had arrived. She pressed the switch to let him in. He came through the front door and followed her into the kitchen, sat down at the table and immediately began asking questions. 'Have you thought how we're going to go about this?'

'We have the address in Fuengirola where he lived. I thought we could start there and check if anyone remembered him or knew where he had gone. We could take it from there.'

'It's worth a try but I wouldn't hold my breath. It's a long time ago, Sandy.'

'There was also the bar where he worked, the Emerald Isle.'

'The same thing applies.'

'If all else fails we could run ads in the local papers asking for information. Maybe offer a reward.'

'That might be worth a shot. However, there's a more obvious place to look. If he lived in Fuengirola and ran a business there, the *ayuntamiento* is bound to have some record of him.'

'What's that?'

'The town hall. Every property owner is obliged to pay taxes. They might have a record.'

She could feel a faint stirring of hope in her breast. 'So we'll go and ask at the town hall?'

'They're going to love you when you turn up looking for

someone who lived there thirty years ago. But if it's got to be done, so be it. Now, where were you thinking of basing yourself?'

'In a local hotel.'

'I've got a better idea. We can stay at Club Atlantic in Marbella. I've checked with my friend and it's free.'

❀

With Sam on board, the task she had set herself didn't seem so daunting. And as her plans began to fall into place, her excitement grew. They checked for flights and decided to go down to Marbella in a couple of days' time. Now that she had made up her mind, Sandy was keen to get started. In the meantime, Sam said he would call a few people he knew in Spain and seek their advice about trying to trace a missing person.

The days were swallowed in preparations and then it was time to leave. Since she didn't know how long she would be in Spain, Sandy packed two suitcases of clothes and a carry-on bag with her laptop computer. They had booked an afternoon flight and Sam had arranged to pick her up by taxi. She rang Patsy to tell her she was going away for a while, locked up the penthouse and went down to meet him.

It was a smooth flight, and by seven o'clock, the plane was landing at Málaga airport. Half an hour later, Sandy was striding out into the bright sunshine and helping Sam load the luggage into the boot of their hired car. Then they were on the motorway, heading for Marbella.

Club Atlantic was quiet when they got there. Evening was coming and the cicadas were chirping noisily in the trees. As soon as they were inside the apartment, Sandy marched into the sitting room, put down her cases and began opening windows to let in the cool air. Now that they had finally arrived she felt a surge of hope and expectation.

Meanwhile, Sam had conducted a quick tour of inspection and returned to report that everything appeared to be in order. 'It's too late to do anything now,' he said. 'I suggest we get unpacked, then go out and eat. We can have an early night and make a fresh start in the morning.'

'Where would you like to go?'

'Why don't we head down to the Paseo Maritimo? There's plenty of choice down there.'

'Good idea. The walk will do us good.'

They changed into lighter clothes and set off down the hill towards the town. As they drew closer, they could hear laughter and singing coming from the bars along the seafront. They found the promenade packed with tourists and holiday-makers and Sandy's memory swept her back to the first time she had come here with Sam. Their love had been in its early bloom and she had been gloriously happy. A lot had happened to her since then.

After walking for a while, they came upon a restaurant overlooking the beach. They went in and were given a table beside the window where they could hear the gentle sighing of the ocean as it rose and fell upon the sand. By now the sun was going down and the stars were peeping out from the dark canopy of the sky.

They gave their order. When the wine arrived, Sam poured some into their glasses and took her hand. 'How do you feel?'

'Eager to get started.'

'Nervous?'

'A little.'

'There's something I have to say, Sandy. I've told you that the chances of finding Alejandro are slim. So don't build up your hopes. But even if you do manage to find him he may not be the idealised figure you have in your mind. He may be an unpleasant man. He may be surly or bitter. He may resent you coming here. He may reject you and send you away. You should be prepared for that.'

'I am prepared.'

'It's not too late to turn back.'

'No, Sam. This is something I must do.'

'So you want to press on?'

'Yes.'

❖

That night, Sandy slept well and was up before eight as the sun was rising. When she had been there before, she had begun the day with a swim in the pool. But this morning she was anxious to get on the road to begin her search. They had a light breakfast of croissants and coffee at Ivy's bar, then set off.

It took forty minutes to reach Fuengirola and park the car. Then they set out through the crowded streets in search of Calle Cervantes. Sandy had already used her map to locate it in the maze of little alleys that ran from the seafront in the old town. But it wasn't easy to find and it took another twenty minutes before they arrived.

Number three was a tiny whitewashed house with pots of flaming geraniums decorating the windowsills. The door was ajar and they could see into the dark little parlour. Sam rapped on the door and called, and a few minutes later, an old lady in a black blouse and skirt answered his call. She looked quizzically at the two strangers standing on her doorstep. Sandy felt her heart quicken its beat.

'*Buenos días,*' Sam began politely.

The old lady peered at him. '*Sí?*'

He launched into a conversation in Spanish, punctuated by frequent finger-pointing towards Sandy, who stood quietly in the background. She watched him take out the photographs of Alejandro. The old lady studied them before shaking her head.

'No,' she said, and looked again at Sandy.

Finally Sam took a notebook from his pocket, scribbled something, tore out the page and pressed it into the old lady's hand.

'*Adiós,*' he said, and the woman retreated back inside the house.

He shook his head as he rejoined Sandy. 'No luck, I'm afraid. It was exactly as I thought. She says she's been living there for twenty years, has never heard of anybody called Alejandro Romero and didn't recognise him from the photos either. However, she's taken my phone number and agreed to ring me if she should remember anything. It's a long shot, Sandy, but it's the best we can do.'

'So what's next?'

'We try to find the Emerald Isle bar.'

They set off again. Sam stopped at every pub and bar they came to and made enquiries. He was received politely but Sandy saw the same routine repeated again and again. The barman would shake his head, whereupon Sam would take out his notebook and write down his phone number. After a couple of hours of fruitless searching they stopped at a café and ordered two coffees.

'It's a waste of time. Nobody's heard of it and I'm not surprised. Pubs like the Emerald Isle open and close all the time and keep changing their names. There must be dozens of them down here on the Costa.'

'Is there anywhere else we could try?'

'We could ask at an *inmobiliaria*.'

'What's that?'

'An estate agency. There's a possibility that one of them may know something.'

They finished their coffee and set off again. A few minutes later, they came upon an *inmobiliaria* on the main road, its windows filled with photographs of houses and apartments for sale. This time, the dark-haired young woman who came to meet them spoke English.

'We're trying to locate a bar called the Emerald Isle,' Sam began. After he had explained their quest, a smile spread across the woman's face.

'Nineteen eighty is a long time ago, *señor*. I wasn't even born.'

'Of course not,' Sam replied politely. 'You look much too young.'

She laughed.

'I thought perhaps the bar might still be operating and you might have heard of it.'

'No, *señor*. However, there is a firm down near the port that specialises in bars and restaurants. There is a possibility that they might know.' She wrote out the name and address and gave it to him.

They set off again in the hot sun. When they arrived at the port, they found it busy with yachts and pleasure boats plying for trade and little cafés bustling with customers. The shop they were seeking was at the end of the quay beside a boatyard. Inside, a plump man in a tight, dark suit sat behind a desk, sweating in the heat. He looked up when they came in. Sam launched into his familiar routine while the man listened patiently.

'*Momento*,' he said, and turned to his computer. He tapped

a few keys then turned to Sam again. 'I have two bars called the Emerald Isle on my list. One is in Benalmádena and the other in Calahonda.'

'The one we're looking for was in Fuengirola.'

'Nothing in Fuengirola.'

'You're sure?'

The man gave him a disgruntled look. 'Absolutely, *señor*.'

'This was several years ago. Perhaps it has changed its name.'

'That is quite possible, *señor*. But, in any case, I cannot help you. I have no record of it. *Buenos días*.'

He turned his attention to some papers on his desk to indicate the interview was over.

Sandy was feeling thoroughly downhearted. It was beginning to dawn on her just how difficult their task would be. But Sam wasn't about to give up just yet.

'We've still got the town hall,' he said. 'Let's see if we have better luck there.'

❀

The town hall was set in a magnificent plaza near the zoo. It was four o'clock when they got there and groups of children were playing happily in the sun. They stopped at an information desk in the foyer and were directed to the foreigners' department on the third floor. Here they were met by a young man in a casual suit, who smiled politely as they came in. Sam began his spiel. He had repeated it so often that he knew it by heart.

The young attendant waited till he had finished. Then he shrugged and began to explain how impossible the task would be. 'Over thirty years ago, *señor*. This is crazy.'

'I know it will be difficult but it's essential that we find this man.'

The attendant glanced at Sandy, then back to Sam. 'You don't understand, *señor*. Where would we begin?'

'Surely you must have records.'

The man gave a loud sigh. 'It will take a long time.'

'We don't mind how long it takes.'

Sandy held her breath. This might be their last chance.

'Okay,' the man said wearily. 'Give me the information. I will see what I can do.'

CHAPTER 34

There was nothing to do but wait. They returned to Club Atlantic and tried to pass the time. Sam sat down with his laptop in the lounge and absorbed himself in business matters while Sandy made some calls to Dublin to keep in touch. One of the calls was to her aunt Betty. When she heard that Sandy was back in Spain, she immediately wanted to know why. But Sandy wasn't about to reveal the reason for the visit. 'I decided I needed a break.'

'You just had a break in London. Why do you need another?' Betty asked suspiciously.

'Why not? I've had a tough time lately, what with Mum and everything. You're the one who's always telling me I should slow down. I'm taking your advice.'

'Well, I suppose it can't do any harm,' Betty said, clearly not satisfied. 'How long do you plan to stay down there?'

'I haven't decided.'

'Hmm,' Betty said. 'It's well for some.'

The weather remained fine, and for the next few days, Sandy took herself to the pool or tried to read a book. But it was difficult to concentrate: her mind kept wandering back to the town hall and she wondered how the search was progressing.

Sam suggested that they take the car for drives along the coast. But it wasn't like the last time she had been there when she had been able to relax. Now she was wound up as tight as a spring. If the town-hall search failed to find Alejandro they had only one option left: to run ads in the local papers in the hope that someone might recognise him.

The tension mounted with each day that passed and with it a growing sense of pessimism. She imagined clerks in some basement at the town hall poring over dusty documents from 1980 while they tried to track down an unknown man. The magnitude of the task was overwhelming. As time went by, Sandy became convinced it was going to fail.

The phone call came a week later as they were having breakfast on the terrace. When Sandy held the phone to her ear she sensed at once that the news was bad. 'I'm sorry, *señorita*,' the man said. 'We have searched and we cannot find him.'

'But he owned a bar in the town, the Emerald Isle,' she pressed. 'That meant he was a taxpayer. Surely there must be a record.'

'Do you know for certain that he owned the bar? Perhaps he was only the manager and someone else owned it.'

The man was right. Betty had told her that Alejandro ran the bar. Sandy had assumed he owned it.

'He lived in Calle Cervantes.'

'But did he own the house or was he merely renting it? It

is quite possible to live in Fuengirola and never come to the attention of the town hall. We have searched our records for 1980 and 1981 and can find no trace of him.'

She had run out of arguments. She thanked the man for his help and terminated the call. Across the table, Sam was watching her intently.

'It's bad news,' she said. 'They can't find him.' She was close to tears. 'What do we do now?'

'We use the option of last resort,' Sam said. 'We hire a private detective.'

She stared at him.

'I've been preparing a fall-back position in case the town hall couldn't find him,' Sam continued. 'I went on the internet and checked out some private investigators. I've narrowed it down to three.'

'Go on.'

'The best prospect is a man called Jorge Sanchez. He's been in the business for fifteen years and has the great advantage of being a former police officer. That means he probably has access to sources of information that we can't get near. What's more, he specialises in finding missing persons.'

Sandy's spirits rose again. They weren't beaten yet. 'How do we get in touch with him?'

'He has an office in Fuengirola, Avenida Jiminez. I have his number.'

'So what are you waiting for?'

Sam picked up the phone and spoke in Spanish for several minutes. At last, he turned to her. 'He'll see us at eleven o'clock.' He checked his watch. 'It's ten now. We'd better get moving.'

The journey through the mid-morning traffic seemed to take for ever. But now Sandy felt excitement take over. An opportunity had opened up again and this time they would have a professional investigator working on the case.

Jorge Sanchez was waiting for them in an air-conditioned office at the top of a building overlooking the bus station. He was a heavy-set man in his mid-forties with sad eyes. He stood up and shook hands, then invited them to take seats across the desk from him. 'Would you like coffee?' he asked. 'Or perhaps water?'

They both chose water and Sanchez smiled. 'The weather, huh? Too hot for you?'

He called, and a moment later a secretary appeared in the doorway with three bottles of water and glasses. 'Now,' Sanchez said, 'tell me what I can do for you.'

'We're trying to locate a man who lived here thirty-three years ago,' Sandy began. 'His name is Alejandro Romero. We have an address where he lived and also where he worked. We also have these.' She took the photographs out of her bag and handed them over.

Jorge Sanchez glanced at them briefly before setting them aside. 'Is this man in trouble? Did he do something illegal?'

'Nothing like that. This is a personal matter.'

'Personal? How do you mean?'

'I believe he's my father.'

Sanchez nodded. 'Are you sure?'

'I don't have DNA evidence. But I have other reasons. He was friendly with my mother at the time she became pregnant.' She explained what Betty had told her about Angela's romance and the letter that had been returned. While she spoke, the detective scribbled notes on a pad.

'What else can you tell me?'

'He was in his late twenties when this happened. That was 1980.'

Sanchez was scribbling again. 'Anything else?'

Sandy glanced across to Sam. 'No,' she said. 'I think that's everything.'

The detective put down his pen and looked at her with his sad eyes. 'It's not much to go on, *señorita*, and the time is so long ago.'

'It's all I have and I'm desperate to find him. Do you think you can help me?'

The detective pursed his lips and shrugged. 'I will try, but I cannot guarantee.'

Before they concluded the meeting, Sanchez outlined his terms. He would charge two hundred euro a day with a bonus payment of three thousand if he was successful. If he hadn't found Alejandro after two weeks, he would terminate the search. It meant another wait but this time it would be limited to fourteen days. Sandy left the office, impressed by the sad-faced detective. Somehow he had given her confidence.

'What did you think of him?' she asked Sam.

'He seemed professional and he was honest. I liked that. He didn't try to hold out false hopes.'

'I thought so too. And I think his fees are reasonable. The most this can cost is six thousand euro. If he finds Alejandro, it will be money well spent.'

Sam stroked her cheek. 'I know how much you care about this. But try not to think about it too much. It's out of our hands now. Let Sanchez get on with his work.'

This time she decided to take Sam's advice and enjoy the fine weather and their beautiful surroundings. She rose every morning around eight when the sun was coming up and began the day with a vigorous swim in the pool. Then she had breakfast on the terrace with Sam while they planned their day.

They spent much of their time in the garden by the pool while they read or listened to an English-language station Sandy had found on her radio. Sometimes, they skipped lunch but they always made a point of going out for dinner, walking down to the Paseo Maritimo or venturing up the coast to the more expensive restaurants in Puerto Banús.

Once they drove past Málaga to the beautiful town of Nerja and stayed overnight in a little hotel perched on a hilltop above the sea. On another occasion, Sam hired a boat and they sailed out until the people on the beach were mere specks and they had only the screeching seabirds for company. Jorge Sanchez never rang to brief them on his search and gradually the obsession with finding Alejandro faded to the back of Sandy's mind.

But the reprieve was short and as the fortnight drew to a close, she felt the tension return. Each time the phone rang, she grabbed it, eagerly hoping for news. When she woke in the morning, Alejandro was the first thought in her mind. No matter how hard she tried, she couldn't shake him off.

She found herself wondering what she would do if the search proved fruitless. Would she give up and accept defeat or would she continue regardless, hiring more and more detectives in her search to find the man she was convinced was her father? She knew it would drive her crazy. But the alternative was just as bad – to go back to Dublin and resume her life with the thought always hanging over her that Alejandro was out there somewhere, waiting for her to find him.

One evening, just before the deadline expired, they were walking along the promenade after dinner when her phone rang.

She clasped it to her ear.

'Sanchez,' the voice said.

She caught her breath. 'Yes?'

There was a group of revellers in a bar nearby. She pressed the phone closer to block out the noise.

'I think I've found him,' the detective said.

CHAPTER 35

She closed her eyes as the news sank in. 'Where?'

'Málaga.'

The noise from the revellers grew louder and it was difficult to continue the conversation.

'Can you be in my office at ten o'clock tomorrow?' the detective shouted. 'I will tell you everything then.'

There was a click and the line went dead.

She turned to Sam. By now, she felt like jumping for joy. 'That was Sanchez. He thinks he's found Alejandro.'

⚫

That night, she could barely sleep for excitement. They were up early, had a quick breakfast and were on the road by nine.

Sanchez was waiting in his office with a sheaf of documents before him on his desk. He paused while they sat down then passed some photographs to Sandy. 'Those were taken yesterday.'

The photographs showed a dark-haired man drinking coffee at a pavement café on a busy street. He was dressed in a lightweight cotton suit and looked to be in his late fifties.

'Compare them,' the detective said and gave her the original photos.

Sandy placed them together and studied them. Immediately she could recognise the similarities – the same dark hair, the same height, the same handsome face. She felt a wave of euphoria sweep through her. She was certain it was him. She passed the photographs to Sam for his inspection. 'Did you speak to him?' she asked.

Sanchez shook his head. 'That is for you to do. I simply undertook to find him. But this man goes by the name of Alejandro Romero. He runs a business selling insurance in Málaga. His address is flat 16B, Edificio Marquez, Calle Valencia. This is his telephone number.'

He gave Sandy another sheet of paper with the information printed on it.

'How did you find him?' Sandy asked.

The detective smiled. 'I have my methods. Let us say that I checked with the police. He has a criminal record.'

Sandy looked up sharply.

'It's nothing serious,' the detective assured her. 'He has a conviction for a minor traffic offence.'

'Did you find out anything more about him? Is he married?'

'He is not married. He lives alone.' Sanchez sat back in his chair. 'Are you satisfied this is the man you are looking for?'

'He seems to be,' Sandy said.

'In that case, I have the pleasure of presenting you with the invoice for my fee.' He slid another piece of paper across the desk.

❖

They left the building and went out into the blinding sunlight.
Sandy's head was reeling. After the weeks of waiting, she felt
giddy with relief that the search had ended successfully.

'What do you want to do now?'

'I want to meet him. I want to talk to him.'

'Remember what I said. He may not want to meet *you*.'

But Sandy was in no mood for doubt. She was seized with
a feeling of hope and expectation. She had found the man she
believed to be her father. And he lived only a few miles away in
Málaga. She couldn't wait to see him and find out all about him.

'How do you plan to approach him?' Sam asked.

'I'm not sure.'

'It might be best to phone him first and ask for a meeting.
You've got his number. It will give him time to get over the
shock.'

'Okay. Let's find somewhere quiet.'

There was a bar nearby. They went there and found a table in
a room at the back. Sam went off and returned with coffee while
Sandy got out her phone. She steeled herself before dialling the
number. The phone seemed to ring for ever before she heard the
call being taken up.

'*Hola*,' a voice said.

'*¿Habla inglés?*'

'*Sí.*'

'Am I speaking to Alejandro Romero?'

'*Sí.*'

Sandy took a deep breath and pressed on. 'My name is
Alexandra Devine. Do you remember an Irish woman called
Angela Cummins? You met her in the summer of 1980 when

she was living in Fuengirola. She was working for a Spanish family called Gomez. You met in a bar called the Emerald Isle.'

There was a pause. 'Yes, I remember Angela.'

'I am her daughter.'

'Oh.'

She heard the surprise in his voice.

'Is Angela still alive?'

'Yes, she is.'

'How is she?'

'She is well.'

'I am glad to hear that.'

'She wrote you a letter. I have it with me. I would like us to meet so I can give it to you. Is that possible?'

'Where are you?'

'In Fuengirola.'

'Do you have a car?'

'Yes.'

'I am working now but I could meet you in Málaga in one hour. There is a café called Bar Jesus. It is in Plaza Victoria. Shall I give you directions?'

Sandy's hand was shaking. 'It's all right, I have a map. I should be able to find it.'

'How will I know you?'

'I'm tall with dark hair. I'll be wearing a white jacket. A man will be with me. He is also tall and has blond hair.'

'Then I will see you at Bar Jesus in one hour.'

Sam had been listening intently. 'So he's agreed to meet you?'

'Yes,' Sandy said, almost laughing with joy. 'Plaza Victoria. We have an hour to get there.'

'Congratulations. You handled it well. I didn't think it would be so straightforward.'

They returned to the car and set off. Once they were on the motorway, they were able to make good speed, and after forty minutes, they saw the spires and rooftops of Málaga shining in the distance. Sandy had the street map spread on her knees and gave directions to Sam as they entered the outskirts of the city. They found an underground garage, locked the car and started to walk. By now, it was almost one o'clock and groups of office workers were packing the cafés and restaurants for lunch.

Plaza Victoria was a quiet little square in a residential district at the back of the cathedral. They found Bar Jesus tucked away in a corner. It was almost deserted. They sat down outside and this time Sandy ordered a glass of white wine to celebrate her success so far. She checked her watch. The hour was almost up.

A few minutes later, they saw a solitary figure approach across the square. He was tall, thin and wearing a light jacket with dark trousers. As he drew closer, she recognised the handsome face of Alejandro from the photographs that Jorge Sanchez had given her. His hair was still dark but speckled with flecks of grey. She felt her body tingle with anticipation. He stopped when he got to their table and bowed politely. 'Señorita Devine?'

'Yes.'

'I am Alejandro Romero. I am so pleased to meet you.'

He held out his hand and Sandy took it. She felt her heart flutter at his touch. This was a big moment in her life. At last, she was in the presence of her father.

He released her and turned to Sam. Sandy made the introductions and the two men shook hands.

'May I sit down?' Alejandro asked.

'Please,' Sandy said, quickly withdrawing a chair so he was sitting beside her. 'What would you like to drink?'

'*Café cortado, por favor.*'

The waiter was back. Sandy gave the order and turned to find Alejandro's twinkling eyes examining her. 'You do not look like Angela,' he said. 'You are darker, more …'

'Spanish?' she said.

'Yes, more Spanish. I am glad she is alive and well. I have many precious memories of her. We were so young then but I can remember that time as if it was only yesterday.'

'It was a happy time for her too, perhaps the happiest time of her life.'

A smile passed across his face.

'I am glad for her. She is married now?'

'Her husband died a few years ago.'

'Oh, that is sad. Did she send you to find me?'

'No, she doesn't know I'm meeting you.'

He looked surprised. 'But you said she had written a letter for me.'

'That is correct. But the letter was written a long time ago. It was written in 1980, soon after she had gone back to Ireland from Spain.'

He looked puzzled. 'I do not understand.'

'It was returned to her.'

'That is very strange. I never received such a letter. May I read it?'

Sandy opened her bag and took out the letter. Alejandro glanced at the address on the envelope and the writing across the front. 'Not Known at This Address. Return to Sender.' He cautiously withdrew the letter and began to read. Sandy exchanged a nervous glance with Sam.

Eventually Alejandro put down the letter. The sparkle had left his eyes and now his face was pale and drawn. 'Forgive me for asking but what is your date of birth, Alexandra?'

'May the twenty-eighth, 1981.'

'Then this letter must mean ...'

'Yes,' she said. 'It means you're my father.'

She watched his face for his reaction. His cheek twitched slightly and his eyes grew moist. He lifted Sandy's hand to his lips and kissed it gently. 'This is a tragedy. If only I had received this letter, it would have changed my life completely.'

'And my life too,' Sandy said.

They sat for a moment without speaking as the significance of what had just occurred began to sink in. It was Sandy who broke the silence. 'You said you never got the letter?'

He shook his head. 'No. I never saw it till now.'

'Angela believed you had returned it to her.'

'That's not true.'

'She rang to tell you she was pregnant but couldn't contact you. She even came back to Fuengirola to find you but the Emerald Isle was closed and boarded up. She went looking for you at Calle Cervantes but nobody knew where you had gone.'

By now, Alejandro had taken out a handkerchief and was dabbing at his eyes.

'Let me tell you what happened.' He paused and raised the coffee cup unsteadily to his lips. 'In the summer of 1980, I was managing the Emerald Isle bar in Fuengirola for a man called Jose Montero. It was very popular with Irish tourists and every night the place was full of people and we would have music and singing. Then one evening Angela came in. The moment I saw her, my heart went to her. She was the most beautiful young woman I had ever seen, so cheerful and full of joy. That summer we fell in love. But eventually her job finished and she had to return to Ireland. I was desperate to stay in touch with her. I said I would write but she said no. It was better if she phoned me at the bar. She said we could speak to each other and hear each other's voices.

'So she phoned me regularly. I lived for her calls. I hoped that maybe she might come back to Spain and we could continue our romance. And then, a few months after she left, disaster struck. One night, someone left a heater on at the Emerald Isle and there was a fire. The bar had to be closed and I was out of work.

'But, worse than that, I had no address for Angela and no way of contacting her. I was desperate. I didn't know what to do. Eventually, I got an offer of a job in Málaga selling insurance. So I gave up the little house I was renting in Calle Cervantes and moved here.

'I kept hoping that somehow Angela would come back into my life. The months passed away and then the years. I wondered what was happening to her. Perhaps she had met another man and got married. Eventually I had to accept that I wouldn't see her again. But I never forgot her.' He stopped and looked into Sandy's face. 'And now you have turned up.'

There was another silence. Out on the sunlit square, the pigeons were fighting over some scraps of bread. Sandy felt her heart swell. Alejandro's story was one of the saddest she had ever heard. She thought of Angela back in Dublin, pregnant and believing he had abandoned her, and Alejandro desperate to contact her but not knowing how.

Eventually, Sam broke the silence. 'Would you like another *cortado*?'

'No, thank you. I must return to my work.' He turned to Sandy. 'I am so glad you have come. It means so much to me. Let us meet tonight for dinner. We have so much to talk about.' He withdrew a card and pressed it into her hand. On it were his address, his phone number and also his email address. He and Sandy stood up. He paused for a moment, then placed his hands on her shoulders and kissed her lightly on both cheeks. '*Cariño*, you are so beautiful. Just like your mother. Thank you for coming. You have brought a light back into my life.'

He shook hands with Sam and started to walk away across the square.

Sandy watched him go as she fought back the tears and the pigeons scattered in his path.

CHAPTER 36

They returned to Dublin two days later. Sam wanted to stay longer, but now that she had accomplished her mission, Sandy was anxious to get back. The first thing she did was visit her mother at Sunnylands. She found her in good spirits, chatting excitedly about the book club.

It seemed to Sandy that she was fitter and more alert, just like the old Angela. She asked about Sam, Patsy and the people at Music Inc, then enquired about the tenants who had moved into her house in Primrose Gardens. How had they settled in? Were they paying the rent on time and taking good care of the place?

Sandy continued to visit her mother often in the coming days and each time she saw an improvement. The move to Sunnylands had worked a great change for the better. She also rang Alejandro to tell him she had arrived home safely. He sounded pleased to get her call and asked after Angela. Soon they were ringing each other several times a week. His insurance business was doing well, he said, but he was thinking of selling it and retiring. Several people were interested in buying it from him at a good price.

A plan began to form in Sandy's mind. One day, she went out to visit her aunt Betty. She found her in the kitchen preparing vegetables for lunch.

'Sit down, sit down,' she said. 'I'll make a pot of tea.' While she was doing so, she asked Sandy about her recent trip to Spain.

'Spain was excellent. I had a very productive visit.'

'Productive? What does that mean?'

'I met someone while I was down there.'

Betty turned and her face fell. 'I knew you were up to something,' she said. 'I knew this was no ordinary holiday. You met Alejandro, didn't you?'

'Yes.'

'How did you trace him?'

'I hired a private detective.'

'Oh, my God, Sandy, I wish you hadn't done that. Why couldn't you leave things as they were? Why did you have to go rooting around in the problems of the past?'

'I had to see my father.'

'Tom Devine was your father. When are you going to recognise that? He looked after you and Angela when no one else would. Tom was a saint.'

'I know that. He was my dad and no one will ever replace him in my heart. But imagine how shocked and hurt I was to discover that he wasn't my real father. That was Alejandro. Can't you understand that I would want to meet him?'

Betty poured the tea and sat down. She stared at Sandy as

if she still couldn't believe what she had heard. 'How did he receive you?'

'Very well.'

'He must have been as shocked as I am.'

'I think he was pleased.'

'Humph,' Betty said. 'And what did he have to say for himself? Did he explain why he returned that letter to poor Angela when she was desolate and in need of help?'

'He never got it. He didn't know she was pregnant. While she was looking for him, he was desperately trying to contact her. Oh, Betty, it's the saddest story you ever heard. Alejandro is a lovely man. He's never married. I don't think he ever got over losing Mum.' She recounted the details of their meeting and what she had heard from Alejandro while Betty sat open-mouthed.

'That's terrible,' her aunt said, when Sandy had finished. 'I had no idea. If that bar hadn't caught fire, none of this would have happened.'

'That's right. And my life would have been completely different.'

Betty regarded Sandy warily. 'What are you going to do now? You're not going to tell Angela, are you?'

'Why not?'

Her aunt's face drained of colour. Her hand trembled as she put her teacup down on the table. 'Sandy, you can't do that.'

'Surely she should know what happened. All these years, she has lived with the belief that Alejandro abandoned us in our hour of need. Don't you think she should hear the truth?'

'But the shock – she wouldn't be able for it.'

'I'm not so sure about that. She might welcome it. I've wondered why she kept the photographs and why she named me after him. I think somewhere deep in her heart, she still has feelings for Alejandro.'

'I don't think this is a good idea, Sandy. I really don't. She's happy out there in Sunnylands. Why drag up all that stuff again?'

'So we can finally put it to rest.'

She left the house after her aunt had extracted an undertaking that she would tell Angela nothing about her role in the events. 'I broke my promise when I told you the background to that letter,' she said. 'She'd be furious if she knew.'

'Don't worry. Your name will not be mentioned.'

Over the next few days, the conviction grew in Sandy that Angela must be told. But the problem remained about how she should break the news. She would have to be extremely careful. If she made a wrong move, the situation could easily backfire.

She decided to take her mother to lunch in some quiet place where they could talk. She chose the Avondale Hotel. It was close to Sunnylands, they had been there before and Angela had liked it.

The day of the lunch arrived and Angela was bubbling with excitement. When they had finished eating, they retired to the lounge for coffee.

'I see a big change in you,' Sandy said. 'Your health has improved enormously. You're a completely different woman since you moved to Sunnylands.'

'Thank you,' Angela said. 'I feel much better. My problem was I became withdrawn after your father died. I can see that now. I should have got out more and mixed with people instead of brooding. That's the great thing about Sunnylands. There's so much to do that there's never a dull moment.'

'I was thinking,' Sandy said. 'How would you like to come away with me for a little holiday?'

Her mother looked up sharply. 'Where to?'

'Spain.'

At the mention of Spain, Angela frowned. 'Why does it have to be there?'

'Well, the weather is sunny, there's lovely scenery and things to do and see. I think you'd enjoy it.' She paused and took a deep breath. 'Besides, I know you've been before. You were there when you were a student, weren't you? You lived for a while in Fuengirola?'

Angela drew back as if she had just been burned by a hot coal. 'How did you know that?'

'It's all right,' Sandy said, reaching out and taking her hand. 'I know all about it.'

'Who told you? Was it Betty?'

'No, it wasn't Betty. I was down there recently and I met someone who knew you back then, an old friend from the past, someone who has never stopped thinking about you.'

She waited for her mother's reaction. Would she explode in fury or break down in tears? But Angela didn't pull her hand away. Instead she sat quietly for a moment, as if digesting this momentous statement. Then she said softly, 'It was him, wasn't it? It was Alejandro.'

'Yes. He's living in Málaga now. He asked after you.'

'How is he?'

'He's fine. I think he's lonely.'

'Did he tell you about us?'

'Yes. He told me everything. Would you like to hear what he had to say?'

Her mother slowly nodded, and for the next few minutes, Sandy told the story of the fire, how Alejandro had never received the letter and how he had hoped desperately that Angela would return some day. 'He never married. I think you were the only woman he ever loved.'

At this, her mother lowered her eyes. 'What does he look like now?'

'He's still tall and handsome. His eyes are still dark and passionate. His hair is still black although there are some streaks of grey.'

'And he asked about me?'

'Yes. He said he had many precious memories of you. He said you were the most beautiful woman he had ever seen.'

'Did he really say that?'

'Yes.'

'I thought he'd abandoned us.'

'No, he didn't. He didn't even know.'

'How can you ever forgive me?'

'What for?'

'For not telling you, for allowing you to believe that Tom Devine was your father.'

'But Tom *was* my father. He was the one who reared me. He was the one who loved me and took care of me.'

Her mother sat in silence. Eventually she sighed. 'I'm tired. I think I should go back now.'

❖

They drove to Sunnylands and Sandy promised to visit the following day. She went home and rang Sam.

'How did it go?'

'Much better than I expected. She listened to everything I had to say. She asked about Alejandro. She didn't react like I had feared.'

'That's progress. So what's the next step?'

'The big part has been done. It's a lot for her to absorb and she's going to need time. I'm seeing her again tomorrow. I suppose I'll just have to be patient.'

'Good luck,' Sam said.

The next morning when she went to visit, she found her mother in the sitting room of her flat with a cup of tea and a book. She took off her reading glasses and offered Sandy a seat.

'How are you today?' Sandy asked.

'Harassed, if you really want to know. We've got the book club this afternoon and I've got to finish this.'

She held up a copy of a novel Sandy had never heard of.

'Any good?'

'I'm finding it very heavy going. Margaret Delaney chose it on her daughter's recommendation. It's a bit too pretentious for my liking, and if I find it difficult, God knows what the rest of them will make of it. I'm expecting fireworks this afternoon.'

Sandy stifled a laugh.

'I enjoyed the lunch yesterday,' Angela said. 'I can't remember if I thanked you. I like the Avondale Hotel. It serves plain old-fashioned food with no frills.'

'It was my pleasure.'

Sandy was expecting her mother to mention Alejandro but she veered off to some other topic. They stayed chatting for an hour and Sandy left without Alejandro's name being mentioned. It was the same each time she visited. A fortnight passed and she began to think that Angela had somehow managed to banish the subject entirely from her mind. She debated whether she should raise it again and decided not to.

Then one morning when she went to visit, she found Angela with a group of her friends watching television in the lounge. As soon as she appeared, she excused herself, stood up and steered Sandy away. 'I've been waiting for you,' she said.

They walked out to the garden and sat down on a bench. A couple of ravens were pecking at the lawn.

'I've been talking to Emily and she says I should do it.'

'Do what?'

'What you suggested. Go to Spain.'

CHAPTER 37

At this announcement, Sandy felt a great relief mingled with joy
and immediately alerted Dr Hyland of her plans to take Angela
to Spain. Now there followed a great flurry of activity. Sam said
he would come with them and arranged for them all to stay
at Club Atlantic. Meanwhile, Sandy got busy with the travel
arrangements and assisting her mother to renew her passport.

It was May – one of the best times to be on the Costa
del Sol. She checked the weather forecast, which predicted
temperatures of twenty degrees and twelve hours of sunshine
daily. That would be perfect. After some thought, she decided
to go for a week. Once she had her mother's agreement, she
went online and booked the flights.

The packing came next. Sandy and Sam were experienced
travellers and knew exactly what to expect but Angela hadn't
been abroad for thirty years. The announcement that she was
going on holiday to Spain had caused great interest among the

residents of Sunnylands and she was inundated with advice. One man who had lived for years in Africa suggested she should bring a mosquito net for her bed at night and watch out for crocodiles if she went swimming. But, finally, with the assistance of Emily Sutherland, she was persuaded that one large suitcase would be more than adequate for everything she would need.

The days ticked away till it was time to go. By now, Angela was totally sold on the idea and eagerly looking forward to the trip. The flight was scheduled for lunchtime, and at ten o'clock, Sam and Sandy arrived at Sunnylands to take her to the airport. They found her waiting patiently in the foyer with her suitcase beside her. Her friends gathered round to wish her well, and once she was seated securely in the back of the car, they set off.

By now, Angela was filled with excitement and seemed to enjoy the whole experience, passing effortlessly through check-in and security. Finally they arrived in the departure lounge where she found a comfortable seat, accepted Sandy's offer of some tea, took a book out of her travelling bag and began to read while they waited to board.

They touched down in Málaga at half past four and the sun was shining. There was a short delay while Sam completed the car-hire formalities and then they were off for Marbella.

Angela gazed from the car window as the scenery flashed by. 'I remember this, the mountains and the sea and the flowers. Everywhere I went in Spain, there were flowers.'

Sandy squeezed her hand. 'This holiday is especially for you. I want you to enjoy it.'

Angela's face flushed with pleasure. 'I've been enjoying it since the minute we left Sunnylands.'

◆

When they arrived at Club Atlantic, Angela went eagerly from room to room admiring the apartment. 'It's magnificent,' she said, finally walking out onto the terrace and gazing over the rooftops of Marbella to the sea. 'Look at that beautiful view. Isn't it spectacular? I can't wait to tell my friends.'

Sandy smiled, happy that her mother's first impressions were positive.

'You'll enjoy the gardens too,' she said. 'But we can leave that till tomorrow. Now I suggest we get our bags unpacked and go out for an early dinner. Are you hungry?'

'A little.'

'We'll leave at six. Would you like me to help you unpack?'

'If you don't mind.'

At six, they set off by taxi to a restaurant Sam had booked. Angela had dressed in a smart jacket and skirt and had even put on a little makeup. When they arrived, they were met by a fawning head waiter, who quickly showed them to a prominent table where they could see over the entire room.

Angela glanced about her, at the gleaming cutlery and the glittering candles, as the dark-suited waiters flitted back and forth about the tables. 'This place is very swish. It must be terribly expensive,' she said to Sam. 'I don't want you spending too much money.'

'Nothing is too expensive for you, Angela,' he said. 'You're a very special lady. You deserve only the best. Now, take your time and have a good look at the menu till you find something you like. I think you'll find the food is very good.'

'Will we be eating here every night?'

He laughed. 'If that's what you want. As Sandy keeps telling you, you're here to enjoy yourself. We want you to have a holiday you will never forget.'

They left the restaurant at nine o'clock and went back to Club Atlantic. By now it was dark and the air was filled with the scent of flowers from the garden. They sat on the terrace and had a nightcap while they gazed at the moon reflecting off the sea.

At ten o'clock, Angela said she was tired. Sandy went with her to her room and helped her get ready for bed. By the time she left, her mother was already sleeping. She rejoined Sam on the terrace.

'That went very smoothly,' he said. 'She certainly seems to be having a good time.'

'Thank God,' Sandy replied. 'But the really difficult part has yet to come.'

He took her hand. 'This trip has reminded me of something I've been intending to do for some time.'

'What?'

'Ask you to marry me.'

She turned to him. He was still as handsome as the day they had first met but now her love for him burned stronger. 'What would you do if I said no?'

He looked a little nervous. 'I'm hoping you won't, Sandy.'

Suddenly she leaned forward and kissed him passionately. 'Does that answer your question? Of course, I'd be delighted to marry you.' She laughed as Sam's arms drew her closer. 'I was wondering if you'd ever ask.'

❀

The following couple of days they spent reading in the garden and doing a little sightseeing. On the third morning, Sandy was awakened by the sound of movement in the kitchen. She got up and found Angela making tea. They went out to the terrace and had breakfast.

'What would you like to do today?' she asked.

Her mother turned to her. 'I'd like to go back to Fuengirola. I'd love to see the town again.'

'Are you sure?'

'Yes. It's where I worked all those years ago when I was young.'

'It doesn't hold sad memories? I don't want you getting upset.'

But Angela had obviously been thinking about this decision. 'It does hold sad memories but there are good ones too. I was very happy there.'

'Okay,' Sandy said. 'You get ready and we'll go.'

She and Angela got into the rented car and set off. All the way on the short journey, Angela stared out of the window as landmarks flashed by. 'There's a lovely little beach down there,' she said, as they passed through Calahonda. 'The family I was staying with took me there for a picnic. Their name was Gomez. I must tell you all about them.'

They parked in the centre of Fuengirola near the station. There was a festival in the town and the streets were gaily decorated with flowers and banners. They started to walk, and every few moments, Angela would point out some place she remembered from the past.

'The town has barely changed,' she remarked. 'It's exactly how I remember it.' As they continued, she gradually took control, directing their footsteps till eventually they found themselves in a narrow little street in the old part of town. She stopped at last when they came to a little bar with tables outside. She stood for a moment, examining the surroundings, then turned to Sandy. 'This is where it was,' she said. 'The Emerald Isle. This is where it all began.'

Sandy's heart skipped. 'Do you want to turn back?' she asked.

'Not at all. This is what I've come to see.'

They sat down and ordered coffee. Sandy looked at her mother. She seemed calm and composed, not at all affected by the momentous discovery.

'You should have seen this bar back then. It had all these posters on the walls with the Cliffs of Moher and Killarney and photographs of James Joyce and other famous writers. And every night it would be packed with people from Dublin and Belfast and Cork singing "The Wild Rover" and other old Irish ballads. It was such a happy place. Everyone was on holiday and having a good time. And I was young and the future stretched in front of me like a golden thread.' She closed her eyes and let the memories flood back.

'So this was where you met Alejandro?'

'Yes. He was the handsomest man I had ever seen. He was so courteous, such good manners. And he paid me such attention. It was no wonder I fell in love with him.'

'Have you thought about what he told me? How he never got your letter? How he had no way of contacting you? How he kept hoping against hope you might come back some day to Fuengirola?'

'He's got his wish at last,' Angela said. 'I *have* come back.'

Sandy took a deep breath. 'Does that mean you're prepared to meet him? He'd love to see you again. I know it would make him very happy.'

Angela opened her eyes. 'Of course I'll meet him. We've got an awful lot to talk about.'

EPILOGUE

It had been another warm day but now the air was cooler as the dusk began to fall. All along the edges of the square, the lights were coming on. Siesta time was over and people were venturing onto the streets again. The shops were pulling up their shutters and opening for business.

That morning Sandy had called Alejandro and told him her mother was back in Spain and would like to meet him. He had been overwhelmed by the news and quickly agreed a venue. Now they sat at a table outside Bar Monica in Fuengirola and drank coffee while they waited. Sandy wore a light summer frock. Her mother was in her best dress and a pretty jacket. Earlier she had been to the hairdresser.

'How do you feel?' Sandy asked. 'Are you nervous?'

'I'm a little apprehensive. You've told me he's still handsome. I wonder what he'll make of me.'

Sandy smiled. 'So you're still vain after all these years.'

'No, just practical. I know what I look like and I'm no beauty queen.'

'Beauty's in the eye of the beholder.'

'So they say. I don't believe it.' She fidgeted with her cup. 'The last time I was here was the night before I left to return to Ireland. He was taking me for a farewell dinner.'

'I know. I think that's why he chose it.'

'I was sad that night. I didn't want to go home.' She glanced at her watch. 'What time did he say? Is he late?'

'Calm down,' Sandy replied. 'He'll come. He was delighted when I told him. He's waited a long time for this.'

Angela glanced away when she heard a guitar start up somewhere nearby, and when she turned back Alejandro was approaching across the square. He was exactly as she remembered him: the same tall figure, with passionate dark eyes. He was like a photograph she had always carried in her heart.

He stopped when he came to the table where she was sitting, then made a formal bow and presented her with a single red carnation. 'So here you are, *cariño*. I never stopped hoping and now you have come back at last.'

ACKNOWLEDGEMENTS

I would like to thank my family as always for their support and encouragement. Take a bow Gavin, Maura and Caroline.

I would like to thank the staff at Hachette Books Ireland, particularly my editor Ciara Considine and copy-editor Hazel Orme. Also Joanna Smyth for being unfailingly pleasant and efficient.

Thanks also to Marc Patton. There is nothing about technology this guy doesn't know.

I would like to thank the booksellers for helping to get this novel into the hands of you the reader. I trust that your good taste and loyalty will continue to be rewarded.